ERLE STANLEY GARDNER

- Cited by the *Guinness Book of World Records* as the #1 bestselling writer of all time!

- Author of more than 150 clever, authentic, and sophisticated mystery novels!

- Creator of the amazing Perry Mason, the savvy Della Street, and dynamite detective Paul Drake!

- THE ONLY AUTHOR WHO OUTSELLS AGATHA CHRISTIE, HAROLD ROBBINS, BARBARA CARTLAND, AND LOUIS L'AMOUR *COMBINED*!

Why?
Because he writes the best, most fascinating whodunits of all!

You'll want to read every one of them,
from
BALLANTINE BOOKS

The Case of the
One-Eyed Witness

Erle Stanley Gardner

BALLANTINE BOOKS • NEW YORK

A Ballantine Book
Published by The Random House Publishing Group

Published in the United States by Ballantine Books, an imprint of The Random House Publishing Group, a division of Random House, Inc., New York, and distributed in Canada by Random House of Canada Limited, Toronto.

Ballantine and colophon are registered trademarks of Random House, Inc.

www.ballantinebooks.com

ISBN 0-345-39225-6

This edition published by arrangement with William Morrow and Company, Inc.

Manufactured in the United States of America

First Ballantine Books Edition: June 1995

Foreword

Twice each year eight or ten of the outstanding experts in the field of scientific crime detection gather at the Harvard Medical School. There, under the auspices of Captain Frances G. Lee, one of the most remarkable characters in the history of crime detection, these experts instruct a hand-picked class. The instruction fills a work-crammed week. It covers everything pertaining to murder, from detection to an actual post-mortem.

There are no more than two dozen pupils. To be enrolled in such a class one must have an okay from the governor of his state, a clearance from the head of the state police, or a special dispensation from Captain Frances G. Lee herself.

In previous forewords to three of my books I have mentioned some of the leading figures connected with these seminars: Captain Frances G. Lee of the New Hampshire State Police; Dr. LeMoyne Snyder, a doctor of medicine as well as a lawyer, who specializes in the field of legal medicine; Dr. Alan R. Moritz of the Western Reserve University in Cleveland, one of the country's leading pathologists as well as one of its cleverest detectives.

In the foreword to this book I want to introduce the reader to Dr. Robert P. Brittain, a Scotsman who is both a barrister and a doctor of medicine. He is a young man of great brilliance who is at present lecturer in Forensic Medicine, in the department of Forensic Medicine at Leeds University in Leeds, England.

Dr. Brittain is quiet and unassuming, a man of small, wiry physique. Intellectually he's a giant.

At his first lecture to a group of the broad-shouldered men who had been carefully selected from the cream of the state police, I felt that Dr. Brittain's youthful appearance, his slight build, would make it difficult for him to hold the interest and attention of his audience. I was never more mistaken.

Earnestness, sincerity and knowledge command respect everywhere. Dr. Brittain aroused the interest of his audience with his first few sentences. He held the men fascinated and there was an underlying attitude of deep respect in their attention.

Midway in his lecture, in illustrating a point on identification, Dr. Brittain asked the members of the group to estimate his height and weight. These men who were carefully trained to give a mere glance and tell the color of a man's eyes, his height, weight, age and complexion, made some very wild guesses about Dr. Brittain. They all estimated him as being heavier than he was and taller than he was.

And at this point I take respectful issue with Dr. Brittain. It wasn't that these trained officers were lacking in powers of observation, it was simply that they became confused in trying to reconcile the man's intellectual stature with his physical appearance.

I know because I was in the room, and while I didn't guess out loud, I'd have been as far off as any of the others if I'd made my estimate.

Later on I was to see Dr. Brittain in his home in Glasgow, to consult with him on a difficult case Dr. LeMoyne Snyder and I were trying to solve. I was then to learn something of his charm, his social grace, his marvelous sense of humor, the poetic side of his nature. But at the time I first saw him I sat spellbound through a technical lecture, my interest so aroused that I can even now repeat almost verbatim parts of that lecture.

I think the true measure of an instructor is whether he can be interesting as well as exact. Knowledge is apt to be ponderous, boring and a bit stuffy. We remember only what interests and impresses us. If, therefore, instructors can make their lectures so interesting they cause pupils to sit forward on the chair edges, there is no need for later "cramming."

And, lest the reader may think I am giving too much emphasis to Captain Lee's program, it is well to remember that the upgrading of our police officers is one of the most important problems in the present-day administration of justice.

Of late, I have been privileged to work with a committee which donates its services for the purpose of freeing innocent men who have been wrongfully convicted of murder. In this manner, I have been brought to a realization that every time an innocent man is convicted it is not only a great tragedy, but the party who is really guilty continues at liberty as a menace to society. This has brought home to me the importance of having crime detection keep pace with the achievements of science in other fields.

We have some remarkably competent investigative officers and we are rapidly getting more. The police officer who has pride in his profession and confidence in his knowledge can tackle his job with the quiet courtesy born of competence. The ignorant officer all too frequently masks his ignorance with brutality and may well send innocent men to prison.

Captain Frances G. Lee is a pioneer in the field of more efficient investigative work, and she carefully selects her instructors at these semi-annual seminars on Homicide Investigation. The sessions run through long hours for six consecutive event-packed days, but one seldom sees a student yawn. Such men as Dr. Richard Ford of Harvard, Dr. Milton Helpern of New York, Dr. Russell S. Fisher, now Chief Medical Examiner of Baltimore, Dr. LeMoyne Snyder of Lansing, and Dr. Joseph T. Walker of Harvard and laboratory consultant for the Massachusetts State Police, make those seminars never-to-be-forgotten events.

So I make a bow to these men who can make learning

so much fun, and I dedicate this book to one of the truly great intellects in the field of legal medicine and of scientific crime detection,

DR. ROBERT P. BRITTAIN.

Erle Stanley Gardner

Chapter 1

The night sky was sodden with low-hanging clouds. Cold drizzle coated the sidewalks with moisture, gave a halo to the street lights, and caused the tires of passing automobiles to hiss over wet pavement.

Most of the buildings in the neighborhood shopping center were dark, but on the corner the drugstore was a blaze of light. Halfway down the block on the same side an all-night café radiated a glow of hospitality. Across the street the motion picture theater had switched out most of the lights in the foyer. The second show was drawing to a close and within five minutes the doors would open to disgorge the audience after the last run of the feature picture.

Over in the drugstore, the prescription clerk in a white smock was making entries in a book. The long soda counter was vacant, but a tired-looking girl was arranging glasses, preparing for the sudden rush of trade which would follow the closing of the motion picture theater. Within seven minutes every stool would be occupied and people would be three deep at the counter. At that time, the cashier would move over to help out, and the prescription clerk would lend a hand.

In the meantime there was a complete lull as the store waited for that last spurt of business which would swell the day's receipts.

The woman who came hurrying down Vance Avenue and turned into Kramer Boulevard paused to glance apprehensively over her shoulder before making the turn, then she rounded the corner. The light from the window of the drugstore splashed her features, showing lines of determination about the mouth, fear in the eyes.

1

She opened the door and walked in.

The cashier, an open book held flat on the desk by the side of the cash register, kept on with her reading. The girl at the soda fountain looked up inquiringly. The prescription clerk put down his pen and started to move forward.

Then it was apparent the woman's interest was in the two telephone booths at the back of the store.

Afterwards, in trying to recall her appearance, they all agreed she was somewhere in her early thirties, with a good figure which even the lines of the dark coat with the fur collar couldn't hide. The cashier noticed that she was carrying a brown alligator-skin purse.

They might have remembered more if it hadn't been that at that moment the swinging doors of the movie theater opened and a stream of people poured out to congest the sidewalks.

The cashier sighed and closed her book. The prescription clerk pushed an advertising display of vitamin pills to the front of the counter, moved a carton of razor blades slightly forward. The girl at the soda fountain wiped her hands on a towel, and started mixing four chocolate malted milks in the electric mixer. She knew she would have orders for those within the next ninety seconds.

The woman disappeared into one of the phone booths, opened her handbag and took out a coin purse.

A frown of annoyance crossed her features. She searched vainly for a nickel, then almost ran to the cashier's desk.

"Can you give me some nickels? Please hurry. Please!"

The cashier would have noticed her then if it hadn't been that the doors of the drugstore were pushed open by a crowd of teen-age students, noisily centered in their own little world, exchanging loud banter, intent upon banana splits, butterscotch sundaes, whipped cream, marshmallow, chocolate syrup, and chopped nuts.

The cashier handed the woman five nickels, sized up the crowd pouring in the door and moved over to the soda fountain to give a hand. It would be another ten minutes before the avalanche would hit the cashier's desk.

2

The woman vanished into the phone booth. No one remembered her after that.

She placed a slip of paper on the shelf by the telephone, stacked the five nickels on top of the paper, picked off the top nickel, dropped it in the coin slot and dialed a number.

The hand which held the receiver to her ear was quivering slightly. Her eyes kept watch through the glass window of the booth, carefully checking the faces of this sudden influx of late customers.

The woman listened anxiously while she heard the sound of ringing coming over the telephone, then the receiver was lifted at the other end of the line, the strains of dance music from an orchestra mingled with the synthetic sweetness of a voice which had been carefully trained in sugary accents, "Yes. Hello."

"Quick, please. Get this right. I want to speak with Perry Mason, the lawyer. Get him to the phone and . . ."

"Perry Mason? I'm afraid . . ."

"Get Pierre, the headwaiter, on the phone. Mr. Mason is with a young woman at a table . . ."

"But Pierre is very busy. There will be a wait. If you are in a hurry . . ."

"Go to Pierre. Ask him to point out Mr. Mason to you. Tell Mr. Mason to come to the phone at once. It's important. At once. Do you understand?"

"All right. Hold the line."

There followed some two minutes of waiting. The woman impatiently glanced at her diamond-studded wrist watch, frowned at the telephone, said at length, half to herself, half to the mouthpiece of the telephone, "Hurry, hurry. Oh, please hurry!"

It seemed an age before the lawyer's slightly annoyed voice came over the wire. "Hello. Yes. This is Mr. Mason."

Her words came out with the staccato force of a sudden burst of machine-gun fire.

"This is important," she said. "You must get it and you must get it straight the first time. I won't have an opportunity to . . ."

3

"Who is this speaking?" the lawyer interrupted.

"I'm the one who sent you the package," she said. "Please listen to what I have to say. Do you have a pencil?"

"Yes."

"Please write down this name and address."

"But why . . ."

"Please, Mr. Mason. I will explain. Seconds are precious. Will you *please* write this name and address?"

"Go ahead."

"Medford D. Carlin, 6920 West Lorendo. Have you got that, Mr. Mason?"

Mason said, "Just a minute. That's Carlin, C-a-r-l-i-n?"

"That's right," she said. "The initials are the same as the abbreviation of a physician and surgeon, M.D. The address is 6920 West Lorendo."

"Yes, I have it."

"Did you receive the money all right?"

"What money?"

"Oh, Mr. Mason, you *must* have received it! That package I told you about. Don't tell me you didn't get it. Oh, I . . ."

Her voice trailed away into a silence of utter despair.

"Will you," Mason asked impatiently, "kindly give me your name and quit beating around the bush? How was I supposed to receive any money and who is this talking, please?"

"I can't tell you my name. It wouldn't mean anything. But the money, five hundred and seventy dollars, was in the envelope I . . . Oh, Mr. Mason, *please* go to see Mr. Carlin, show him the clipping which is in the package with the money and . . ."

"But I tell you I haven't received any package."

"Then you will. It's coming. Tell Mr. Carlin that under the circumstances he's going to have to get another partner. Mr. Mason, I can't begin to tell you how important this is. It's a matter of life and death. Don't lose a minute when . . . *Oh! Oh! OH!*"

Her voice froze in her throat as the dark, apprehensive

eyes, which had been watching the front door of the drug-store, spotted a tall man in his early thirties. He was just entering the door.

He walked with the long, easy stride of a person who has never known anything except good health, and stood, with a slightly quizzical expression in his eyes, surveying the faces of those who occupied every available stool at the lunch counter.

The woman's reaction was instantaneous. The receiver dropped from her hand to dangle at the end of the cord, knocking a few times against the side of the telephone booth, then swinging gently.

She glided out of the booth, inched along behind a display rack, then stood with her back turned to the soda fountain, apparently completely engrossed in a study of the magazines which were grouped in long lines of display.

She managed a start of surprise as the man's fingers closed on her elbow. Her head jerked back. Indignation on her face suddenly melted into a seductive smile. "Oh," she said, "you!"

"I wondered if you were here."

"I—you're finished?"

"Yes. It didn't take as long as I thought it would."

"Oh, I hope I haven't kept you waiting. I wanted a tube of toothpaste and while I was here I got started looking at the magazines. It's only been just a second or two and I . . ."

He placed an athletic arm, hard with muscle, around her waist, swung her over toward the lotions counter. "Come on. Let's get that toothpaste and get out of here."

5

Chapter 2

Perry Mason, holding the receiver of the telephone in his left hand, held his right index finger pressed against his ear to shut out the sound of music which came from the night-club orchestra.

Della Street, Mason's efficient secretary, seated at the table which Mason had vacated, caught his eye and correctly interpreted the quick, nodding gesture of his head. "What is it?" she asked, moving rapidly to his side.

"Something funny about this," Mason said. "Get on one of the other phones, see if that telephone supervisor friend of yours is on duty and if they can trace this call, will you? Tell them to rush it. It's a woman. She sounds terrified."

Della Street whipped out a notebook, leaned toward the celluloid circle on the front of the telephone on which Mason was talking, and noted the number. Then she rushed to a phone in the women's powder room.

Mason was still holding the receiver when she returned.

"It's a pay station, Chief, at a drugstore on the corner of Vance Avenue and Kramer Boulevard. Apparently the receiver has been left off the hook."

Mason slipped the receiver back into place.

"What was it?" Della Street asked.

Mason returned the notebook to his pocket. "Someone wants me to contact an M. D. Carlin immediately. Address is 6920 West Lorendo. Look him up in the book, will you, Della?"

Della Street's swift fingers turned the pages of the telephone book. "Yes, here he is. M. D. Carlin, 6920 West Lorendo. Telephone is Riverview 3–2322."

"Make a note of the number," Mason said.

"Do you want to ring him?"

"Not yet. It's late. I want to know more about this before I take any action. But it's something mighty important to that woman. I wish you could have heard her voice over the telephone, Della."

"Upset?"

"More than upset. She was in a blue funk."

"What did she want you to do?"

"To tell this Carlin that he was going to have to get another partner."

"She has been working with him on some scheme?"

"I don't know. She gave me that message and said that a package of money was on its way to me. Ordinarily I'd toss an offer of anonymous employment to one side, but I can't get over the note of terror in that woman's voice. When she left that telephone she'd worked herself up to a pitch where she was frightened to death. You could hear the bang when the receiver dropped and then hear it thumping from time to time against the wall as it swung back and forth. I thought perhaps she had fainted."

"So what do we do now?" Della Street asked.

Mason said, "We wait for a few minutes to see if this package that the woman referred to shows up."

"And in the meantime?"

Mason escorted Della Street back to their table. "We finish our after-dinner coffee, perhaps have a dance and act as though nothing had happened."

Della Street said, "Don't look now, Chief, but the telephone call seems to have attracted attention."

"In what way?"

"We seem to be the subject of a whispered discussion over there in the corner."

"Who are they?"

"The hat-check girl, the girl who has the photographic concession, and the cigar and cigarette girl. Wait a minute, here comes the cigarette girl now."

Mason sipped his coffee.

The girl with her cigarette tray made a perfunctory canvass of the people at the adjoining table, then turned to Perry Mason. "Cigars, cigarettes?" she asked, her voice caressing and lingering.

Mason smiled and shook his head.

Della Street nudged him.

"Well, give me a package of Raleighs," Mason said.

She selected the package, tore off the corner, tapped out a cigarette, handed it to Mason, then bent to hold a light.

She was an olive-complexioned girl with rather high cheekbones, and a good figure. The costume exhibited soft, rounded shoulders from the daring low neckline, and good legs in opera-length nylons.

Mason handed her a dollar. She started to make change.

"That's all right." Mason smiled warmly.

"Oh, you are—so generous."

"That's all right."

"It is so good of you to—to give me this. . . ."

"What's the matter?" Mason broke in, looking at her sharply. "Don't you ordinarily get tips?"

"Ten cents, fifteen cents, perhaps twenty-five cents," she said, and suddenly her eyes filled with tears.

"Hey, wait a minute," Mason said. "What's the idea?"

"Oh, you will forgive me. I am so upset and on edge that when someone is kind I have no control of myself. I am not myself . . ."

"Here, sit down," Della Street said.

"No, no, I will lose my job. I cannot sit with the customers. I . . ."

Mason watched her face convulse with emotion, saw the tears start trickling down, leaving streaks through the makeup.

"Here," Mason said, "sit down."

He arose to hold a chair for the girl, and after a moment's hesitation she turned the chair so that her tray could balance itself on her lap, and sat down at the table.

"Now then," Mason said, "what you need is a brandy and . . ."

8

"No, no, please. That I cannot do. To drink with the customer is against the rules."

"What's the trouble?" Mason asked.

Della Street flashed him a warning glance.

"Something wrong with the job?" Mason prompted.

"No, no. It's all right. Just a private matter and nothing new. But every now and then like a wave it . . ."

She broke off and almost savagely turned on Della Street. "Your husband would not understand, but you, yes. You can know how a woman feels about her baby."

"What about your baby?" demanded Mason.

She shook her head. "I am foolish to intrude upon you in this way. Please will you pretend to be selecting something from my tray? It—the headwaiter can be very disagreeable."

Della Street fingered the various small souvenirs and gadgets.

"Go on," Mason said.

"It is nothing. After all, it will work out all right. My child is probably in good hands. Only I wish I knew. Oh, how I wish I knew."

"Knew what?" Mason asked.

"Where my little girl is. You see, it is very difficult and complicated. I am—I am part Japanese."

"You are?"

"Yes. You probably don't notice it unless you look sharply, but you can see the eyes, the cheekbones."

Mason studied her for a moment, then nodded, and said, "Yes, I see now. I thought there was a certain exotic something about you. Now I see what it is. There's a definite Oriental cast to your features."

"Only partially Japanese," she said, "but I'm an American. I'm as good an American as anyone. Only do you think anyone else thinks so? No. To most people I am Japanese, and that makes me taboo, an outcast."

Mason said, "There was something about your baby."

"I had a child."

"You are married?"

"No."

"Go on."

"That is it. I had the child, and the child's father managed to steal her from me. He sold her. When I heard she'd been released for adoption I was frantic. I tried in every way to find out what had happened, to do something, but there was nothing I could do."

"*Was* this man who took your baby really the child's father?" Mason asked.

She hesitated a moment, her eyes lowered, then she raised the lids and looked Mason full in the face.

"No," she admitted. "The father—died."

"Why don't you do something to find your baby?" Della Street asked.

"What *can* I do? I have Japanese blood, and people do not go out of their way to help the Japanese unless they have much money, and I have none. I do not even know where my child is, but I am sure she was released for adoption. This man who posed as the father of the child and signed papers has disappeared and . . ."

"How old is your child?" Mason asked.

"She would be four years old now. She was just a baby when . . ."

Pierre, the headwaiter, glancing around the crowded dining room, suddenly spotted the cigarette girl seated at the table. "Cigarette girl, this way," he called sharply. "At once!"

"Oh," she said, "I shouldn't have done this. Pierre is angry."

She produced a handkerchief from the V-shaped opening of the strapless costume which hardly seemed adequate to afford sufficient concealment for a postage stamp, hurriedly wiped her eyes, gave her face a quick dab with the powder puff from a make-up compact.

"Cigarettes!" Pierre called, his voice harsh with impatience.

She flashed Della Street a quick smile, for a moment

10

placed her hand on Perry Mason's arm, gave it a little squeeze, said, "It gets me down once in a while."

"Don't let it," Della Street said. "You should . . ."

"Cigarette girl. Here, at *once*," Pierre called.

"Thanks for the buggy ride," she said, patting Mason's shoulder, and was gone.

"Poor kid," Della Street said.

Mason nodded.

"Babies are worth money," Della Street pointed out. "I suppose by posing as the father and saying that the mother was dead or had skipped out, he was able to release it for adoption and got probably five hundred or a thousand dollars."

"A Japanese baby?" Mason asked.

"Who was going to know it was Japanese?" Della Street asked. "You wouldn't have known that girl was Japanese unless she told you. There's something about her eyes, just a faint suggestion in the contours of her face. She is a lot more American than Japanese."

Again Mason nodded.

"You seem rather unimpressed," Della Street said irritably. "Why don't you *do* something about her baby? *You* could do it, Chief. You could find that child and see that justice was done."

"To whom?" Mason asked.

"To the mother, to the child."

"How do you know it would be justice to the child? The child may be in a good home. The mother is working in a night club with just about enough clothing to keep her from being arrested for indecent exposure and . . ."

"What difference does that make? She loves her child."

"Maybe she does," Mason said, "but it's strange to think that she loves it *that* much."

"What do you mean?"

"It must be more than three years since the child disappeared," Mason pointed out dryly. "She walks up to a couple of total strangers in a night club, suddenly bursts into tears and violates the rules of the place to sit down and pour out her troubles."

"Well, of course," Della Street admitted, "when you look at it that way. . . . But it was so spontaneous! You just had the feeling she had been keeping her troubles to herself until finally they had piled up on her and she just couldn't contain herself any longer."

"You overlook the significance of the conference which took place over there in the corner, Della, after I had been called to the telephone."

"That's right. Then she *must* have known who you are."

Mason nodded.

"And then tried to interest you in coming to her rescue. And yet it was done so convincingly—and those were real tears, Chief." .

Mason glanced at his wrist watch, said, "Well, if there are going to be any further developments they'd better show up. It's going to be too late to do anything tonight. I can't forget that note of urgency, of sheer terror in the woman's voice. I'd like to know what happened at the other end of that telephone to cause her to . . ."

"Here's the headwaiter coming this way," Della Street said.

The headwaiter, a rather short, stocky, middle-aged man, was suavely apologetic with his bow and his voice. His eyes, however, indicated definite purpose.

"You will," he said, with a shrug of his shoulders, "pardon the interruption, Monsieur."

"Yes?" Mason asked.

"But is it that you should be Perry Mason, the lawyer —no?"

Mason nodded.

"I am so sorry. I did not recognize you when you entered, but you were pointed out to me. I have seen your pictures in the paper many times, but"—he moved his hands in an expressive gesture—"when I see you, you are younger than I expect."

"All right," Mason said, somewhat impatiently. "The

food is fine, the service is excellent. Please don't apologize for not recognizing me and don't tell anyone I am here."

The headwaiter glanced just for one fleeting moment at Della Street. His smile indicated that he could be the soul of discretion. "But certainly, Monsieur," he said. "This is not a place where we point people out. Monsieur's business is his own—no? The reason I am intruding upon the privacy of Monsieur is that an envelope has been given to me by a messenger for Monsieur Perry Mason, the lawyer. It is of the greatest importance that the envelope is to be delivered only to Monsieur Mason."

His hands made a swift motion. The envelope was produced with something of a flourish, something of the skill of a magician bringing a live rabbit from a coat tail pocket.

Mason didn't reach for the envelope immediately. He studied it lying there on the table. It was long, manila, and the "Mr. Perry Mason" had been hastily written. Then his eyes, cold and granite-hard, turned up to the urbane, smiling headwaiter.

"Where did you get this?" he asked.

"It was delivered to the man at the door by a messenger."

"Who was the messenger?"

"But I do not know. One does not know the names of messengers. The doorman, perhaps. If you wish, shall I send him?"

"Send him."

For a moment their eyes locked, the lawyer's probing, insistent, impatient, Pierre's smiling with what might have been a slight touch of mockery. Then the headwaiter averted his eyes.

"He shall be sent to you at once, Monsieur, and I hope you find everything satisfactory." The man bowed, turned away and walked toward the door of the night club.

"Somehow," Mason said, watching the man's back, "if you're looking for an explanation of how our whereabouts was discovered by our mysterious would-be client . . ."

He broke off and tore open the heavy envelope.

13

"This is it, all right," Della Street said as she saw the currency, the newspaper clipping.

Mason looked through the assortment. "A collection of everything from five-dollar bills through one-dollar bills, up to a couple of fifties," he said.

He raised the bills to his nose, then handed the packet to Della Street.

She smelled it, said, "Rather a strong scent."

"Oh, certainly," Mason said. "Dollars and scents."

"I should kill you for that," Della Street said, smiling. "That would be justifiable homicide in any court in the land."

"Well, forget the dollars," Mason said. "Let's talk about the scents."

Her eyes became serious. "It's a nice scent," she said, "but strong. You know, Chief, it might be that some woman had been saving this money, a dollar or two here and there, then perhaps five dollars, then by a lucky break a fifty-dollar bill, placed in a bureau drawer where she kept her handkerchiefs, the whole thing being saved for an emergency."

Mason nodded, his face thoughtful. "Only," he said, "the fifty-dollar bills represent an opportunity she's had to change a lot of ones and fives. After she scraped that much money together there was a chance to go to a bank and get the lot changed into something that didn't take so much room and—here comes the headwaiter and the doorman. Della, get the money back in the envelope."

"There's no name?" she asked.

"No name," Mason said. "And no note. Just the money and a newspaper clipping. That's why she had to call me on the phone to tell me what she wanted me to do.

"Apparently she didn't have time to write a note. She just put this stuff into the envelope and . . ." He broke off as the headwaiter escorted the doorman to the table.

"The doorman, Monsieur." Pierre stood waiting, somewhat expectantly.

14

Mason handed him a ten-dollar bill. "The service," he said, "has been excellent."

Deft fingers folded the bill and palmed it. It was as though the money had been swallowed up into nothing. There was no hint of sardonic amusement in the man's eyes now. His manner was deferential. "It is a pleasure to serve you, Monsieur. Any time that you wish to come here ask only for Pierre and the table will be waiting."

He managed to make the message a personal one for Perry Mason but to include Della Street by a swift, almost surreptitious, glance. Then he was bending suavely over another table. "Everything is satisfactory?" he murmured.

The doorman, a big man in an ornate uniform, seemed in a hurry to get back to his post, but his quick eyes had apparently caught the denomination on the bill which had been given Pierre, despite the latter's swiftness in folding the bill. He seemed properly impressed.

"That envelope," Mason said. "Can you tell me about it?"

"Not too much," the doorman said. "The car was just average. Not too new. To tell you the truth I didn't pay much attention to it. There was a rush on at the time and both of the lads who handle the parking were busy. I stepped up and opened the door and saw there was a lone man in the front seat who didn't look like he belonged. I knew he wasn't going to get out as soon as I opened the door. I thought he was a moocher who'd ask for directions. We have a few of them. Fellows pull up to the curb and want to know how to get some place, or where such and such a street is.

"You don't mind it if you're not busy and if they'll just roll the window down and let you know what they want, but when they sit there and wait for you to open the door, it makes you sore. I've never had a tip from one of those guys yet."

"And this one?" Mason asked impatiently.

"Well, like I say, I knew he wasn't going to get out. I

opened the door and he pushed the envelope into my hand and said, 'Give that to Perry Mason. He's inside.' "

"Yes?" Mason asked.

The doorman said, "I remember handling your car but I didn't recognize you, Mr. Mason. I've heard the name enough but—I guess it's your first time here, isn't it?"

Mason nodded. "Go ahead. What about the person with the envelope?"

"Well, that's all. I stood there sort of dumb, I guess. The man said, 'Go ahead. Get the lead out of your . . .' "

He stopped abruptly.

"Pants," Della Street finished.

"Thank you, ma'am," the doorman said, grinning. "That's what he said, and then he said, 'Give it to whoever's in charge in there and tell him it's important and it's for Mr. Mason.' So I passed it on to Pierre."

"And what did the man do?"

"Slammed the car door and drove away."

"You didn't get the license number or anything?"

"That's right," the doorman said. "I didn't get *anything*. I'd say it was a Chevvie—about five or six years old. Dark color, a four-door sedan, and that's just about all I can tell you about it."

"Can you describe the man?"

"Sort of a grayish suit, his shirt collar was rumpled. He was maybe, oh, six or eight years older than I am, and I'm—let's see, fifty-three. . . . He didn't look like a customer."

"A working man?"

"Well, not so much a working man. The kind that would have a little business of his own. He looked—well, he was seedy, but he was shrewd. A guy who has some money but doesn't spend it on clothes and cars, or throw it away in . . ."

"Night clubs?" Della Street prompted.

Once more the man grinned.

Mason produced a second ten-dollar bill. "Try and remember something else," he said. "You're missing tips out

16

at the door and it's on your mind. You'll do better later on, if you keep your mind on it. This is Miss Street, my secretary. You can ring my office any time tomorrow and ask for her and let her know in case you think of something else."

The doorman's attitude was entirely different from that of Pierre, the headwaiter. In place of swiftly folding the bill and getting it out of sight, the doorman made it a point to look at the denomination, then nodded and beamed approvingly.

"Say," he said, "don't worry about me passing up tips outside. Now if there's anything . . ."

"Just think it over," Mason said, "and you might get my car. It's . . ."

"I remember your car," the doorman said, "and I'll remember *you* next time, Mr. Mason. Anything you want . . ."

"That's fine," Mason interposed. "Right at the moment all I want is to find out more about the messenger who sent this envelope to me."

"I'll keep thinking. If anything comes of it I'll telephone you tomorrow afternoon. I'm on duty until two o'clock in the morning and I don't get up until around noon. I may think of something."

Mason nodded to Della Street, said, "All right, Della, we'll ring Carlin."

"If he's in bed he'll be mad," she warned.

"I know," Mason told her, "but it's a chance we'll take."

"You don't think it can wait until morning?"

"You didn't hear that woman's voice over the phone, Della. Whatever it is, it has to be handled right now. At least I'm going to make a stab at it."

Mason accompanied Della Street to the telephone. She dropped the coin, dialed the number, glanced inquiringly at Mason. "Do you want to take it from here?"

"No," Mason told her, grinning. "Use your most seductive voice until he gets over being peeved at the late call, Della. See if you can soothe his feelings."

"Do I tell him who we are and why we're calling?"

"Not why, just who. You can . . ."

Della Street jerked her head back toward the transmitter and said, "Yes, hello. Is this Mr. Carlin?"

She waited a moment, then smiled sweetly and said, "Mr. Carlin, I hope you will pardon the intrusion at this late hour. This is Miss Street talking. I am Mr. Perry Mason's confidential secretary and it is very important that we see you at the earliest possible moment. . . . I trust you weren't in bed. . . . Oh, that's fine. . . . Yes. If possible. . . . Yes, I know it's unusual. I'll put Mr. Mason on the line."

She cupped her hand over the transmitter and said, "He wasn't in bed. Sounds polite. I think it's all right."

Mason nodded, took the receiver from her hand, placed it to his ear, and said into the telephone, "Hello. This is Perry Mason talking, Mr. Carlin. I'm very sorry to bother you at this late hour."

"So your secretary told me," the man's voice announced over the wire. "However, you don't need to worry about that. I seldom go to bed before one or two o'clock. I'm quite a reader and very much of a night owl."

"I want to see you upon a matter of the greatest importance."

"Tonight?"

"Yes."

"How long will it take you to get here?"

Mason said, "I'm phoning from the Golden Goose, and I have one other minor matter which I have to see about and it'll probably take me—oh, perhaps thirty or forty minutes."

"I'll be waiting for you, Mr. Mason. Now, let's see, you're Mr. Perry Mason, the attorney?"

"That's right."

"I've heard about you, Mr. Mason. I'll be very glad to meet you. I'll make some hot coffee."

"That's fine," Mason said. "I feel that this is something of an imposition, and I certainly appreciate . . ."

"Not at all, not at all. I'm rather a lonely bachelor here,

18

and I like company. It's definitely not an imposition, Mr. Mason. I'll be glad to see you. Are you bringing your secretary with you?"

"Yes. She'll be with me."

"That's fine," Carlin said. "I'll be very glad to see you, Mr. Mason, in about half an hour."

"That's right," Mason said. "Thank you," and hung up.

"Seems to be rather affable," Della Street said.

"He does indeed."

"What's the newspaper clipping, Chief?"

"I've only had a chance to glance at it," Mason said. "It's just a few paragraphs, evidently from a New York newspaper, mentioning that a certain Helen Hampton had been convicted of blackmail and sentenced to jail for eighteen months. It seems that she and some male accomplice, who was not named, were engaged in a sort of shakedown racket, but it seems to have been rather hush-hush. She pleaded guilty and the judge mentioned in passing sentence that the scheme of extortion was so diabolically ingenious that he did not care to have it made public through the press because of the possibility that others might put the same plan into operation."

"Nothing else?"

"Nothing else," Mason said.

"What was the date of the clipping?"

"There's no date on it," Mason said. "It's just a clipping from a paper. It's begun to turn slightly yellow, which might mean either that it's old or that it has been left in the sun. Newsprint turns yellow rather quickly under those conditions."

"Well," she said, "we'll probably know more when we talk with Carlin. What was the other matter you said you had in mind, Chief?"

"I want to go out to that pay station," Mason said. "I presume it's open until midnight. I want to see if we can find out anything more about the woman who telephoned."

"Well," Della Street said, "your friend Carlin sounds casual enough. I rather took a fancy to him."

"He certainly seemed to be affable and matter-of-fact," Mason said, "and relatively devoid of curiosity."

"That's it," Della Street remarked. "I was trying to put my finger on what it was that impressed me about him. He seems to have complete poise. The average person would have been burning with curiosity and perhaps a sense of guilt. I can imagine most people would have said, 'Well, why on *earth* would Mr. Mason want to see *me* at *this* hour? What *is* it you have in mind?' and stuff like that. Mr. Carlin wasn't like that at all."

Mason thought it over. "Seemed to be affable and devoid of curiosity," he repeated slowly.

"As though perhaps he'd been expecting the call?" Della Street asked, cocking her head on one side.

"Well," Mason told her, "I'm not going that far, but he certainly seemed to take it very much in his stride. Come on, Della, let's get out of here and hunt up that phone booth."

Chapter 3

Driving out to the drugstore on Vance Avenue and Kramer Boulevard, Mason said, "Della, just how do you suppose this woman knew I was at the Golden Goose?"

"Why," Della Street said, "a person of your prominence is pointed out everywhere and . . ."

"Then you have to start with the assumption she had been there at the Golden Goose."

"Not necessarily. She—wait a minute—yes, I guess you do have to figure it that way."

"Of course," Mason went on, "she *could* have had a friend who rang her up and said, 'Look, Mr. Mason is here at the Golden Goose. Now's your chance. All you have to do is get in touch with him.' Or the headwaiter . . ."

"Yes, that *could* have happened."

"But, somehow," Mason said, "I don't think it did. Then there wouldn't have been that note of urgency or that abject fear in her voice. . . . No, she must have been someone who was at the night club, who saw us there, and then went out and telephoned."

"No one could have known you were going to be there?"

"We didn't even know it ourselves," Mason said. "You remember we finished interviewing our witness and it was on the way back that you remembered Paul Drake had recommended the Golden Goose. He said there was excellent food and a pretty good floor show and . . ."

"That's right," she said. "We went there on the spur of the moment, and no one knew where we were."

"With the single exception of the Drake Detective Agency," Mason said. "You remember we called Paul from the night club and told him we had the statement of that

21

witness and that we'd see him in the morning, and I think I told him we were trying out the night club he'd recommended."

"That's right. I remember hearing you say that."

"But," Mason said, "Paul Drake wouldn't have told anyone where we were. After all, he's a detective. He knows how to keep his mouth shut. Oh, well, we'll probably find out a lot more when we talk with Carlin. It'll probably turn out to be one of those routine affairs. No reason to get excited about it, and probably no reason to do all this night work.

"However, I can't get over the idea that this woman had been carefully saving money against an emergency, and when that emergency arose she went to the place where she had been hiding her money and . . . Well, here we are at the drugstore. Let's see what we can uncover here. Coming in?" he asked her.

Della Street already had the door open. "Try and stop me."

The man in charge was just getting ready to close up. Four youths, who were gossiping over gooey concoctions of thick syrups and ice cream, were being courteously but pointedly reminded of the time. The soda clerk was dispiritedly plunging glasses into hot water filled with a detergent, and the cashier was making up totals.

The prescription clerk listened listlessly.

"Can't remember very much about her," he said. "They kept ringing the phone in the other booth and we were too busy to answer. Finally I got over there and Central told me someone had left the receiver off the hook in the other booth. I saw they had, and reached in and put the receiver back on the hook. That's all I know about it. You might ask the cashier."

Mason crossed to the cashier's desk.

Yes, she remembered a woman vaguely. She had changed a quarter. Perhaps thirty or thirty-five years old, with a dark coat and a fur collar, and a brown alligator purse. No, she couldn't describe her more accurately. The

22

receiver had been left off the hook. No, she hadn't seen the woman leave. They were busy and . . .

"Which booth did she use?" Mason asked.

"The one on the right, over nearest the magazine stand."

"I'll just take a look," Mason said.

He walked over to the booth, Della Street at his side.

"The prescription clerk is certainly watching you, Chief," she whispered.

"Probably thinks I'm FBI," Mason said. "I don't suppose there's one chance in a thousand we can find out what frightened her, but we'll take a look just the same. If she had to leave so suddenly there might be something left behind, a handkerchief, a purse, a . . ."

"There's a paper on the shelf and some nickels," Della Street said, looking through the glass oblong in the door.

Mason pulled the door open. Della Street glided into the telephone booth. "Four nickels stacked here on a piece of paper," she said.

"What's the paper?"

Della Street said, "There are just numbers on it, scrawled in pencil. Here's a number, Main 9–6450."

"Call it," Mason said. "See who answers."

Della Street dropped a nickel and dialed the number, said, "We probably won't get any answer this time of night. It—oh, yes, hello, hello, yes, oh, thank you—no, never mind, I called the wrong number by mistake."

She dropped the receiver back into place and smiled at Perry Mason. "That," she said, "was the number of the Golden Goose!"

"The deuce it is! I'd give a lot to know how she knew we were there. Anything else on that paper?"

"Some numbers on the other side. They're neatly written, the way a woman who had been a bookkeeper would write them."

"What are they?"

"It looks like some sort of a complicated license number."

The numbers were written in a string. 59-4R-38-3L-19-2R-10L.

Mason stood frowning down at the paper.

The prescription clerk moved over rather rapidly. "Find anything?" he asked.

Mason smiled and shook his head. "I was making a note of the number here."

"Oh," the clerk said.

Mason slipped the piece of paper in his pocket, yawned ostentatiously and said, "It's nothing particularly important. I have a cousin who has amnesia. For some strange reason she seems able to remember my telephone number even when she can't remember who she is, or my name, or anything about her family."

"I see," the clerk said in a tone of voice which indicated he did not see at all.

Mason piloted Della Street toward the door.

The drizzle had developed into a cold, driving rain. Della Street jumped into the car and slid across the seat to come close to Mason. "Brrrrr," she said. "I'm cold. The human ankle really needs more than sheer nylon to protect it in weather like this. Did you have some idea about that string of numbers on the paper, Chief?"

"The string of numbers," Mason said, producing the paper from his pocket, "is the combination to a safe. Four times to the right to fifty-nine, three times left to thirty-eight, twice to the right to nineteen, then turn to the left and stop at ten."

"The clerk is moving casually toward the door," she said. "I think he's interested in your license number just in case . . ."

Mason stepped on the throttle. The car hissed into motion, the windshield wipers beating a monotonous protest against the pelting rain which drove against the windshield and streamed down in rivulets.

Mason said, "That headwaiter at the night club could know a lot more than he told us."

Della Street said, "Well, I hope he looks you up and

finds out you're a bachelor with a perfect right to take a secretary to a night club. He may have known who *you* were but he certainly didn't know who *I* was. He took you for a married man out on a surreptitious round of revelry."

"And you?" Mason asked.

"I," she said, "was the siren, the voluptuous seducer of virtue."

Mason said, "I think that Pierre's reaction to you was because of the way he sized me up."

"That's it," Della Street said bitterly. "Never give the woman any credit. The man always wants to preen himself on being the big bad wolf."

"Or," Mason said, "you can look at it the other way. Pierre decided you were the expert vampire and I was the mere plodding businessman suddenly swept off my feet by the glamour . . ."

"Stop it," Della Street said, laughing. "As a bookkeeper, how am I going to enter this five hundred and seventy dollars on our books?"

"I guess," Mason said, "you'll have to enter it as a credit to Madam X until we find out more about our client.

"However, let's go see what M. D. Carlin has to say for himself. Perhaps he can enlighten us."

"What are you going to tell him, Chief—about your client, I mean?"

"Not one single thing," Mason said. "And I do hope he wasn't kidding about the hot coffee."

They were thoughtfully silent until Mason, turning into West Lorendo Street, found himself in the sixty-eight-hundred block.

"Turned too soon, Della," he said. "This will put us on the wrong side of the street."

He drove across the intersection, slowed as he studied numbers, then said, "There it is, directly across the street."

"What an old-fashioned house!" Della Street exclaimed.

Mason nodded. "Probably this was the residence of a man who had a ten-acre tract twenty-five years ago. Then the city started expanding and finally he decided to subdivide, but you can see he kept plenty of elbow room.

"That lot must run thirty or forty feet on each side of the house. Probably tied up in an estate somewhere. You can see the evidence of lack of care. It's been a long time since it's been painted, and all that gingerbread trimming certainly is a relic of the dim and distant past. Well, here we go, Della."

Mason swung the car into a swift U-turn, parking it directly in front of the house. "How are your legs?"

"Still wet."

"I was hoping the car heater would dry them. Don't catch cold."

"I won't. How are your feet?"

"All right. I have heavy shoes."

Mason switched off the lights, shut off the motor, walked around the car to open the door for Della Street.

"Okay, Della," he said. "Here we go on the run."

They sprinted up the cement walk to the creaky, unpainted porch supported by round wooden pillars, and ornamented by a wooden scroll design.

Mason was groping for the doorbell when the front door swung open. A man's quiet, calm voice said, "I'm sorry. There's no porch light. You're Mr. Mason?"

"That's right. I assume you're Mr. Carlin?"

"Yes, sir. Won't you and the young lady come in?"

Carlin pushed the screen door open. Della Street entered, followed by Perry Mason.

"Rather a bad night," Carlin said. "A cold rain."

"It *is* rather disagreeable," Mason admitted, cautiously noncommittal for the moment, sizing up both the man and the surroundings.

The dim light in the hallway disclosed a man somewhere in the early sixties, a bullet-headed individual, quiet-voiced, with protruding gray eyes behind thick glasses, who regarded his visitors with a certain whimsical patience.

His clothes were as antiquated and as shabby as the outside of the house. A single-breasted coat was cut on a

26

bygone pattern. The trousers were badly in need of pressing. After long months of hard usage, the leather in the shoes had broken down and spread out to conform to the contours of short, broad feet.

He said, "This is a bachelor establishment. I live here by myself. A housekeeper comes in once a week, but I don't go around picking things up and sweeping and dusting. You'll have to take things as they are."

"Quite all right," Mason assured him. "We owe you an apology for intruding at this late hour. However, the nature of my business is such that it couldn't wait."

Carlin adjusted his glasses, peered up at Mason thoughtfully. The left side of his face was long and placid. The right side had a little twist from the upturned corner of the mouth to a quizzical droop at the corner of the eye. The combined effect gave him the appearance of regarding the world with lopsided appraisal.

"My house," he said, "is at your disposal. I know only too well how crowded your days must be, Mr. Mason. Now please come on in to the living room. I have some hot coffee on the stove."

"That," Mason announced, "is going to hit the spot."

"With cream, with sugar, or black?"

"Both with cream and sugar," Mason told him.

The living room strongly reflected Carlin's personality.

There were three old-fashioned cloth-covered platform rockers, two wooden chairs with rounded arms of a type formerly classified as barroom chairs. In the wooden seats of these two chairs holes had been bored in the design of a star. There were no floor lights and apparently no wall outlets. Extension connections had been screwed in the sockets of a chandelier which hung in the center of the room. The result was a spider web of wires and several drop cord lights, shaded by conical sections of pasteboard, green on the outside, white on the inside.

A small table in the center of the room was piled high with books, magazines and newspapers. There had been an overflow down on to the floor, and a pile around one of the platform rockers indicated the man seated there had read things and then disposed of them by simply dropping them on the floor.

"Make yourselves comfortable," Carlin invited. "I'll be back with coffee in just a minute."

Carlin retired to the kitchen. Mason and Della Street looked around the room. Della smiled at Mason. "Problem, find the guy's favorite chair." She indicated the rocker around which the litter of books, magazines and papers had been scattered.

Mason smiled, moved over to look at the books in the age-darkened mahogany bookcase. "By George, Della, some of this stuff is interesting. Our man does some real reading. And just take a look at these bindings."

"What about them?" Della Street asked. "Don't try to lure me away from here, Chief. I've found a gas radiator and this warm air feels good."

Mason turned to look over his shoulder. Della Street was standing on an ornamental grating. The warm air which came drifting up from below was gently billowing her skirt, raising it a few inches, spreading it out.

Mason laughed.

"You'd have to wear a dress on a cold rainy night to know how good this feels," she said. "What about the books?"

"Various subjects," Mason said, "but quite evidently they're special editions of some sort with fine bindings, and . . ."

Shuffling steps sounded from the direction of the kitchen and Carlin brought in a big tray on which was a huge granite coffeepot, some cups and saucers, a pint bottle of cream about half full, and a big cut-glass sugar bowl.

He glanced somewhat hopelessly at the table.

"Just a minute," Della Street said. "Perhaps I can help."

She stacked the books and magazines. Carlin smiled his thanks, placed the tray on the table, started pouring coffee.

The cups were of various patterns and showed evidence of hard usage.

28

"I'm afraid I can't do anything about the chips," Carlin apologized whimsically, "but you will, of course, understand that the one without any handle is for the host. And that's the last apology I'll make for the hospitality I have to offer. This is my bachelor home. Such as it is, you are welcome. Now let's have coffee and get acquainted."

Mason stirred his coffee, glanced at Della Street, sipped the hot beverage and nodded approvingly. "You certainly do make good coffee!"

"Thanks. I'm glad you enjoy it."

"You do all your own cooking?" Della Street asked, and then added hastily, "I'm sorry, I don't mean to pry."

"Quite all right," Carlin said. "I like to cook. My meal hours are irregular and my tastes are unorthodox. When I get hungry I go fix myself something to eat. When I'm not hungry I don't eat. One of the curses of our so-called civilization is that we are dominated by clocks. We have invented wheels that go around and our lives are dominated by the revolutions of those wheels.

"Many and many a man who is overweight is a slave to the custom of having dinner at a certain time. He may not be hungry, but unless he wants to seem churlish he has to sit down at the table with his family or with his friends, and shovel in food."

Mason said, "You have some very interesting books."

Carlin's face twisted into a lopsided smile. "Mr. Mason, let's dispense with pretext and politeness. I know that you didn't come here at this hour to talk about the weather or the coffee or my books. You're curious. I'll satisfy your curiosity. Then you can satisfy mine.

"I'm a widower. I've been living here for five years. I have a small income which enables me to be relatively independent of economic worries, provided I watch my expenditures.

"I'm something of a hobbyist. In the basement, I have a little printing shop and a small stock of very choice paper. From time to time when I find something in literature which I like, I set it in the type which appeals to me and

29

print and bind it in very fine leather. From time to time when I find some book that I think is deserving, I remove the old binding and rebind that book in hand-tooled leather.

"I'm something of a photographer. I have a dark room and a very good enlarging camera. I like to prowl around with a camera and take such pictures as appeal to me. Interesting bits of light and shadow. The various moods of nature. The morning sunlight filtering through an oak tree. The turmoil of a breaker as it hisses up on a sandy beach after a storm.

"I think it is given to all men to appreciate beauty and while I'm willing to admit that my appreciation of art in my younger years was for more animate objects," and Carlin smiled reminiscently, "I now have adopted a philosophic attitude and worship a more impersonal beauty.

"And now, Mr. Mason, *I've* been frank with *you*."

Mason said, "I'm a lawyer. I'm trustee for the secrets of my clients. Many things I'd like to reveal, I can't tell."

"I understand that," Carlin said. "But let's hear the things you *can* tell."

Mason said, "I'm going to tell you very frankly that I don't know the identity of my client."

"The deuce you don't!"

"That's right."

"And do you accept clients under such circumstances?"

"Not as a rule. This case is different. I have a message for you."

"What is it?"

Mason took the newspaper clipping from his pocket. "First of all, I was asked to show you this clipping."

Carlin arose from his chair, walked across the room, took the clipping from Mason's hand, and said, "This means nothing to me. However, let's see what we have here— Hmmmmmm— Well. . . . Seems to have to do with some young woman who was arrested for cutting corners."

"Do you know her?" Mason asked.

"Good heavens, no!"

"Or perhaps you at one time had something to do with—

well, you'll pardon me, Mr. Carlin, but perhaps at one time there was an attempt made to blackmail you?"

"Definitely not. Perhaps, Mr. Mason, the message you were to deliver will clarify the situation."

"The message," Mason said, "was that under the circumstances you would have to get another partner."

Carlin frowned. "Who gave you that message for me?"

"Frankly, I can't tell you."

"Can't or won't?"

"Either way you want to take it."

"The message is as it was given to you?"

"Exactly."

"In writing?"

"No."

"The words 'under the circumstances'—what did they refer to?"

"I don't know."

"They were part of the message?"

"Very definitely."

Carlin frowned thoughtfully, then, after a moment, shook his head. "Mr. Mason, I have no partners."

"Isn't there perhaps some joint venture, some . . . ?"

Carlin interrupted. "Mr. Mason, I have no partners, no intimates, no associates."

Mason said, "Perhaps the message refers to some business deal, some . . ." He broke off as he saw expression suddenly flood into Carlin's eyes. "There *is* a business deal?" Mason asked.

Carlin waited for the space of a deep breath. "No."

Mason watched the man. "You're certain?"

"Yes."

"Well," Mason said, "that's my errand."

"I see nothing particularly urgent about that," Carlin told him.

"Circumstances made it seem urgent to me," Mason said.

"What circumstances?"

Mason smiled. "I told you I was a lawyer and, as such, trustee for my clients' secrets."

"And a good trustee you are, too."

Mason said nothing.

"Since you can't or won't tell me more, I'll be forced to speculate."

"Go ahead."

Carlin, holding the cup without a handle in his stubby-fingered hand, said abruptly, "It may take me a little while, but I'll come up with the answer."

"And then?" Mason asked.

Carlin merely smiled.

"Will you tell *us* the answer?" Della Street asked Carlin.

"How do I know? I'll have to find out what the answer is first." He sipped more coffee from the cracked cup.

Abruptly Carlin said, "The human mind is a wonderful instrument. We would be able to solve many mysteries if only we would concentrate. We could solve the riddle of life and death if we'd really try, but we are afraid, Mr. Mason; we are terribly afraid. Our whole lives are ruled by fear."

"You mean of death?" Della Street asked, her glance at Mason showing she would try to draw Carlin out.

"I mean fear of ourselves," Carlin said. "Man is more afraid of himself than of anything that can possibly happen to him. He's afraid to be alone with himself. He's afraid to get to know himself. He's afraid to search himself."

"I hadn't noticed it," Della Street said.

Carlin regarded her speculatively. "When people get together for an evening, they bring out a deck of cards and start playing gin rummy, or canasta; or they turn on the radio; they watch television; or perhaps they dash out to a movie."

"Don't you think all normal people crave companionship?" Della Street asked.

"Yes. Only this is not a craving for companionship. It is man's fear of being alone with himself. So people huddle together. The babble of voices drowns out thought.

"However, I digress. Yet it was in an attempt to answer your question. I shall concentrate on certain pertinent mat-

32

ters pertaining to this message. In the end, if it really concerns me—which I doubt—I shall know the things you are not at liberty to divulge, Mr. Mason."

"You still feel the message has no significance for you?" Mason asked.

"Yes. Actually I think your client has the wrong Carlin, Mr. Mason."

"No," Mason said, "you were described to me. Your name, the address . . ."

"Certainly," Carlin interrupted. "I credit you with having made your part in the affair absolutely certain. The mistake is on the part of your client."

"In what way?"

"Suppose your client had a message to be delivered to an individual by the name of Carlin. That client is not certain of the initials, but, let us say, uses the telephone directory, and perhaps due to some complicating factor, which you do not realize at the present time, gets the wrong Carlin. Therefore the mistake is, so to speak, passed on to you and. . . . Well, you are a very distinguished man and a delightful visitor, Mr. Mason. It has been an opportunity to spend an enjoyable half-hour, to meet you and talk with you. I am very much afraid your visit has been mutually unprofitable otherwise." And Carlin gravely handed Mason back the newspaper clipping.

Mason said, "I was hoping you could give me some information about . . ."

"About your client?" Carlin asked, smiling, as Mason hesitated.

"Perhaps."

"I gather your employment, if one might so describe the relationship of an attorney to a client, is something rather recent," Carlin said. "Quite obviously you haven't had an opportunity to talk with this client, therefore some message must have been delivered to you. On account of the lateness of the hour I assume the message was not delivered to your office. Because Miss Street is with you I assume that the message was not delivered after you had gone to your apartment. Therefore it was a message you must have received while at a late dinner at the Golden Goose, which is where you said you were when you telephoned."

Mason smiled. "You seem to enjoy deductive reasoning."

"I do," Carlin said. "After all, man was given a mind. Why shouldn't he use it? . . . However, I'm remiss in my duties as host. Do let me fill up these coffee cups."

He moved with alacrity, filling the coffee cups, passing the cream and sugar, then he sat down, adjusted his glasses on his nose. His face twisted into a whimsical smile.

"Remarkable characters," he said, "if you don't mind my saying so. Your faces would photograph well. I don't usually do portrait work. I like to express the things I see in terms of light and shadow. I like the long shadows of morning, the slanting of the sun's rays in the afternoon, but occasionally I do a bit of portrait photography. I like to figure out how shadows and highlights can express the personality on a man's countenance, how a trick of lighting can bring out the delicate feminine charm of a woman. I should like to photograph you sometime when the occasion presents itself, when it is—not so late."

Mason glanced at Della Street. They sipped coffee. Mason said, "Well, we must be on our way. It's quite late and . . ."

"I could have bitten my tongue off after I'd said that," Carlin said contritely. "I don't know why a person so frequently says things which require explanation and then realizes that the explanation has a tendency to overemphasize the error.

"The hour is not late for me. I was thinking only of you and—if you'll pardon me, a photographer who doesn't rely heavily on retouching, who likes to embody true character in his pictures, prefers to have his subjects fresh in the morning rather than catching them at the close of a long and arduous day.

"Personally, Mr. Mason, I hate retouching. I feel that everything can be done with lights and shadows."

Mason glanced at his wrist watch. "Please don't feel I

34

was referring to your remark. It's well after midnight. We must be on our way, otherwise we wouldn't be fresh enough for a photograph in the morning, and . . ."

"You mean you'll come in the morning and give me an opportunity . . . ?"

Mason laughed. "It was just a generality. Perhaps some day, Mr. Carlin. Well, thank you very much for your hospitality. Some other time I'd like to discuss your philosophy of life at greater length and to look at some of your photographs."

"It would be a pleasure," Carlin said, moving slightly forward in his chair as though waiting for them to arise.

Mason got to his feet.

"Thank you very much for coming," Carlin said, and then smiling at Della Street, added, "Just when a man thinks he is entirely self-sufficient in a masculine world and has learned to appreciate the beauty in nature rather than in more animate forms, something happens to show him how wrong he is."

"Thank you," she smiled, getting up from her chair and walking toward the hallway.

"You would make an excellent photographic subject," Carlin said hopefully. "I trust that before too long you and Mr. Mason will find time in your busy schedule to drop by. It won't take more than—oh, shall we say half an hour? Fifteen minutes apiece will do the job very nicely. And you must see some of my photographs and look at my studio. But now I know it's late and you doubtless have had a hard day. I realize that the life of a prominent and busy attorney is very exacting."

Carlin opened the front door. "Well, well, here's good news! It's breaking away. You can see the edges of clouds scudding across the heavens, and—look at that moonlight on the cloud. Notice that silvery sheen. It's one of my trials and tribulations as a photographer that so far no lens and no film have been made fast enough really to photograph the spell of moonlight. However, we're progressing very rapidly.

"Of course, you understand that all of the commercial moonlight photographs are taken at very high speed in sunlight. The camera is pointed directly toward the sun and the lens stopped way down and the shutter speeded up. Sometime we'll be able to get a true picture of the delicate charm of moonlight and not the harsh effects of sunlight.

"However, I mustn't keep you. It's turning cold and I know you're anxious to get started. Be careful. At this hour there are quite a few drunken drivers tearing through the intersections."

"We'll be careful," Mason promised.

"And you *will* come back and let me . . . Well, I am not going to ask for a promise because I realize how difficult it is at times to keep promises, but the invitation is open and my name is listed in the telephone book as, of course, you know, since you called me. Good night, and it was a real pleasure to meet both of you."

Mason and Della Street said good night, thanked him for his hospitality, watched the door swing slowly shut, then groped their way through the dark, down the cement walk to the curb where Mason's car was parked.

"Well?" Mason asked.

"He frightens me," Della Street said.

"Why?"

"I don't know."

"Womanly intuition?"

"I guess so."

Della Street reached out before Mason could grasp the door handle, pulled the door open, jumped in with a quick swirl of skirts and a flash of leg. She pulled the door closed, said, "Let's get away from here."

Mason walked around the car, climbed in behind the steering wheel, said, "Tell me more about the feminine intuition, Della."

"I think *he's* frightened, too."

"You believe that our message meant something to him?"

"I think it meant a great deal to him."

36

Mason started the motor, eased the car into motion and said, "He gave himself away just once."

"How? I didn't notice it."

"When I handed him that clipping," Mason said, "he didn't more than glance at it before saying that it meant nothing to him. If he had been really trying to ascertain what was in the clipping he would have read it through before expressing himself. As it was he took it and said almost immediately that it meant nothing to him. However, if he was acting, you have to admit it was a marvelous job."

Della Street nodded. "He didn't turn a hair. Afterwards he didn't seem nervous or hurried, yet somehow he managed to get rid of us very adroitly by calling attention to the lateness of the hour."

"But you think he was disturbed?"

"Chief, I think that man is as badly frightened as it's possible for him to be."

"All right," Mason said. "I wouldn't be prepared to go that far, but I'll agree with you that the message was for him and meant a lot to him."

"Why are you slowing down, Chief?"

"We're looking for the first public phone we can find."

"Better swing over to the boulevard then," Della Street said. "You'll find some all-night cafés catering to the through traffic, and nearly all of them have pay phones. Whom are we calling?"

"The Drake Detective Agency," Mason said. "We'll see if Paul happens to be around. If he isn't, I'm going to use his private number, get him out of bed and start him on the job."

"Doing what?"

"I'm going to put a tag on M. D. Carlin."

Mason turned into the boulevard and within four blocks found a café from which he was able to get Paul Drake on the phone.

"Have a heart, Perry," the detective protested. "I'm dog-tired. I'm just winding up a case and for two hours now have been looking forward to crawling into bed. I'm all in."

37

"This is nothing that needs to worry you personally," Mason said. "Do you have some men you can send out on a job right quick?"

"What do you mean by quick?"

"Right now."

"No. Wait a minute. One of these men who's been working on this other job might like to work. He's only had three or four hours."

Mason said, "Okay, Paul. Get this. Medford D. Carlin, 6920 West Lorendo. Telephone Riverview 3–2322. A man around sixty, bullet-headed; face absolutely devoid of expression except when he gives a peculiar lopsided smile; about five feet six and a half, or seven inches; weight about a hundred and seventy-five or a hundred and eighty pounds; living alone.

"I want men to cover that house. I'm particularly interested in finding out who may come to call on him."

"Anything else?"

"In case he goes out, I want to know where he goes."

"You think he's going out?"

"I have an idea he is. How soon would it be possible for you to get someone on the job?"

Drake said, "What's that address? 6920 West Lorendo. Let's see, it'll take . . . If this man wants to work on the job he should get there within fifteen to seventeen minutes, Perry. But he's already had one case today, and . . ."

"That's fine, Paul. Let's start with him. How long will it take to get another man on the job?"

"That's a question," Drake said. "Just hold the phone a moment."

Mason could hear Paul Drake talking to someone who apparently was seated near the telephone, then Drake said, "Hello, Perry. I've got one man on the way. I'm instructing him to follow Carlin if Carlin leaves the place. Is that right?"

"That's right."

"On a plant of this kind," Drake went on, "we usually have one man watching the front door, then we have a man

38

out where he can watch the back, and one man held in reserve. In case someone comes to the place and leaves by the front door, one of the men in front follows him. If the party should leave by the back door the man in back will follow. Then the man in reserve in front would move around to the back and in case someone else comes . . ."

"I'm not interested in the mechanics of the thing," Mason interrupted. "It's about twelve-fifty now, and I want action. I think Carlin is going places. I'm afraid he may go before your man can get on the job."

"He'll have to work fast if he does. Remember I have one man on his way. This chap's a good driver and there's not too much traffic right now. He'll be there. Soon as you hang up I'll get started on the others."

"Okay," Mason said. "Give me a report in the morning."

He hung up the telephone, said to Della Street, "How about something to eat?"

She shook her head. "Not me. How about you?"

"I'm fine."

"I could use quite a bit of shut-eye," Della Street said. "It's been a tough day. In case you're interested, the exact time of your conversation with Paul Drake was twelve-fifty-two A.M."

"Make a note of it," Mason said.

"I already have," she told him, smiling.

Chapter 4

Mason heard the steady rhythm of the bell on his unlisted telephone breaking through his slumbers. He fought his way back to consciousness, groped for the chain on the bed light, closed his eyes against the dazzling brilliance, picked up the receiver and said, "Hello."

Paul Drake's voice over the wire sounded crisply businesslike. "Hate to bother you, Perry," he said, "but they woke *me* up and I decided I'd pass the buck to you."

"Shoot."

"Carlin's place is on fire."

"How serious?"

"Apparently it's pretty serious. There was sort of an explosion at five minutes past three and . . ."

"What time is it now?"

"Three-twenty."

"You mean it's been going on for fifteen minutes," Mason asked, "without . . . ?"

"Keep your shirt on, Perry," the detective told him. "My man had to drive half a mile to an all-night service station. He telephoned the fire department, then he telephoned me and made a report, and I telephoned you. All of that took time."

"All right," Mason said. "I'm going out there."

"I'll meet you there," Drake told him, and hung up.

The lawyer jumped out of bed, starting to peel off his pajamas almost before he hit the floor. He dashed to the closet, jumped into a pair of slacks and golf shoes, pulled on a heavy turtle-necked sweater, made certain he had his keys and wallet, and didn't even take time to switch out the lights as he left the apartment.

Some ten minutes later a patrol car pulled alongside Mason's speeding automobile. A belligerent officer rolled down the window. "Hey," he yelled, "where the hell's the fire?"

Mason, keeping his foot on the accelerator, barely turned his head. "6920 West Lorendo."

The officer consulted a chart of fire calls. "That's the address all right," he said to his companion.

The driver shook his head sadly. "In twelve years on the force," he said, "that's the first time a speeder ever gave the right answer to *that* question."

Within a dozen blocks of the Lorendo Street address, Mason was able to detect a faint ruddy glow in the sky, but by the time he had arrived at the fire lines, he realized the fire department was rapidly getting the fire under control.

Paul Drake, who had already made contact with the officers and arranged for Mason to go through the fire lines, led the lawyer to within some fifty feet of the burning building.

Standing in back of one of the fire wagons, listening to the hiss of water on live embers, the rhythmic throbbing of the fire engines and the sound of solid streams of water impinging on the walls of the building, Mason looked at Paul Drake inquiringly.

"Want it now?" Drake asked.

Mason pulled up his sweater collar. "Gosh, it's turned cold! Okay, Paul, let's have it."

The detective looked carefully around to make certain that their actions were unobserved. "I couldn't get all three men here at the same time. I felt you wanted action so I rushed them out as I was able to pick them up."

Mason nodded.

"The first man on the scene," Drake said, "got here at seven minutes past one. He started watching the front door. The house was dark. Shortly before one-thirty (my man clocked it at one-twenty-eight) a woman turned the corner up there, hurried down the street, then walked up the steps and entered this house."

41

"Ring the bell?"

"She *seemed* to have a key that fits the lock or else the door was open. My man couldn't be certain which."

"What did the woman look like?"

"Around thirty to thirty-five, apparently a nice figure. Hard to tell much because of the raincoat."

"She went in?"

"That's right."

"When did she come out?"

"Now there," Drake said, "you have us stumped. We don't know that she came out."

"Go ahead. What happened?"

"At one-fifty my second man got here, and at two-five, or a minute or two before, the third man arrived. His notebook says two-o-three A.M.

"The second man took up his position where he could command a view of the alley and the back of the house, and the third man was to act as general relief, a tail on anyone who left, and be ready to carry messages.

"This third man cased the joint before he got on the job. He knew that the other two would be out there ahead of him and he wanted to get a description of Carlin. He located an all-night service station about half a mile down the boulevard and, as luck would have it, struck pay dirt right away. Carlin trades there. He has a credit card and charges his purchases. He has a Chevvie that he bought in 1946, right after the restrictions were loosened on the buying of automobiles."

"What's the description?"

"About sixty-one or sixty-two; high cheekbones; bullet head; wears glasses; lopsided smile; about five feet seven; weighs about a hundred and sixty-five pounds."

"That's our man all right," Mason said. "What else?"

"Well, my third man came out and reported on duty. They kept the place pretty well sewed up. The man in front reported that there was a woman in the house who might or might not be living there. They arranged a series of signals so they could pick anyone up for a shadowing job from either the back door or the front door."

"And this woman didn't come out?"

"Not unless she went out the back door before my second man got on the job."

"No sign of life inside the house?" Mason asked. "That is, when the fire broke out?"

"No sign of life then or up until the present time."

"Not so good," Mason said.

Drake nodded.

"Tell me about the fire."

"Well, just about five minutes after three there was the sound of a muffled explosion from the inside of the house. For two or three seconds nothing happened and then all of a sudden a glow began showing in the windows.

"My man jumped in his car, raced to the service station, called the fire department, called me and then came back here. The other two men kept their stations at the front and rear of the house. No one came out. Of course, it took a little dodging to keep from being conspicuous, but after the flames attracted attention and people began to leave adjoining houses it wasn't too difficult."

"They're certain the woman didn't come out?"

"She's still in there unless she left by the back door before one-fifty."

"Police talk with you?" Mason asked.

"Not yet, but they will—if it's a police job!"

"Okay," Mason said. "Tell your men not to volunteer any information."

"They won't."

"I mean about how long they were here."

"They won't tell anyone anything, Perry. You can trust these boys."

Mason paused to study the situation. "They're getting the fire under control, Paul?"

"Very rapidly," the detective said. "Ten minutes ago it looked as though the whole house was going, but now

43

they're going to save the walls and probably quite a bit of the downstairs."

"Where did the fire start?"

"Apparently on the second floor. The place is a firetrap. If it hadn't been for my men being on the job and getting in such a prompt alarm there wouldn't be anything there right now except a pile of embers. In another five minutes the firemen will go in. They're drenching it down with water. Men are on the roof now. That shows they have the interior fire pretty well under control and don't think there's any chance of a collapse. The east side of the roof is pretty well gone, but this west side is all right. The whole fire seems to have centered on the east side of the house."

Mason said meditatively, "I'd certainly like to see the inside of that house."

"It'll be a mess," Drake warned. "Water will have drenched everything and the inside will be all soggy, water-soaked embers and charred wood. You get in there now and your clothes would stink for a month. You couldn't get that smell out of them."

"Nevertheless," Mason said, "I should like *very* much to get in there."

"I can fix it up," Drake said. "It'll take some sort of a story. Suppose you're the man's lawyer, making a will and . . ."

"No," Mason interrupted, "that won't do."

"Well, you think up one that *will* do."

"That's what I'm mulling over in my mind. It isn't going to be easy."

"Why not tell them the truth for a change?" Drake asked.

"The truth is that a mysterious woman client wanted me to give a message to Carlin. I don't want the police to know about that—not just yet."

"Why?"

"I don't know what we're going to find on the inside."

"Would that make any difference?"

"It might."

"What other reasons?"

"I'm not certain my client wants the police to know that she was interested."

"Who is your client?"

"I don't know."

"Then the police won't."

"The police might be able to find out, and then there would be embarrassing questions."

"Well," Drake said, "if you're going to concoct a story, for heaven's sake get one that will sound reasonable. Here's the deputy fire chief working over this way. We're going to have to do something fast. He'll turn back here, spot us and—oh-oh, here he comes now."

The deputy chief came slogging over toward the two men.

Drake said, "Hi, Chief, how are you? Do you know Perry Mason?"

"The lawyer?"

"That's right," Mason said, shaking hands.

"Well, I'll be damned. What are *you* doing here?"

"Watching the fire. It looks as though you have it about under control."

"It's all finished now. Just a question of soaking the thing down and seeing that there are no latent sparks to catch later on. Sometimes when the floors drop you get a pocket of embers that'll break out after a while, so we just make it a rule to give the thing a good soaking and then go in and look it over."

"You're going inside?"

"Very shortly."

"Looking for anything specific?"

"Bodies."

"Oh," Mason said, his voice indicating interest, "like that, eh?"

The deputy chief looked at him sharply. "In a dwelling house at this time of night, when we find a fire with no one around on the outside, there's always the possibility that someone hoisted a few drinks too many, decided to light a cigarette, went to sleep and set the bedding afire. It's happened thousands of times before and it'll happen thousands of times again."

Mason, glancing at Paul Drake, said, "I'm interested in your technique of fighting a fire of this sort. Now, as I understand it . . ."

"It's a technical subject," the deputy chief interrupted, "just as technical as practicing law, only you don't have so much time to fool around making up your mind. What *I'm* interested in is how *you* two happen to be on the job, particularly in view of the fact that we can't seem to find who turned in the alarm."

"Probably one of the neighbors," Mason said.

"You still haven't answered my question."

Mason said, "As a matter of fact I'm not exactly in a position to answer your question."

"Why not?"

"Well," Mason said, smiling affably, "let's just suppose that I had a client who wanted to buy this property and had asked me to look up the title. The fire could be a very important development, yet I could hardly state my interest."

"You got a client who wants to buy this property?"

"Don't be silly. I was merely pointing out that *if* such *were* the case I could hardly communicate the fact."

"Then I take it that *isn't* the case."

"I didn't say it was."

"I'm not asking you if it was, I'm asking you if it isn't."

"All right," Mason said, grinning, "it isn't. You shouldn't have been a fireman, you should have been a lawyer or a detective."

The man's steady, intense eyes studied Mason's poker-faced immobility of expression.

"We have to do lots of detective work in our line," the deputy chief said. "Why do you suppose I'm out here?"

"To put out the fire."

"That's why my men are here. *I'm* here because the report was flashed into headquarters that it was an arson—an inside job, an explosion of gasoline or something of the sort. I want to take a look inside."

46

"So do I," Mason said.

"Me too," Drake chimed in.

"Nope. Too dangerous. Anything's apt to happen in there. Timbers will be weakened and falling, floors and stairways have been weakened by fire and may collapse. I'm going in alone."

"Of course," Drake pointed out, "you could outfit us with helmets and . . ."

"I could," the officer told him, "but I'm not going to."

One of the firemen winked a flashlight and the deputy chief said, "That's the signal. I'm going in. You two better stick around. I want to find out a little more about this."

He walked away.

"Hang it," Drake grumbled, "I know the man in charge. If it hadn't been for the deputy chief showing up we'd have been sitting pretty. Now the deputy chief knows you're here and he knows I'm here and if it's an incendiary fire he's going to be *plenty* suspicious."

Mason said, "Paul, have your men start working on the neighbors and see what they can uncover."

"How're you going to find the neighbors in this mob?"

"Easy. You're a hell of a detective. The neighbors will be standing around with overcoats thrown over pajamas, talking excitedly to each other. The neighbors will know each other. People from farther down the street are more apt to be strangers. Have your men spot the groups that are talking and . . ."

"Okay," Drake said, "I'm on my way. You wait here."

Mason stood watching the house, which was now illuminated only by the powerful searchlights from the fire-fighting apparatus. There was no longer any glow of flames. A steamy smoke emanated from the building, carrying the characteristic smell of wet, charred wood mingled with the odor of burned upholstery.

For the moment there were no streams of water playing on the outside of the building. Two lines of hose had been snaked in through the windows and from the interior came the flicker of lights as powerful flashlights moved around the inside of the building.

The rain had ceased and it had turned cold. Mason, standing there in the damp chill of early morning, wished that he had brought a heavy overcoat. The spectators, now that there was no longer the warmth of the burning building and the excitement of action, began melting away.

Drake came back to Perry Mason and said, "Okay. My men are working under definite instructions. All three of them are rounding up people, finding out all they can learn, and then they're going to beat it by the time the deputy chief comes out of the building. It might not be a bad idea if you and I were out of the way where *we* couldn't be questioned. I've arranged to get a report on anything new at my apartment and I have some things up there I think you'd be interested in."

"What?"

"Some hot water, spices, a cube of butter, a little sugar, and a big slug of rum. A fine hot buttered rum about this time would . . ."

"What the deuce are we waiting around here for?" Mason inquired.

"That," Drake said, "is the point I was trying to make."

"You've already made it," Mason told him.

Chapter 5

The steam heat was off in Drake's apartment, but by lighting the oven of the gas stove in the kitchenette and turning on a small electric heater, Drake managed to get a small area of reasonable warmth.

"That's my kick about California," Drake complained. "You get colder here than any place in the country. They rave about the mild climate. They turn the heat on at six in the morning, shut it off at eight-thirty, turn it on again from four-thirty until nine-thirty, then shut it off for the night. . . . Here, try this."

He poured a steaming hot rum mixture into a mug in which there was a big chunk of butter, stirred it with a spoon, handed it to Mason, and poured a steaming drink for himself.

They lit cigarettes, sat smoking, and sipping their drinks, waiting for the telephone to ring.

Mason shifted his position in the straight-backed kitchen chair and said, "That certainly does hit the spot, Paul."

"Best thing on earth," the detective said, "when you've been out on a cold assignment. Other drinks don't mean so much to me, but hot buttered rum is a lifesaver. Here, let me fill it up."

He reached for the container, refilled Mason's mug, then filled his own.

"What is this? A secret formula?" Mason asked.

"Oh, it's something I've worked out by rule of thumb," Drake said. "A little cinnamon, a little sugar, lots of rum, butter, water, and then I put . . ."

The telephone rang.

Drake abruptly put the mug down on the drainboard of

the sink, walked into the other room, lifted the receiver and said, "Hello."

He waited a moment, then nodded to Mason and said into the transmitter, "All right, Pete, go ahead."

Drake listened for something over a minute, then he said, "No one spotted you? . . . Well, I guess that's all you can do for tonight. . . . Where are you now? . . . Okay, I'll call you back inside of ten minutes. Wait there for my call. It'll be within ten minutes. Let's make sure I've got that number right. Give it to me again."

Drake copied the number on a scratch pad which was affixed to the telephone, said, "Okay. I have it. Thanks."

He hung up, walked back into the kitchen and said to Mason, "They found a body."

"Burned to death?" Mason asked.

"That," Drake said, "is the question. Probably not."

"How can they tell?"

"Thanks to our men, the fire department got on the scene sooner than would otherwise have been the case. The boys at the fire department aren't sticking their necks out, but they don't think the victim was burned to death. The fire seems to have been in an adjoining room and this corpse is burned but not charred."

"You know this deputy chief pretty well?"

"Sure," Drake said. "He's a smart guy."

"Think he's apt to be right?"

"He's apt to be right."

"That," Mason said thoughtfully, "complicates the situation."

"Of course," Paul Drake pointed out, "it's just his opinion. We'll see what the doctors say."

Mason said, "A burned body assumes what they call a pugilistic attitude. Looks as though it had been standing in the ring, fighting, when it was suddenly enveloped by flames. The firemen must have had a lot of experience. Would they move the body, Paul?"

"Not this body," Drake said. "They telephoned for the homicide squad. They evidently have some pretty good lead. Lieutenant Tragg was on his way out when my men ducked for cover."

"Where is your man now—the one who phoned?"

"At an all-night café."

"Find out anything from the neighbors?" Mason asked.

"Quite a bit of stuff. He's going to type a report and have it on my desk in the morning."

"What was this body, man or woman?"

"Man," Drake said. "About sixty. Physical description seems to match the description of Carlin."

"I was afraid of that," Mason mused.

"My operative," Drake went on, "gave me just a thumbnail report. There's a lot of stuff he wants to put in writing. He'll have it on my desk at eight-thirty in the morning. He says it was an incendiary fire all right. It had been touched off with a time bomb. The police think this was worked through an electric clock that was plugged in on the lower floor."

"The *lower* floor?" Mason said.

"That's right. It's one of those clocks that's designed to turn on a radio. You know, you can plug it in, fix the hands for any particular time and promptly on that hour the clock will turn on the radio. You have to turn it off by hand."

"Go ahead," Mason said.

"They found a clock connected on the lower floor with wires that had evidently been running upstairs. The clock had been set for three o'clock."

"Oh-oh," Mason remarked, and then added after a moment, "Where does that leave your woman visitor?"

"Probably right in the middle of a very complicated situation."

"What time was it she showed up?"

"One-twenty-eight."

"And no one knows how long she was there?"

"She couldn't have been there after one-fifty. That's when my man took up his station at the back door. From that time we had the house watched both front and back."

51

"When she entered, was she carrying anything with her? A suitcase, or anything?"

"Not a thing."

"Then she could hardly have carried a clock into the building, a jug of gasoline and all the other stuff."

"That's right."

"On the other hand, when she entered the house she must have found everything all set ready for the fire."

Drake nodded. "She was the last one in the house, all right."

"So she must have gone in the front door and out the back."

"That's right. . . . What about my operative? He's waiting out there at this café."

Mason said, "Telephone him to go home and type that report, then to keep out of circulation and not talk with anyone."

"We should report this to the police," Drake said.

"I'm representing a client."

"I have my license to think of," Drake pointed out.

"You're working for me, Paul."

"Just the same, we're supposed to let the police know what happened out there."

"How are you going to explain the fact that you had men on the job?"

"That's something I *could* hold out on," Drake said. "I could refuse to divulge the name of my client."

Mason grinned and said, "That would be like a candidate for office refusing to divulge whom he voted for when he walked out of the voting booth."

"Want some more hot rum, Perry?"

"No thanks. Guess we'd better get some more shut-eye. Lieutenant Tragg will be hot on our trail. He'll find out that we were out there and he'll be after both of us. Gosh, I got chilled out there."

"Ain't that liquor warming you up?"

"A little bit. Tell you what let's do, Paul, let's go up to the club and take a Turkish bath."

52

"You shouldn't take a Turkish bath right after you've had a hot toddy."

"It'll wear off by the time we get there. No one will think to look for us there."

"Tragg'll have kittens."

"Let him have them."

"Well," Drake said, "I'll call up my operative. Oh, say, Perry, there was one more thing."

"What?"

"In that house," Drake said, "there was something that didn't register. The police think it may have been mixed up in some dope-running, or something of that sort."

"How come?"

Drake said, "Remember that it was an old, ramshackle, rambling house. It had evidently been sparsely furnished, but there was one son-of-a-gun of a big fireproof safe on the lower floor, a regular humdinger of a safe."

Mason's eyes lit up. "Gosh, Paul, I'd sure like to take a look at the inside of that safe."

"So would the police."

"I wonder what the chances are of being on hand when the police get it open."

"Just about one in a million," Drake said.

"But suppose a man could furnish the police with the combination?"

Drake looked at him sharply. "The combination to that safe?"

"The combination to that safe."

"You're holding out on me?"

Mason pushed back the mug half full of unfinished hot buttered rum. "Okay, Paul," he said. "Call up your operative and tell him to make himself scarce. You and I are going to the club for a Turkish bath where Lieutenant Tragg can't find us."

Drake said, "I hate to dump good liquor down the sink, Perry. I . . ."

"Don't dump it down the sink," Mason told him. "Leave it there so we can point out to Tragg that I was chilled to the bone. It was only when the hot buttered rum didn't have any effect that I suggested we go to a Turkish bath. That'll make our story sound plausible."

"Oh yeah?" Drake asked skeptically, moving over to pick up the telephone.

He dialed the number of the all-night café where his operative was waiting, then said ominously over his shoulder, "If you have the combination to that safe, Perry, there isn't time enough between now and noon tomorrow to think up any story that'll make Lieutenant Tragg ... Hello.... Oh, hello, Pete. This is Drake. Okay. Go on home. Put all that stuff on paper and have it on my desk by eight o'clock. No one saw you down there? No one that recognized you?... Didn't know any of the firemen?... Okay.... Oh, sure, they'll spot you as one of my men but they won't know which one. Keep under cover until you hear from me.... Okay.... Good-by."

Drake hung up the telephone, said wearily to Mason, "Come on. I don't know why you're complaining about the cold. You're in hot water and it's going to get hotter from now on."

Chapter 6

Mason and Paul Drake were the only men in the hot room at this hour of the morning. They sprawled out on wooden deck chairs, sheets underneath them, wet towels wrapped turban-wise around their heads, their feet in tubs of warm water.

A huge bank of radiators around the side of the room kept the temperature high enough to start perspiration almost immediately on entering the room. The wood of the chairs was almost too hot to touch save where it was cooled by the perspiration-soaked sheets.

"This," Mason announced, "feels good. Gosh, I got cold standing out there on the wet pavement. My feet got so cold they were numb."

"*My* feet are still cold," Drake said gloomily. "I'd like to know just what you're getting me mixed up in."

"Why," Mason said, "my cards are on the table, Paul. I told you . . ."

"That combination of the safe," Drake said. "You didn't tell me anything about that."

Mason hesitated. "Well, Paul, it was—oh-oh!"

Drake followed Mason's glance through the heavy plate glass of the swinging doors.

A tall, well-knit man, whose shoulders bore the unmistakable stamp of a trained boxer, his back turned to the hot room, was talking with the attendant.

The attendant jerked his thumb in the direction of the hot room and the man turned, regarded the two nude, perspiring figures, grinned, and pushed the door open.

"Well," he said, "you fellows don't seem glad to see me."

55

"What's all the excitement?" Mason asked.

Lieutenant Tragg slipped off his coat. "You fellows made a tactical error. The last time you ducked out of sight I made it a point to check back and find out where you'd been. I found you were here, so I thought I might . . ."

Mason interposed hastily, "I got completely chilled. I was out at a fire tonight and never got so cold in my life. Neglected to take an overcoat and . . ."

"I heard about it," Tragg said. "You had a golf sweater on. Must have got up out of bed and dressed rather hastily."

He took a handkerchief from his pocket, wiped his forehead, said, "How about you fellows coming outside?"

"Couldn't think of it," Mason told him, glancing at Paul Drake. "We'd catch cold now. We've just started to sweat. How about taking your clothes off and having a Turkish bath, Lieutenant?"

"I have work to do. You know damn well *I'd* catch cold if I stayed here and then went out without taking time to cool off."

"Well, that's too bad," Mason said, "but go ahead, Lieutenant, we'll be glad to answer any questions."

Tragg said irritably, "Dammit, I can't stay in *here*!"

"Well, we can't go out," Mason told him.

Tragg ran the handkerchief around the inside of his collar, again mopped his forehead. "What were you two doing out there at the fire?"

"Watching it."

"Don't be smart. How did you know the house was on fire?"

"Paul Drake telephoned me," Mason said.

"How did Paul Drake know?"

"One of his men told him."

"Which one?"

"The one that was watching the house," Mason said.

"And why, may I ask, were you so fortunate as to be watching the house, waiting for the fire to break out, and . . ."

"Oh, we weren't waiting for the fire to break out," Mason said. "That was a complete surprise."

"All right," Tragg said irritably, "you two guys are up to something. Drake had a man out there watching the house. I want to know what happened. I want to know how long he was there. I particularly want to know who came and who went."

Drake said, "My man hasn't filed his report yet, Lieutenant."

Tragg said, "Hell, I can't stay in here. I've got work to do. Give me the name of the man. Where can I find him?"

"I don't know where you can find him," Drake said. "He's one of my night operatives. He's making out a report somewhere now. I told him he could go on home. But he's going to type out a report."

"When are you going to get that report? Come on, snap out of it. Kick through with whatever information you have. He must have told you all the important stuff."

Drake looked appealingly at Perry Mason.

Mason said suavely, "Drake is acting under my orders and I'm completely responsible."

"You're not responsible as far as the police are concerned," Tragg said grimly. "Paul Drake is running a detective agency. He has a license. I presume he wants to keep that license. That's okay by us, but when he has information in a homicide . . ."

"In a homicide?" Mason interrupted.

"Homicide," Lieutenant Tragg said. "Now look, I want the low-down on this thing, and I want it now."

Mason said, "It's a long story."

Tragg squirmed in anguish. "Hang it, I can't stay in here. You fellows come outside."

"I told you we couldn't go out now. We've just begun to sweat."

Tragg once more wiped his soggy handkerchief over his perspiring forehead, around the collar of his shirt and said, "All right. You win. I can't get all sweaty and then go out in this cold wind. When are you going to have this report, Drake?"

"In the morning."

"What time?"

Drake glanced at Mason.

"Eight o'clock," Mason said.

Lieutenant Tragg said, "If you know anything that'll help me find out who murdered Medford D. Carlin I want to know it now."

"I'm sure I don't know who murdered him," Mason said. "As I told you, Lieutenant, my connection with Carlin is a long story and . . ."

Tragg interrupted, "All right. I'll be at your office at eight o'clock, Mason. You be there, Drake. If you had any men covering that Carlin house, you have them there. If you're not there and the men aren't there, you'll be summoned to the district attorney's office, and if that doesn't work you'll be subpoenaed before a grand jury. I don't want any more funny business."

Tragg turned abruptly on his heel and pushed his way out of the hot room.

Mason looked at Drake. "The police are supposed to sweat the information out of witnesses, but this is one time we sweat the hell out of the police."

"It gives us about three hours," Drake said moodily, "and then we're really going to have to let our hair down."

"You'd be surprised at what you're going to do in three hours," Mason told him.

"Have a heart, Perry. You know damn well we can't work up a sweat and then go out in this cold wind without . . ."

"You can work up a sweat, take a cold shower, then sit down at a telephone and do a lot of telephoning," Mason told him.

Drake shook his head. "He's caught us with the goods, Perry. You know and I know he's right. He can force me to have those men there and he'll ask questions and they'll have to answer. You can protect your client, that's a profes-

58

sional privilege a lawyer has, but I can't protect anything. I've got to put my cards on the table."

"That's right," Mason told him, "the cards that you're holding as of now."

"As of now?" Drake repeated. "What do you mean?"

"We've got to have a fistful of trumps we can play immediately *after* we see Tragg this morning."

"Such as what?"

"Oh, several things. This mysterious client called me at the Golden Goose, that's the night club you recommended."

"Uh-huh," Drake said dispiritedly. "Good food, pretty fair dance music and good floor shows. A small place but . . ."

"I know," Mason interrupted. "The point is that you recommended it to me. Della and I went there on the strength of that recommendation. We went on the spur of the moment. Someone knew we were there. Now how would anyone know we were there?"

"You must have been shadowed."

"I don't think so, Paul. We'd been all over hell's half-acre hunting a witness and getting a statement. I think we'd have spotted a tail."

"Then someone must have been planted at the club to telephone when you came in there and . . ."

Mason shook his head. "They couldn't have done that because no one knew I was going to be there. I didn't even know it myself."

"Then how did this client know you were there?"

Mason said, "It had to be someone who was already at the club, Paul. Someone who was there when we walked in. Someone who had me pointed out, and *then* went out and called me."

"That sounds logical."

"And," Mason said, "the person who pointed me out may have been the headwaiter."

"And you think he'd remember?"

"I think he'll remember, but he may not want to talk. This woman saw me there, Paul. She left the place, drove home, opened a handkerchief drawer where she kept a nest egg for use in an emergency, put the money in an envelope, and rushed it to me at the night club by messenger. Then she went to a telephone and called me."

"Why did she do all that? Why didn't she just walk up to you and . . ."

"Because," Mason interrupted, "a woman wouldn't be at the Golden Goose without an escort. This woman didn't want her escort to know anything about her interest in me. She made some excuse to get out of there and go home. It has to be that way."

Drake nodded. "Well?"

"That means she was there with her husband."

"I don't get it. She could have told her boy friend she had a headache. . . ."

"Not to get rid of him that fast. And if it had been a boy friend, *after* she got rid of him, she'd have called the Golden Goose from her apartment, asked for an appointment, or tried to get me to go out there. I'm betting that she was with her husband, that something happened to frighten her, that I was pointed out to her, and that gave her an idea."

Drake ran a towel over his body. "It could be," he admitted.

"The woman," Mason went on, "made some excuse: that she'd left the gas on, or had forgotten to lock a door. She got out of there and went home. Her husband, of course, was with her. After she got home, she 'remembered' something she wanted to get at the drugstore before it closed. My client is a married woman, Paul, and she's living within a short walk of that drugstore. I want your men to have her located by eight-thirty, and not a minute *before* that time."

"That's a tall order," Drake said, rubbing a hand along his red torso. "I can't stay in here much longer, Perry."

"We've got to stay in here," Mason said, "until we're certain that Lieutenant Tragg has left and gone about his business. Then you're going to get on the telephone. By eight-thirty this morning I want to know who my client is."

"But Tragg's going to be in your office at eight, Perry."

"That's it," Mason said, grinning. "I don't want to have the information while Tragg is there, but I do want to get it just as soon as he leaves."

Drake adjusted the wet towel on his forehead. "You do give me the damnedest time schedules," he said irritably.

Chapter 7

Promptly at eight o'clock Tragg entered Mason's private office to find Perry Mason, Della Street and Paul Drake huddled in conference.

Mason seemed quite cheerful. Drake was definitely worried and Della Street, seated at her secretarial desk, a pencil poised over an open shorthand notebook, glanced up at Lieutenant Tragg with a smile of greeting which somehow seemed forced.

"Hello, Della," Lieutenant Tragg said. "Considering the elaborate preparations for this interview it must be even more important than I thought."

"Am I an elaborate preparation?" Della Street asked.

"Darned if you aren't," Tragg said, seating himself and abruptly losing his manner of easy banter as he turned to Mason and Drake. "A murder's been committed. I find you two guys were at the scene of the crime shortly after three o'clock in the morning. How come?"

Mason's voice was casual, but his words were carefully selected, as one who is giving a written statement that may be of the greatest importance.

"So far as Paul Drake is concerned, Lieutenant, I take entire responsibility for his being there. He was there at my request and under my orders."

"And your interest in the matter?"

"My interest in Carlin was due entirely to a client."

"What client?"

"I can't tell you."

"We keep going around this ring-a-rosy," Tragg said irritably, "and I don't like it. I know you're supposed to protect . . ."

"Please understand me," Mason interrupted. "I said that I *couldn't* tell you, Lieutenant, not that I *wouldn't*."

"Why can't you?"

"Because I don't know."

"The hell you don't."

"That's right."

"How did this client contact you?"

"Over the telephone."

"Man or woman?"

"Confidentially, it was a woman, but I don't want that given to the press. I don't want to read about it in the papers."

"And what did she say that put you in such a dither to get Paul Drake on the job?"

"Now that's something I *won't* tell you," Mason said.

Tragg thought that over for a moment, then turned to Paul Drake. "I don't like these lawyers with their professional privileges and all that stuff. Suppose you and I have a little heart-to-heart talk, Drake. You had men on the job. What time did those men go on the job?"

Drake pulled a notebook from his pocket. "The first one got on the job at seven minutes past one."

"There were others?"

"Yes, one at one-fifty."

"Did you have any more than these two?"

"I had three."

"What about the third?"

"He arrived at three minutes past two."

"Why three men on the job?"

"I wanted to have a shadow for anyone that left the house."

"Why all those elaborate precautions?"

"Those were my instructions."

"Anybody leave the house after your men got there?"

"After seven minutes past one, no one left by the front door."

"How about the back door?"

"After one-fifty, no one left by the back door."

"The fire started shortly after three?"

"That's right."

"Where were your men when the fire started?"

"Right there on the job."

"Why didn't they turn in an alarm?"

"They did."

"Why didn't you tell me?"

"You didn't ask me."

"All right," Tragg said, "I'm asking you now. I'm asking you for every single thing of any importance. One of your men made a report?"

"Yes."

"Where is it?"

"I have it here."

"Let's take a look."

Drake took the folded report from his pocket, handed it over to Lieutenant Tragg.

Tragg turned the typewritten pages, said in an aside to Perry Mason, "These guys always make it sound as though they were a whole secret service. These reports certainly are impressive. I wish I could get by with turning in stuff like this. Listen to this choice bit: 'Knowing that two other operatives were on the job, sewing the place up, I desired to get a physical description of the subject and case the neighborhood, so I located the service station where subject buys gas and oil on a credit card, and, by judicious inquiries, solicited the information that . . .' "

Tragg looked up and grinned. "You know what that really means, that when he got within a few blocks of the place he happened to see a service station that was open. So he stopped in and asked if the guy knew Carlin. The chap said he did, that Carlin got his stuff there, and this detective took five or six minutes to tell him that he'd gone to college with a man by the name of Carlin and knew he lived out in the neighborhood some place but didn't know exactly where; that he'd looked through the telephone book, found this man's name and address, and that he didn't want to disturb him unless it was his old college chum.

"So then the service station attendant tells him that that can't very well be because this Carlin is probably thirty years older than the guy who is making the inquiries. So the bird asks a few more questions and . . ."

"Have a heart," Drake interrupted, grinning. "You're spilling all this stuff in front of a cash customer. He probably thinks my man went through the district with a fine-tooth comb to find the place where Carlin got his gasoline, and then . . ."

"Yeah, I know," Tragg interrupted, "and still managed to get on the job only thirteen minutes after the second man arrived. Now what about this jane that went in at one-twenty-eight?"

"There," Drake said, "you've got me. She must have gone out the back door before one-fifty."

"And no one else came in after that?"

Drake said, "There's one possibility. It's just a possibility. This woman could have gone out before one-forty, say, and shortly after that someone could have gone in through the back door, stayed inside for ten minutes and still got out of the back door before my operative came on duty at one-fifty."

Tragg said to Mason, "Why all the rush, Perry?"

"I was protecting my client's interests."

"How does it happen you start spending money for all this high-priced detective service if you don't know the person who is your client?"

"She sent me a retainer."

"How?"

"By messenger."

"Where?"

"At the night club where we were dining."

"Which one?"

"The Golden Goose."

"What time?"

"Oh, I would say somewhere around ten minutes after eleven."

"What time was the call?"

"Right around eleven o'clock. Perhaps five or ten minutes afterwards."

"All right," Tragg said, "that's last night. You've heard from her again this morning?"

Mason shook his head.

"Don't hand me that line of talk, Mason. You know damn well she read the early morning edition of the paper, found out about Carlin being found dead and rang you up."

Mason shook his head. "I haven't heard a word from her."

"You will."

"Perhaps."

"If you do, I want to know who she is. I want to talk with her."

"That, of course," Mason said, "will depend on whether she wants to talk with you."

"This is a murder case, you know, Mason."

"What makes it look like murder?"

Tragg grinned. "The Chief is narrow-minded in such matters, Mason. He has the old-fashioned idea that the function of a police force in murder cases is to gather information rather than to distribute it."

"How quaint!" Mason said.

"I know, but he happens to be running the department."

Mason said very casually, "I understand there was a rather expensive safe in Carlin's residence."

Tragg paused, surveyed the lawyer with searching eyes. "What's that leading up to?" he asked.

"I was just asking."

"All right, you've asked the question—or was it a question?"

Mason said, "I might be able to help you out there."

"In what way?"

"How is the safe? Damaged by the fire? I mean, is it pretty hot?"

"No, it's on the first floor. The fire did most damage to the upper floor and the roof. What do you know about the safe?"

"I may not know anything about it," Mason said, "but there's just a chance, mind you, Tragg, it's just one chance in a hundred, that I might have the combination to that safe."

"The hell you might!"

"I mean I might be able to turn the dials and . . ."

"Never mind all that stuff. I want to know how you happened to get this combination."

"I don't know that I have it."

Tragg said angrily, "Look here, Mason, that safe is an important factor in the situation. We want to get it open and fast. I've had one man doing nothing but working on that since four o'clock, telephoning." Tragg grinned. "The officers of the company that made that safe haven't had much sleep since four. They've been down at their office looking up records. And their local representative, with all the dope, should be out there before long. But time is an important factor. If you're sitting there with the combination to that safe . . ."

"I don't know that I have it."

"Well, how the hell are we going to find out?"

"By trying it on the safe."

"How did you get it? Where did you get it? When did you get it? Why was it given to you?"

"You've complicated the situation now, Lieutenant."

"You're damn right I have."

Mason said, "Well, Lieutenant, when you do get the combination to the safe I'll be glad to sit down and discuss it with you. For instance, if it should appear that the first figure is fifty-nine four times to the right—well, then, I might be able to help you."

"And how do you expect us to find out if the first figure is fifty-nine four times to the right?"

"What about your factory expert?"

Tragg grunted. "I don't know that he'll have the combination. He'll probably have to drill into the lock and take the thing to pieces. No one knows how long it's going to take him. Come on, Mason, you're going for a ride."

"Where?"

"Obviously," Tragg said, "I can't lug that safe in here and dump it in your lap, so you're going out to the safe."

"And then what?"

"You're going to give me the combination and I'll try it out."

"I can't give it to you. I'm not at liberty to. It's confidential."

"All right," Tragg said, "you'll try out your combination on the safe. Come on, you're going places."

"How about the men who are waiting in Drake's office?" Mason asked.

"To hell with them," Tragg said. "This is a lot more important."

Mason arose with every suggestion of weary reluctance. "Oh, all right," he said. "I suppose that's what comes of trying to be helpful. Now I've got to lose a morning going out to try to open a safe for the police department."

He glanced at Della Street, lowered his right eye in a swift wink.

Chapter 8

The interior of the house was dark and gloomy. The odor of charred wood, of fire which had been extinguished by tons of water, clung to the place as an unpleasant aura.

The big safe stood in the far corner of what had evidently been a workroom.

The room contained furniture which had been shoddy even before black water, soaked with charcoal from the burning timbers above, had riveted through the holes in the ceiling, to soak the upholstery to the point of saturation.

Tragg indicated the safe and said, "Go ahead and open it."

Mason took a small fountain-pen flashlight from his pocket, moved over to the dials of the safe.

Lieutenant Tragg crowded closer.

"Don't breathe down my neck. You make me nervous," Mason said.

"I want to see what you're doing."

"I can't work that way."

"Do the best you can."

Mason leaned so close to the big combination, held the small flashlight cupped in his hand so near the dial that it was impossible for Lieutenant Tragg to see the figures as Mason rapidly spun the dial through the series of numbers which had been on the slip of paper he had picked up in the telephone booth.

The lawyer finished the last spins of the dial to number nineteen, twice to the right, then turned to the left until the combination stopped at ten.

He surreptitiously brushed his hand against the handle. It didn't budge.

"You finished?" Tragg asked.

"I haven't even started," Mason said. "I can't handle this combination with you standing there, all but pushing me to one side so you can see what I'm doing."

"Well, you tried hard enough. What happened?"

"I think I missed a number."

"You haven't tried it to see if it'll open."

"I'm certain I missed a number."

Lieutenant Tragg said, "I get you. Since I was watching to see what the combination was, you decided to send me on a wild-goose chase."

A siren sounded. Tragg and Mason moved over to a window.

Outside, a police radio car pulled up at the curb, two radio officers escorted a tall, gaunt man in his sixties into the house.

"This is Corning, from the safe company," one of the radio officers said.

"Glad to see you, Corning. Can you get this thing open without having to blast it?" Lieutenant Tragg asked.

"I think so."

"Just by fooling with the locks?"

"I don't think we'll have to do that, Lieutenant."

"Why not?"

"The safe has a number. A combination was set on the lock before the safe left the factory. My people have checked on our records of the billing of this safe, right through the jobber and dealer. The sale was made to Carlin about six months ago.

"A provision is made by which the dealer can change the combination on safes when they are sold. In this instance no request was made that the combination be changed. The factory had a record of the original combination. I doubt if the combination has been changed."

"Give it a whirl," Lieutenant Tragg said.

Corning stepped gingerly across the charred rubble on the floor. "Always afraid of sticking a nail in my foot," he said. "I had a friend one time who . . ."

"I know," Lieutenant Tragg interrupted, "died of lockjaw. Let's get the safe open."

They watched in silence while Corning took a small leather-backed notebook from his pocket, twisted the dial experimentally, then, with long, sensitive fingers, started twirling the combination.

There came a reassuring click from the interior mechanism. Corning twisted the twin handles on the safe, stepped back and jerked open the double doors.

The officers crowded forward.

"Well, I'll be damned!" Lieutenant Tragg said.

Mason moved forward to look over their shoulders at the interior of the safe.

It held nothing save a pile of charred papers.

"That's a hell of a safe," Tragg said. "A tin box would have been as good. This fire . . ."

"Don't be silly," Corning said. "The fire didn't even blister the paint on the safe. These papers were burned and put in the safe *after* being burned, unless . . ."

"Unless what?" Tragg asked.

"Unless they were coated with some chemical before being put in the safe, so there'd be a spontaneous combustion, or unless someone managed to work out a scheme by which . . ."

Tragg abruptly signaled the man to silence, turned to Perry Mason. "I don't think we'll need you any more, Counselor," he said. "In fact I'm quite certain of it."

Chapter 9

Mason called Paul Drake from a drugstore.

"Okay, Paul," he said when he had the detective on the line. "What have you found out? Who's my client?"

"What about the safe?" Drake asked. "Did you . . ."

"No," Mason interrupted, "I didn't. That can wait. What about my client?"

Drake said, "I put men to work on that Golden Goose. Those people go to bed about three o'clock in the morning and don't get up until afternoon. Trying to rouse them up and get information was a terrific chore. You can't find out where some of them live and . . ."

"Never mind all your hard luck," Mason interrupted. "You'll tell me about that when you present the bill. I want to know who my client was."

"Well, there are lots of things you should know in addition to my best guess on that," Drake said. "To begin with, this fellow Pierre, the headwaiter, whom you wanted investigated. He's a chunky Swiss, about sixty—and I can't get to first base with him."

"Won't he talk?"

"I can't find him."

"You mean he's skipped out?"

"He left the club around midnight last night, and no one has seen him since. We just can't find him, period. No one knows where he lives. There's an address listed on the employment register and he gets mail there, all right, but it's one of those places where you can have a cover-up address, a place where desk space and office facilities are rented, or you can have mail come there at so much a letter and telephone service if you want it."

"All right. What did you do with the others?"

"I got my only lead from the hat-check girl. Following your hunch, I told her I was interested in couples who came there regularly, who knew Pierre, who were probably married, and who had left early.

"Well, after we'd taken a tongue-lashing for disturbing her beauty sleep, given her twenty dollars to salve her injured feelings, and refresh her recollection, we secured the information that two couples had left rather hurriedly. Her description was more or less vague but we did know that two couples who were more or less regular customers left the place at about the time we mentioned.

"Now I'm not going to bore you with all the details. She didn't know their names. She knew one man was called a doctor and thinks he was an M.D. I found that the car hops who park the cars pool their tips with the doorman and make notes of the license numbers of the cars they park— well, anyway, I have a couple of names and addresses for you. Now, one of them is an M.D."

"Live anywhere near the drugstore at Kramer Boulevard and Vance Avenue?"

"No, he lives at the other end of town."

"Of course," Mason said, "my theory is that the woman must have walked to the drugstore unless they had two cars, and she was able to get a car out without attracting attention. Even so, she'd have been in a hurry and gone to the nearest telephone. But give me the dope, Paul."

"Dr. Robert Afton," Drake said, "residing at 2270 Evenrude."

Mason wrote down the name and address.

"You've checked him, Paul?"

"Checked the address. He's listed in the phone book."

"All right. What's the other?"

"Now this one," Drake said, "I'm not so sure about. The man goes alone to the Golden Goose quite a bit. The hat-check girl has seen him frequently. She thinks the woman with him last night was his wife. The car is listed in the name of Myrtle Fargo. I can't get the address. I can't find

73

Myrtle listed. She doesn't vote. There are a couple of dozen persons by the name of Fargo listed in the telephone book, but no Myrtle. The car is a Cadillac convertible, so it looks like we're dealing with money, but so far I can't find any Myrtle.

"The car registration lists Myrtle's address as Sacramento, so she must have left there within the last year. Now, if you want to stand the expense, Perry, I can put men on the job in Sacramento and check her from there, but I don't know just how strong you want to go on the thing."

Mason said, "The hell of it is I don't know, myself, Paul. Her name is Myrtle Fargo?"

"That's right. So far we've drawn a blank, but remember it's still early in the morning. She may have moved here a short time ago. She may be living in an apartment hotel where they have a switchboard and she gets her telephone service that way. The man who was with her may have been her husband or just a friend, and they were using the Golden Goose as a rendezvous."

Mason said, "Check all the Fargos in the phone book. Check them for addresses. See if there's a Fargo listed with an address near Vance Avenue and Kramer Boulevard."

Drake said, "I already have one of my girls doing that. Wait a minute, here's the answer I think. Hold the line . . ."

There was silence for a moment, then Drake said, "There are two in the neighborhood, Perry. There's an Arthman D. Fargo living at 2281 Livingdon Drive, and there's a Ronald F. Fargo living at 2830 Montcrief."

"Take a look at a map," Mason said. "Which one is closer to the drugstore on the corner of Kramer Boulevard and Vance Avenue?"

"Arthman D. Fargo is three blocks, and Ronald F. Fargo is about eight blocks."

"All right," Mason told him, "I'll take Arthman D."

"Going to walk right in and play it straight?" Drake asked.

"I don't know, Paul. I'll take a look at him and then play my hunches. I'll be seeing you in an hour or so."

Mason hung up the receiver, drove to the address on Livingdon Drive. A neat stucco house was fronted by a small but well cared for lawn, in the middle of which a sign mounted on a sharp steel spike bore the legend ARTHMAN D. FARGO, REALTOR.

Mason parked the car, walked up to the house and rang the bell.

It was a moment before he heard any motion, then he heard steps, the door opened and a man who was almost as tall as Mason, with the build of an athlete, said, "Good morning."

Mason couldn't see the faintest change in his expression. "I'm looking for Mr. Fargo."

"This is Mr. Fargo."

"I wanted to talk about some properties."

"Come in, please."

The man held the door open, and Mason entered.

Mason's nostrils detected stale tobacco smoke and the faint odor of cooking. The living room was simply but tastefully furnished. There was something about the way the newspapers were lying half-opened and propped up against a chair which made it seem they had been there for only a minute or two.

"My office is this way," Fargo said. "A little room I've fixed up."

He turned to the left, into what evidently had been designed originally as a downstairs bedroom, and opened the door, disclosing a small office in which there was a couch, a desk, a safe, a few chairs, two filing cabinets, and a typewriter perched on one corner of the desk.

The room was cold and dark, with the Venetian blinds tightly closed.

Fargo made haste to apologize. "I was doing some work in connection with listings this morning and the place hasn't warmed up yet. It rained last night, you know, and was cold. I'll switch on the electric heater and it will only take a second or two to warm it up."

He clicked a switch and almost immediately a concealed fan began gently circulating a current of warmer air.

"It'll only take a minute," Fargo apologized. "Sit down and tell me just what you had in mind."

Mason said, "I've got some free capital. I want to buy a place if I can find one that's a good bargain."

Fargo nodded.

"I want to get something that's priced well below the market. I want to be sure it isn't being sold because the neighborhood is going to pot, or because there are termites or dry rot, or anything of that sort."

"How high did you want to go and just what sort of a place did you have in mind?"

Mason said, "I'm buying for speculation. I have no particular limit except that I want to get something that is very definitely underpriced. Otherwise I'm not interested."

"Of course, such a thing as you want isn't going to be easy to find," Fargo said, "although I have some very good bargains listed. Did you intend to rent the property or live in it while you were holding it for an advance?"

"Rent it."

Fargo seated himself at the desk and started running through some cards.

"I have some good buys listed but not anything you might call a steal. When would you have an opportunity to look at some properties if I could get the listings together?" Fargo asked.

Mason consulted his watch, said, "As it happens, I have a little time on my hands this morning. Ordinarily I'm rather busy."

"I see. Would you care to leave your name, Mr. . . er?"

"Not yet," Mason said. "Perhaps a little later on. Nothing personal, you understand, but in the real estate business . . ."

"I understand," Fargo interrupted hastily. He glanced at the telephone on the office desk, said, "If you wouldn't mind waiting for just a few minutes, sir, I would like to check on one listing, but the data is in another part of the house."

"Quite all right," Mason said.

Fargo arose. "I won't be long. If you'll make yourself comfortable, please. I'll be right back."

He hurried from the room.

Mason stepped to the window, tilted the Venetian blind so he could look out at the front of the house to where he had left his car parked.

When he saw Fargo, who had evidently slipped out of the back door, tiptoeing toward his car, Mason, having taken the precaution of removing the registration certificate before he had parked the car, swung around to the safe back of Fargo's desk.

The safe was locked.

Mason spun the dial through the figures of the combination on the slip of paper he had found in the telephone booth in the drugstore. He tried the handle on the door. The bolts clicked back.

Mason heard steps and had just time to get back to his seat when Fargo entered the room, saying, "I've just checked up on a listing I have. The house has been withdrawn from the market. I'm sorry."

"That's too bad," Mason said.

Fargo's eyes met his. "How'd you like to buy this place?"

"You own it?"

"Yes."

Mason shook his head. "I told you I'm looking for bargains. You'd hardly offer this place on the terms I want."

"What makes you think I wouldn't?"

"Because you're in the business."

"You can steal this place—for cash."

"How much?"

"Eighteen thousand, just as it stands, including furniture. I'll just walk out."

"That's too much. The place is worth it, all right, but I'm after places that are priced so low ..."

"Seventeen thousand—furnished."

"That's a good price, but . . ."

"Sixteen thousand five hundred, and that's rock bottom."

"Let's take a look at it."

"I can be ready to show it in an hour, and . . ."

"I'm here now. Why can't I look it over right now?"

Fargo hesitated. "You're really interested in it at that price?"

"Furnished, yes."

Fargo hesitated. "My wife is in Sacramento, visiting her mother, and I am not much when it comes to housework. I . . ."

"I'm interested in the building," Mason said, "not in your neatness as a housekeeper."

"Well, if you'd like to look it over, come ahead."

Fargo led the way through the door, across the living room, and into the kitchen. "Nice big kitchen," he said. "Quite modern, good icebox, electric stove, electric dishwasher . . ."

Mason interrupted. "You say your wife's away?"

"Yes. She left this morning for Sacramento. She took the six o'clock plane. I drove her to the airport."

"Are you sure she'd agree to the sale?"

"Oh, yes, as it happens, we've been discussing this for some time, and I have her signature already appended to a deed and bill of sale."

"Wouldn't that signature require a notarial acknowledgment?" Mason asked.

"I can fix all that," Fargo said.

"Let's look some more," Mason told him.

Fargo showed Mason around the lower floor, then, starting up the stairs, paused to say, "There's one room I can't show you."

"Why not?"

"One of the bedrooms. It's my wife's room and things are in disorder."

"What's the matter with that room?" Mason demanded coldly. "I'd want to see the whole house before I decide."

78

"Certainly, certainly," Fargo said ingratiatingly. "Of course you would. You'd want to see it all, but this one room you would have to see a little later. It's—well, my wife packed very hurriedly and—you know how it is, catching a plane early in the morning. Her intimate garments and things are ... I'm quite certain she wouldn't want anyone to see the room at the moment. You could make an appointment to return. I'll show the other rooms to you now."

Fargo turned away with an air of finality, showed Mason the two upstairs bathrooms, three of the four bedrooms.

Mason made a point of regarding the door of the one closed bedroom with frowning disapproval, but Fargo remained firm. The door of that bedroom was closed, and it remained closed.

"Well, we'll take a look around the outside," Mason said. "The place looks good. I may make an offer."

"I'm afraid I won't consider an offer," Fargo said, trying to keep his tone firm. "I have made a bedrock price. It's a question of taking it or leaving it."

"Well, we'll talk about that when I've seen the place," Mason said.

He went down the stairs, followed Fargo out into the back yard, down into the basement, and around to the driveway at the double garage. There was a Cadillac convertible in the garage.

"I only have one automobile," Fargo said, "but there's ample accommodation here for two cars."

"I see," Mason said. "Those Cadillacs certainly are grand, aren't they? That's yours, I suppose."

"Yes, yes, of course. It's registered in my wife's name, but it's mine. Now if you're looking for bargains you can't beat this place."

Mason said, "I have another party—well, that is, I *might* live here myself. In that event I . . ."

"You mean your wife would want to see it?"

"Not my wife," Mason said, "the young woman who— well . . ."

"I understand," Fargo said.

"I'm not certain that you do."

"Does it make any difference if I don't?"

"No."

Fargo smiled.

Mason said, "I could bring her out here a little later on."

"I might be out," Fargo said. "I'm in and out all day."

"That's all right. I'll phone for an appointment."

"That will be quite satisfactory. Would you let me have your name, now?"

"Not yet," Mason said. "In real estate transactions I have found that it is a good idea to remain anonymous."

"But I should have some name so that when you telephone I . . ."

"You may call me Mr. Cash," Mason said, "and the initials are C. H."

"Mr. C. H. Cash," Fargo said.

"That's right, and the initials C. H. stand for cold and hard, so that the full name is Mr. Cold Hard Cash."

He shook hands with Fargo, walked rapidly to his car, drove to the drugstore at Vance Avenue and Kramer Boulevard, and, from the same telephone booth from which he had received the mysterious phone call the night before, called Paul Drake.

"Hello, Paul," Mason said, keeping his voice low and speaking rapidly. "You got some men all ready to put out on a job?"

"That's right. I'm holding some reserves here in the office."

Mason said, "I've struck pay dirt."

"With Fargo?"

"Yes."

"Which one?"

"The realtor on 2281 Livingdon Drive."

"His wife is your client?"

"Apparently so," Mason said. "I didn't see her."

"How do you know she's your client, then?"

"Because," Mason said, "I have the combination to the safe in Fargo's office."

"Oh-oh."

Mason said, "Get some men out here right away, Paul. I want Fargo's place covered. I want enough men so that you can tail anyone who leaves the place, and you're going to have to hurry."

"You think someone's going to leave?"

"I think he is."

"Know where he's going?"

"He's just going away," Mason said. "He wants to sacrifice his house, furniture and everything, and be on his way. I made a noise like a sucker and he tipped his hand. He thinks he's going to sell me the whole shooting works."

"Well, he won't get away then before you give him an answer," Drake said.

"I'm not certain just what he will do. He sneaked out and tried to look at my registration certificate. When he couldn't find that, he took the license number of my automobile. He'll look that up. The answer may start him moving."

"But look here, Perry, if you were pointed out to him in the night club he must know who you are and . . ."

"I evidently wasn't pointed out to *him*," Mason said. "The one I was pointed out to was his wife. I'll swear he doesn't know me. His face didn't change expression by so much as the flicker of an eyelash when he opened the door and saw me standing there on the threshold."

"But you must have been pointed out to the wife."

"That's right."

"Where is she now?"

Mason said, "Fargo *told* me that he had taken her in to the airport this morning to catch a six o'clock plane for Sacramento. She was going to visit relatives."

"You don't think he did?"

"I don't think he did."

"Why not?"

"Because," Mason said, "there was a cold drizzle up until midnight. I don't think he would have left his car parked at the curb. There's a door leading directly from the garage to the kitchen of the house."

"Well, what are you getting at? Didn't he drive the car into the garage?"

"If he did," Mason said, "he drove it in just once. There's a gravel driveway going up to that garage. It's quite soft. The car was in the garage and there was only one set of tracks going in. If he'd taken the car out to drive her to the airport and then driven it back, there would have been three sets of tracks."

"Where do you think the wife is?"

"She could be dead."

"In the house?"

"Could be," Mason said. "I talked him into showing me around. One room was closed, but as we stood in front of the door I distinctly heard someone breathing on the other side of the door, someone who was listening with an ear at the keyhole."

"The wife?" Drake asked.

"I don't know why, but I don't think so," Mason said.

"Okay, we'll get on the job."

Mason said, "I'm going back to keep an eye on that house. Get your men out there just as fast as you possibly can. They'll find me parked where I can tail the car in case it drives out. We're going to have to work fast. He doesn't know who I am now but he will by the time he gets my license number looked up."

"Okay," Drake said, "I'll tell my men to look out for you."

Chapter 10

Mason eased his car around the corner and parked at the curb. From that point he couldn't see the door of Fargo's garage but he could see the driveway.

Mason lit a cigarette and settled himself to wait until Paul Drake's men would come to take over.

He had hardly taken the first puff from his cigarette when a car backed rapidly out of the driveway. As it entered the street it turned so that the rear end was toward Mason, then the exhaust emitted a few puffs of smoke and the car moved rapidly down the street.

Mason pushed on the starter, gunned his motor into life and took after the Cadillac. There was no opportunity for finesse, no chance to disguise the fact that he was following the machine.

As Mason pushed his car into speed the car ahead of him increased its own pace until they were going some sixty miles an hour through a suburban residential district, showing only too well that the driver was aware of the following car and was trying to get away from it.

The top of the convertible was up, and the relatively narrow rear window was insufficient to give Mason any opportunity to get more than a vague glimpse of the driver.

The car drove smoothly through a boulevard stop without even pausing. Mason followed. He heard the scream of sliding tires as a car on the boulevard slewed around, trying to stop.

Mason kept his eyes on the car ahead. It swung into an abrupt skidding turn and vanished. At that instant a motorcycle pulled alongside Mason's car. A siren growled ominously.

"Pull over."

Mason said, "Look here, officer, I'm after a car ahead and . . ."

"Pull over."

"I'm chasing another car. I . . ."

"Pull over."

The lawyer, face red with anger, pulled over.

The officer pulled the motorcycle in to the curb, came alongside and said, "You can't hog the traffic like that. I watched you . . ."

"I'm chasing a car ahead. It may be . . ."

"Who's in it?"

"Someone who has to do with a case I'm investigating."

"You a detective?"

"No. I . . ."

"Connected with the Department?"

"No."

"Let's take a look at your license."

Wearily Mason produced his driving license, said, "I'm an attorney."

"Oh, Perry Mason, eh? Well, under the circumstances I'll let you go with a warning, Mr. Mason, but, regardless of the circumstances, you have to be more careful at intersections. You were taking all sorts of desperate chances there. People had to slam on brakes in order to avoid hitting you. Don't let it happen again."

"Thank you," Mason said. "Can I make a U-turn here?"

"I thought you said you were chasing a car?"

"I was," Mason told him with elaborate sarcasm.

The officer said, "I *could* give you a ticket, you know."

"I know," Mason told him.

For a moment there was silence, then the officer returned to his motorcycle, eased in the clutch and roared away down the block.

Mason made a U-turn and returned to the Fargo residence.

Cruising around the block, he had no difficulty in picking

up one of Drake's men parked in almost the same position where Mason had left his own car.

Mason swung in ahead of the detective's car and walked back to the man who was seated behind the steering wheel of the nondescript sedan.

The man rolled down the window.

"You're Drake's man?"

The man regarded Mason in thoughtful silence.

Mason produced his driving license. "I'm Perry Mason, the lawyer. I'm employing the agency to cover this case."

"Okay," the man said.

"How long have you been here?"

"About five minutes."

"Any sign of activity?"

"No one in, no one out."

Mason said, "The car I wanted to have followed made a getaway. I tried to tail it, but I got a bad break."

"It'll happen all right," the man said sadly. "Once a person knows he's being followed he can almost always lose a shadow. All he has to do is get into traffic and keep moving until he gets a break on a signal, then give it the gun and leave the other fellow behind to argue with the traffic."

"In my case," Mason said, "the argument was with a traffic officer."

The man's eyes regarded him sympathetically. "Well, you have one advantage."

"What's that?" Mason asked.

"You don't have to try to explain how it happened to Paul Drake and listen to him tell you what a job it's going to be explaining it to the client."

"Yes, I suppose so," Mason said, smiling. "I think the horse has been stolen but we'll watch the stable anyway."

He drove to the drugstore, telephoned his office, and when he had Della Street on the line said, "Want to grab a taxi and come out here and join me?"

"Where are you?"

"At that drugstore on the corner of Vance Avenue and Kramer Boulevard."

"Right away?"

"Right now."

"I'll be out within ten minutes," she said.

"Okay," Mason told her. "I'll be having a cup of coffee at the counter. What else is new? Anything?"

"Nothing too important."

"Okay. Pick me up out here."

Mason hung up, picked up a magazine at the newsstand, moved over to the counter, ordered a cup of coffee and killed time until a taxi deposited Della at the door of the drugstore.

Mason paid his check, moved out to join his secretary.

"What's the pitch?" she asked.

Mason said, "I'm buying a house. You're to be the bride."

"Oh-oh!"

"You won't make me a very good wife," Mason said.

"You underestimate me! What's wrong with me?"

Mason grinned. "You're too critical."

"Oh, is that so? Of what am I critical?"

"Of everything."

"I don't like the character you're sketching for me. It isn't bridal."

"I know," Mason said. "You're planning to string me along until you have me safely hooked. You want to get married, but you're nervous, cross and irritable.

"Now that we're just engaged, whenever you find yourself being a little too peevish you catch yourself at it and make up for it with some affectionate little gesture. After we're married you're going to start nagging. Nothing that I do will be right. Think you can portray that sort of young woman?"

"I hate even to think of the pattern."

"Particularly," Mason went on, smiling, "if we find one of the bedrooms locked, you're going to be *very* annoyed. You simply have to see the inside of that bedroom before you can make up your mind on the house."

"We're planning on buying a house?"

86

"Yes."

"Whose?"

"Arthman D. Fargo's residence. We're going to get it furnished and we're going to get it cheap."

"And right now we're inspecting the premises?"

"That's right—provided we can get in. A car left the place a short time ago. Fargo may have been driving, or it may have been someone else—maybe his mistress—checking out."

"Is he married?"

"Yes."

"Where's his wife?"

"He *says* she's visiting her mother in Sacramento. However, her body *could* have been in the trunk of the Cadillac that was driven from the place a few minutes ago."

"What a perfectly *divine* house for a newly married couple!" Della Street exclaimed. "I'm enchanted with it already. Let's go!"

They drove to the Fargo residence. Mason parked the car directly in front of the house, said to Della Street, "Remember this is during the period of courtship and engagement. We haven't as yet got to the point where we hurl barbed remarks at each other except inadvertently, and then we always make up for it with a little affection, so sit still and wait for me to run around and open the door."

Mason jumped out from behind the steering wheel, ran around the back of the car to open the door and helped Della Street to the sidewalk.

She smiled up at him, snuggled her hand into his.

Hand in hand they walked up the sidewalk.

Mason said, "It'll be in order to look around a little bit before we go in, Della, noticing the advantages of the place. And, incidentally, giving me an opportunity to study the wheel tracks in the driveway in front of the garage."

Mason led Della Street around to the graveled driveway.

"A soft spot directly in front of the garage," he said. "There was only one set of wheel tracks when I was here a short time earlier. Ah, yes, there are two sets of tracks now. I'm afraid our bird has flown."

"What bird?" Della Street asked.

"Well, let's say Fargo's mistress."

"He brings her here to the house?"

"That would be my guess. He told me his wife had taken the six o'clock plane to Sacramento."

"The mice didn't lose much time playing, with the cat away," Della Street said.

"But," Mason went on, "these car tracks indicate to me that he didn't take his wife to the six o'clock plane.

"Moreover," Mason went on, "there's something about Mr. Fargo that I definitely don't like. He impresses me as a man who has a great deal on his mind. Well, let's walk back to the front of the place now, Della. We'll ring the bell and you *may* have an opportunity to form your own impressions of Mr. Fargo."

Mason slipped his arm around her waist, said suddenly, "Della, you know, we don't need to play-act on this thing. We *could* really play for keeps."

There was something wistful in her laughter. "And then I'd be staying home in this house and you'd be going to the office and hiring another secretary to run your business and . . ."

"No," he said, "you could continue to be my secretary."

"Phooey! That never works out and you know it."

"Why doesn't it work out?"

"Darned if I know," she said, "but it doesn't. I suppose a man can say things to his secretary he wouldn't dare say to his wife and . . . You know it doesn't work. Are you going to ring the bell or are we going to stand here and . . . Chief, the door isn't closed. There is a half-inch crack between the door and the jamb."

Mason nodded, pressed his thumb against the bell button. After five seconds he rang the bell again, waited another five seconds, then held his thumb against the button.

From the inside of the house they could hear the noise of the bell.

Mason frowned. "You know, Della, it's the strangest co-incidence that I have the combination to his safe in the office."

"Oh-oh."

Mason said, "Of course, I wouldn't take a chance on opening it in the absence of Mr. Fargo, but since the door is partially open we *might* just peek through the crack and see if . . ."

Mason fitted his eye to the crack in the door, then suddenly gave an exclamation and pushed his shoulder against the door.

The door moved only a scant inch, then hit an obstruction which kept it from moving farther.

"What is it?" Della Street asked.

Mason said, "It seems to be the foot of a man who's lying on his back and is very, very inanimate. I guess we'd better try the back door, Della."

A cheery voice behind them said, "Well, well. What seems to be the trouble with mother's little angels? Having some difficulty with your housebreaking?"

Lieutenant Tragg, taking advantage of their preoccupation at the partially open door, had walked quietly up behind them.

"What the devil are *you* doing here?" Mason asked irritably.

"Well," Tragg said, smiling, "as it happened I wanted to get in touch with you, Mason, and since you seemed to be a little difficult to corner, I decided that I would keep a routine watch on Miss Street and see if perhaps she left the office rather hurriedly. When my shadow reported that she was evidently speeding on her way by taxicab to an appointment, I instructed him to follow and relay directions to me. These two-way radio cars are a great invention. And so you're having some trouble getting in. What's the matter? Won't the man on the other side of the door cooperate, or are you afraid of a charge of housebreaking?"

Tragg eased his way past Perry Mason, placed his hand

on the doorknob, peeped inside, then suddenly stiffened to attention. "Well, I'll be damned!"

Mason said, "We just came here, Tragg, and . . ."

"I know you just came here," Tragg said. "I've followed you all the way from the drugstore where Miss Street met you. My car is parked just around the corner. Were you ringing the bell?"

"We rang the bell," Mason said, "before Miss Street noticed that the door was unlatched. I pushed it open just to see . . ."

"Just to see what?" Tragg asked as Mason hesitated.

"Well," Mason said, "I wanted to make sure the bell was working and I wanted to see if anyone was at home."

"Yes, yes," Tragg said. "It's very interesting. Suppose we go round to the back door, Mason."

"Will you want me with you?"

"Right with me, Mason. I wouldn't want you out of my sight now. It would certainly seem that there's a man's body lying there on the floor blocking the door."

"Perhaps a case of heart trouble," Mason said.

"Oh, undoubtedly," Tragg said, "or perhaps he could have fallen asleep just casually, you know. But you'll probably notice that car over on the corner, Mason. One of my men is shaking the driver down. I wouldn't be at all surprised to find the driver was one of Paul Drake's operatives. In fact, I thought I recognized him as we drove by. And he made frantic signs when he recognized me, trying to catch your attention, waving his hand and turning his headlights on and off. As it happened, you were quite preoccupied in your conversation with Miss Street, so didn't notice. I'm going to have to ask him just what his idea was in trying to give you those furtive signals.

"You know, Mason, you're developing the damnedest habit lately of hiring Paul Drake's men to watch a house and almost invariably the occupant of that house dies about the time the men get there. If this keeps up we'll have to communicate with the insurance companies. They'll want to change their statistics, or mortality tables, or whatever it

90

is they call them. . . . Let's see, I guess we go around this way. You were also looking at the garage, Mason. What was the idea?"

"Just looking the place over," Mason said. "Actually I was thinking of buying it."

"Oh, you were! Well, you didn't tell me that you were interested in making real estate purchases out here."

"I'm sorry," Mason said, "very, very sorry. We've been awfully busy up at the office and I neglected to notify you. Now I've been thinking of buying some railroad stock and I believe we've been putting some money in Government Bonds. Do you think that's all right? Is that a good investment?"

"Sarcasm doesn't bother me at all," Tragg told him. "In fact I like it. Now let's get this all straight, Mason, you wanted to buy this house?"

"Yes."

"Had you met the owner?"

"Yes."

"When?"

"This morning."

"What time?"

"Shortly after I last saw you."

"I see. You had an appointment with me to discuss a murder case, and then you rushed out here to buy this property."

"I was looking for investments."

"Then you've been in this house?"

"Yes."

"While this man—what's-his-name was with you?"

"Yes."

"No funny stuff?"

"No funny stuff."

"He was with you all the time you were inside the house?"

"Yes."

"He wasn't a client of yours? He didn't send for you and ask you to come out here?"

"No. I came to see him. I told him I was looking for investments. I didn't even give him my name. He didn't know who I was."

"Well, that sounds fishy as hell, Mason, but we'll let it ride at that for the moment. Now let's take a look at that garage. We may be able to get in through there."

They walked up the driveway and Tragg said, "A car was either driven in or driven out a short time ago."

"How do you know?" Della Street asked.

Tragg said, "Elemental, my dear Miss Street. You'll notice there's a low place in the driveway here. The gravel has been pretty well thinned out at this place, what you'd call a regular mud puddle, and you'll notice that the water is muddy. If those tracks hadn't been made recently the water in the puddle would have been clear. You see, it hasn't been raining since midnight.

"Now let's see, Mason, this door is one of the kind that lowers automatically to close. You evidently press this button to open the door and then after an interval of about two minutes the door automatically closes. A new gadget they're putting out for garage doors. Very nice."

Tragg pressed the button and the garage door swung upward on a hinge against a counterweight, disclosing an empty garage.

"I suppose, under the circumstances," Tragg said, standing to one side, "I should be the host. If you'll walk right in, please."

They entered the garage. Tragg looked swiftly about him and said, "A two-car garage. Evidently only one car is kept here. The other side of the garage is used for storage. Now I suppose that door goes directly into the house. Let's try it. . . . Ah, yes, it's unlocked."

Tragg paused to look swiftly around the garage and while he was doing so a clockwork mechanism clicked an electric connection and the garage door slowly and ponderously swung shut, cutting off a good part of their light.

Tragg opened the kitchen door and said, "And from here on, Mason, I think you and Miss Street had better follow me. Now please be very careful not to touch anything. Keep your hands off of everything. You understand?"

Mason said, "As a matter of fact, Lieutenant . . ."

"Let's not engage in conversation right now, if you don't mind, Mason. I want to get through here to the front hall. I want to take a look at this man who's blocking the doorway."

Tragg opened the swinging door from the kitchen into the dining room, went through the dining room to the living room, then paused suddenly as he looked through the open door into the downstairs front bedroom which had been fixed up as an office.

"Well, well," he said, "there seems to have been rather a hurried search."

Mason looked past Tragg and saw that the door of the safe in the corner of the office was wide open. A litter of papers and books had been spewed out in a pile on the floor. Account books were lying opened, or partially opened, face up and face down, some of them standing on end. Great piles of canceled checks had been scattered over the floor. There were letters strewn around and a tray, which had evidently contained cards of property listings in alphabetical order, had been dumped carelessly so that the cards were strewn all over the floor.

"Very, *very* interesting," Tragg said. "Now quite evidently someone was looking for something in very much of a hurry. No time to be orderly."

Tragg turned suddenly to Mason. "Perhaps you can tell me exactly what they *were* looking for, Mason."

The lawyer shook his head.

"Well, well, we'll look around," Tragg said. "At the moment the gentleman who's lying in the hallway in front of the door seems to take precedence. He . . . . Oh-oh, notice the stairs, Mason."

They had entered the reception hallway.

A wide trail of blood ran down the stairs. Blood which as yet had only begun to dry and retained its brilliant red color rather than the darker, more brownish hue which would come later.

Tragg said, "Now you and Miss Street had better stand right there, Mason. Don't move. Don't touch a thing."

Tragg stepped forward, looked down at the body that was lying on its back, sprawled out in the hallway on the waxed hardwood floor.

"You seem to have moved the body just a bit, Mason, when you opened that door. That is, you moved the left arm, and there's just a little smear indicating you may have moved the body an inch or so."

Tragg bent to feel the wrist. "Not much chance of life after a hemorrhage like that. . . . No, as I suspected, he's quite dead, but he hasn't been dead long. You recognize him, Mason? Just step forward so you can see the face."

Mason looked down at the death-colored features of Arthman D. Fargo.

Mason said, "That's the gentleman who seemed to live here. He told me his name was Arthman D. Fargo when I talked with him a short time ago."

Tragg looked up the stairs, following the trail of blood. "Evidently he was stabbed up there on the second floor. There's not a sign of a weapon here. Nasty cut in the neck. Then he tried to run out of the front door, perhaps seeking help, perhaps trying to escape, hit the top of the stairs, tumbled down and was dead by the time he hit the bottom.

"And now, I am very sorry, but I think we have some work to do, Mason, and if you and your estimable secretary will just turn right around, being very careful not to touch anything, I'll escort you out of the house the same way we came in, and then I'm going to ask you to wait in your car, if you don't mind, until I can ask you a few questions.

"Before I can talk with you, Mason, I want to look around here. I'm going to have to notify headquarters and get some photographers out here and a deputy coroner. And by all means we want to interview Mr. Drake's detective who happens to be so opportunely posted out there at the corner. Tell me, Mason, do you arrange for these murders on some sort of a schedule? A very, very interesting coincidence, isn't it?"

"Very," Mason said.

"And so you were interested in buying this house?" Tragg went on, with his voice showing the extent of his keen interest. "I suppose that you rang up Drake and asked him to put an operative out here to make certain that no other customer came in and raised your bid. I think, Mason, that for a person who doesn't know who his client is, you certainly have an uncanny ability to determine where the next murder is going to take place. Right this way, please. I'll signal my driver and get him over here, and then after a while we'll have a nice little heart-to-heart chat, Mason, but first I want to know a little more about the situation here in the house, if you don't mind."

"Not at all," Mason said. "There are days when I don't have anything to do at my office. Nothing at all."

"I'm sure that's right," Tragg said, "so just to keep yourself amused you pick out the places where murders are going to be committed and have Paul Drake post men there. You're a regular bird dog, Mason."

Chapter 11

Mason had an opportunity for a few hurried words with Della Street as Lieutenant Tragg moved out to the curb to give secret instructions to the officer who had accompanied him to the Fargo house.

"Do we talk?" Della Street asked.

"Not yet," Mason said.

"He'll want to know how you located the place, he'll want to know . . ."

"I can't tell him, not yet."

"Why not?"

Mason said, "Apparently my client is Mrs. Fargo. My best hunch is that she's going to turn up missing, but I can't be certain."

"You think he killed her?"

"That's what I did think. Now I'm not certain. Someone stuck a knife in him. It just might have been that his wife found out he was intending to murder her, and beat him to it. In that event it was self-defense, but we'd have one hell of a time proving it. Or he may have killed his wife, sent for his mistress, told her what he'd done and asked her to run away with him. She might not have been willing under the circumstances. She might have told him she wouldn't go for that at all, and threatened to tell the police; so he began to get rough—and got stabbed—self-defense again. No one knows—not yet."

"Can't you tell Tragg that much?"

"Suppose I should be wrong."

"Then what?"

"I can't tell Tragg anything my client told me in confidence."

"Is the wife your client?"

"We took money from someone, presumably the wife. She . . . Hold everything, Della, here he comes."

Lieutenant Tragg said, "Just get in the car with the officer, if you will, please, Miss Street, and you too, Mason. We'll try not to detain you any longer than is absolutely necessary, but there are a few facts I want to find out just as soon as I finish with my examination in here."

"Always glad to accommodate you, Lieutenant," Mason said cheerfully.

He and Della Street entered the car. There followed a long wait, during which official cars came siren-screaming out to the house. Reporters showed up, news photographers took pictures for their papers, the "meat wagon" from an undertaking establishment drove up to remove the body, and then Lieutenant Tragg came hurrying down the driveway, the gravel crunching under his energetic feet. "Sorry to keep you folks waiting," he said briskly, "but there were quite a few angles I had to check on. Now we'll go to headquarters, if you don't mind."

Mason said, "Why don't you question us here, Tragg, and save . . ."

"No, thank you, Mason. I think headquarters is the place. We have all of the stenographic facilities there in case you care to make a statement."

"I'll make a statement right here."

"Headquarters," Tragg said, nodding to the officer who was driving the car, and jumped in, slamming the door behind him.

Mason knew that protests were out of order, so he sat quietly while the siren screamed for a right of way through traffic.

Tragg ushered his visitors into his office at the department devoted to homicides, called in a police stenographer.

"Sit right down and make yourself comfortable," he said. "Now, Mason, I'd like to know just what happened."

"I gave you a general sketch earlier in the day."

"About Carlin?"

"That's right, about having been retained."

"Yes, yes, I understand. Some mysterious client. You don't want to mention who it was. A woman, I believe. Could it have been Mrs. Fargo by any chance?"

"I don't know."

"How did you happen to be out there, Mason? How did you happen to have one of Drake's men on the job?"

Mason said, "I was trying to find out something about my client, the person who had telephoned me."

"And did you?"

"Frankly, I don't know."

"Why not?"

"I didn't have a chance to develop the information."

"But you did have a lead to Fargo?"

"That's right."

"How did you get it?"

"A little detective work."

"Mind telling me how you got the lead?"

"Pure deduction, Lieutenant. I couldn't trace the phone call over the telephone, but I had another way of tracing it and—well, Fargo was one of the possibilities."

"Fargo himself?"

"Perhaps his wife."

"And where's his wife now?"

"My best guess," Mason said, "is that she's dead."

Tragg's eyes for a moment were hard as gimlets. "Another one?"

"Another one."

"You seem to be leaving a trail of murder this morning, Mason."

"Following a trail of murder, Lieutenant."

"Yes, I stand corrected. Tell us about Mrs. Fargo."

Mason said, "I talked with Fargo earlier in the day. I pretended that I was in the market to buy his house. As a matter of fact, Della and I were going out there posing as a prospective bride and groom who were interested in getting a house where they could set up housekeeping."

"Most commendable," Tragg said. "Am I to offer congratulations?"

"Not yet. I haven't been able to sell Della on the idea."

"You might do worse," Tragg said to Della Street. "But I certainly wouldn't advise you to say yes until you hear the outcome of this latest scrape, because he may be in a little more serious trouble than he realizes."

Mason lit a cigarette.

"Why do you think she's dead?" Tragg asked.

"Fargo told me that his wife had taken the six o'clock plane to Sacramento. I don't think she did."

"Why not?"

"I don't think the car had been out of the garage."

"The car had been out sometime this morning. It . . ."

"Sure," Mason said. "The car was gone. It had to go out."

"And, by the same token, someone had to drive it out."

"That's right."

"Any idea who?"

"As to identity, no. As to general classification, I might say yes."

"Who?"

"Fargo's girl friend, perhaps."

At that moment a sergeant entered Tragg's office, laid a folded piece of paper on the Lieutenant's desk, and without a word turned and left the office.

Tragg opened the paper and studied it frowningly.

"Fargo's girl friend," he repeated slowly. "Find the woman, eh?"

"That's right."

Tragg's eyes were cold, hard, and penetrating. "Did Fargo have something you wanted, Mason?"

"What?"

"A paper, for instance?"

Mason shook his head.

"You're certain you're not holding out on me?"

"I'm telling you everything I can."

"That means everything you want to."

"Well, perhaps."

"Isn't it possible that Mrs. Fargo employed you to handle her affairs, that you were particularly anxious to get some paper Fargo had in his possession and . . ."

Mason shook his head.

"Careful, now," Tragg said. "I'm going to check up on you."

"No, absolutely," Mason said. "That's not the case."

"Told you she'd gone to Sacramento, eh?"

"That's right."

"And you don't think she had?"

"No."

"You don't think she'd left the house?"

Mason said, "I haven't the faintest proof, Lieutenant. I wouldn't want to be quoted on it. I would be very much embarrassed if you released any statement to the press which indicated I had said anything of the sort. But if *I* were in your shoes, if I were in charge of the homicide detail, I'd get the license number of Arthman D. Fargo's automobile, which incidentally, is registered under his wife's name, and I'd throw out a state-wide broadcast. I'd try to find that automobile just as soon as possible and then I'd make it a point to look in the trunk."

"Well, thanks for your advice," Tragg said. "It's appreciated. It shows you're developing a professional mind, Mason. We've already done that. Now if you were in my shoes, what would you do with one Perry Mason who seems to have certain information that he's holding out?"

"What do you think I'm holding out?" Mason asked.

"The thing you're not telling me."

"I have virtually all my cards on the table, Lieutenant. The only things that I can't give you are certain confidential matters which may have something to do with my client."

"You've told me everything?"

"Everything."

"Then," Tragg said, suddenly leaning forward, his voice taking on the edge of authority, "will you kindly tell me how, according to this report that was just given me, it happens that your fingerprints are all over the combination of that safe? Will you kindly tell me how it happens that when you tried to open the Carlin safe you turned the combination four times to the right and stopped on fifty-nine as your first move? How it happens that the Fargo safe has a combination which starts with fifty-nine four times to the right?"

Mason took a long drag at the cigarette.

"Well," Tragg said, "I'm waiting for an answer."

"I'm afraid," Mason said, "that I can't tell you any more than I have."

"Did you or did you not open Fargo's safe, either before or after the murder?"

"I did not even look inside the safe," Mason said.

"Your fingerprints are all over the combination."

"I can't help that."

"You may wish you could," Tragg told him. "I'm giving you your chance right now, Mason, to come clean. If you're representing a woman who wanted some documents out of Fargo's safe, now is the time to say so."

"That isn't the case—at least not so far as I know."

"I think you lifted a paper out of that safe, Mason."

"I told you I didn't as much as look inside the safe," Mason said, his voice cold. "Go ahead and prove the contrary."

"I think I can," Tragg told him. "That's all. You may go now."

Chapter 12

Within a block of police headquarters, Mason stopped to telephone Paul Drake's office.

"You familiar with the developments in that Fargo matter, Paul?"

"Sure," Drake said. "My operative managed to get word through to me before the police sewed him up. I put some other men on the job just in case. Where are you now, Perry?"

"Within about a block of police headquarters. They've just finished giving Della and me a going-over."

"Okay," Drake said. "Get up here. I have some information for you."

"All right, you're going to have to get some more," Mason said. "I want to find out who Fargo's girl friend was. I want to find . . ."

"I have most of the stuff you want," Drake said. "I've found that the investigation I was doing in that other matter led directly to . . ."

"Who's his girl?" Mason interrupted.

"Celinda Gilson," Drake said, "at the Farlowe Apartments. She's the Golden Goose girl who has the concession for taking flashlight photographs of people who want to have it appear they're near-celebrities, or who would like to perpetuate the occasion of a darned good binge."

"The Farlowe Apartments?"

"Yes."

"Anything else you have will keep," Mason told him, "I'm sending Della to the office. Make a complete report to her. She'll get it all classified and tabulated for me. I'm going to try to beat the police to Celinda Gilson."

"You think the police are looking for her?"

Mason said, "I think she may have killed Fargo when she found out that Fargo had murdered his wife, and had also killed Medford Carlin. I'm mixed in this thing deep enough so I want to find out what it's all about before the police sew everything up. I inadvertently left a set of fingerprints on Fargo's safe, and that could prove rather embarrassing."

"How the devil did you happen to leave prints on his safe?" Drake asked.

"I was trying to check a combination I had, Paul, in order to find out if Mrs. Fargo was really my client."

"And you did open the safe?"

"Now don't make the same mistake Lieutenant Tragg did," Mason said. "He kept asking me if I *opened* the safe. I didn't. I *did* unlock it. That's something entirely different. Tragg neglected to ask me that question."

"Okay," Drake said, "you want me to put a shadow out on this Gilson girl?"

"Good heavens, no," Mason said. "If you put a shadow on her and the police find it out, you'd never get a license again as long as you lived. We've had too many coincidences now, Paul. I'm on my way."

"Think she'll be home?" Drake asked dubiously.

"It's my only chance. If she's driving around, the police will pick her up. They have broadcast a description of the Fargo car and it should be only a matter of minutes until it's located. Now, Paul, I want to know all you can find out about Mrs. Fargo. I think she really has a family in Sacramento. I want to find out who they are and where they live. Get busy on that stuff because we're just one jump ahead of the police and I have to stay that way. There's some tie-up between Carlin and the Fargos. I'd like to find it. . . . Okay, Paul, get busy. I'm on my way."

Mason hung up the telephone, said to Della Street, "You have plenty of money in your purse, Della?"

She nodded.

"Grab a taxi to the office," Mason said. "Paul Drake's

there. He has some information for you. Get him to run over everything he has. Separate the wheat from the chaff. Get him to find out who Mrs. Fargo's relatives are in Sacramento. I don't think there's one chance in ten thousand she took the six o'clock plane, but check into it and make sure. I'll be back at the office just as soon as I can get there. And in case this Gilson girl makes a confession I want you to be ready to jump in a cab, join me there and take down what she says. Keep plenty of cash on hand. We may have to go underground for a while."

"On my way," Della Street told him. "Where does the Gilson girl live?"

"The Farlowe Apartments."

"You know where they are?"

"No."

"I'll look them up," Della Street said.

"You get to the office," Mason told her. "I'll look them up. Grab yourself a cab. You can get one out front."

"I'm on my way," Della Street said, and hurried out of the door. Mason thumbed through the telephone directory, found the address he wanted, all but ran to his car and made time through traffic until he reached the Farlowe Apartments, a medium-sized, unostentatious apartment house which presented a locked door to the street. On the left-hand side of this locked door was a series of cards with the names of the various tenants, with buttons to the left of each card, and individual speaking tubes just to the right.

Mason found a name which had been cut from an engraved visiting card. Celinda Gilson Larue. Two ink lines had been drawn through the last name so that the words Celinda Gilson remained.

Mason held his finger against the button by the Gilson card.

He rang three times before there was a whistle in the speaking tube and then a woman's sleepy voice said, "Who is it?"

"A friend," Mason said.

"Oh, yeah."

"That's right."

"What do *you* want?"

Mason said, "I want to talk with yoú before the police do."

"What in the world are you talking about?" the voice asked down the speaking tube.

Mason remained silent.

There was a pause of several seconds, then the buzzer made noise, indicating that the door was being unlatched by a button from above.

Mason noted that the apartment number was 325, pushed the door open, went in, and didn't bother to wait for the wheezy automatic elevator, but took the stairs two at a time.

The corridor on the third floor was a replica of thousands of other corridors in similar apartment houses. Mason had some trouble adjusting his eyes to the dim light, but finally found the apartment he wanted and tapped on the door.

The young woman who opened the door was knuckling her eyes and yawning as she studied Mason with a certain quizzical humor.

She was attired in a housecoat and slippers. Her face wore no make-up. She said, "So you're supposed to be a friend. And getting me up at *this* hour!"

"Oh, come," Mason said, "this is late."

"Not for me it isn't. What do you want?"

"I want to talk with you."

"Go on and talk."

"I hardly want to stand here and talk."

"This is a one-room apartment. I'm in bed. Be your age."

"I don't want to talk out in the hall," Mason said. "Be *your* age."

"Just because you want to talk doesn't mean you're going to come barging into my place . . . What do you want to talk about?"

"Fargo," Mason said.

There was not enough light to show the expression in her

eyes. They regarded Mason steadily for a moment, then she stepped back from the door and said, "Come on in."

Mason entered and she closed the door behind them.

It was a plain, small, furnished apartment with kitchenette and bath. There was a dispiriting lack of individuality about the place and it was singularly uninviting, with the furniture moved to one side of the small room to make way for the wall bed which had been lowered into place. A single electric floor lamp gave a feeble amount of subdued illumination.

"The chairs are all shoved up against the wall," she said. "That overstuffed chair isn't too uncomfortable. Swing it around and sit down."

She kicked off her slippers, jumped up on the bed, curled her feet under her, pulled the covers over her knees, patted the pillows into a pile against the foot of the brass bedstead, said, "All right, go ahead and shoot."

"You knew Fargo was married?" Mason asked.

She hesitated a moment, then met his eyes, and said, "Yes."

"When did you see him last?"

"Last night."

"What time?"

"About ten o'clock. He was at the place where I work."

"The Golden Goose?"

"Yes. You were there, too. I saw you there with a young woman. I know who you are. You're Perry Mason. Let's quit beating around the bush. What do you want? You're a lawyer. Do you represent the wife?"

"I'm not prepared to state."

"What does she want?"

"I'm not prepared to state that."

"What do you want?"

"Information."

"About what?"

"Mind if I smoke?" Mason asked.

"Not at all," she said, indicating a brass bowl which did

106

duty as an ash tray and which was about half-filled with cigarette butts.

"Join me?" Mason asked.

"I . . . Okay."

Mason took his cigarette case from his pocket, gave her a cigarette, took one for himself and held the match out to her.

She took a quick drag at the cigarette, then put it down, exhaled twin streams of smoke and said, "Let's get on with the inquisition."

"You're friendly with Fargo?" Mason asked.

She hesitated, then met his eyes. "Yes."

"Quite friendly?"

"Intimate, if that's what you're after."

"How long have you been—intimate?"

"Is that any of your business?"

"I think it is."

"About six months."

"Has he talked about marrying you?"

"Don't be silly. He's married."

"What does that make you?"

"You're a lawyer. You can answer that question."

"Smart, eh?"

"It doesn't look like it, does it?"

"Just what did you expect to get out of the companionship?" Mason asked.

"I'll bite."

"Surely you expected something?"

"That's up to him."

"Did you ever discuss it with him?"

"No."

"Is he happily married?"

"No."

Mason said casually, "You knew he was dead?"

She jumped convulsively on the bed as though there had been an explosion near by and she was bracing her nervous system against the shock.

"Did you?" Mason asked.

"Is this a gag? Are you kidding me?"

"He's dead," Mason said. "I think he was murdered."

"Then she did it," Celinda Gilson said with a note of finality.

"Why do you say that?"

"Because she would do it. He—he expected her to."

"How do you know?"

"He told me so."

"Then he'd been having trouble?"

"Yes."

"What sort of trouble?"

"I don't know," she said wearily. "What sort of trouble do you call it when people are married and live together until they get so damn tired of each other they want to break away but there's no opportunity to break away? You get on each other's nerves, you start jawing at each other, you probably loved the guy at one time, but that's all worn off and he irritates the hell out of you just because he's draped around your neck day and night—and he feels the same way about you.

"You say things that hurt his feelings, he says things that hurt your feelings.

"He's always jumping on you, and you get to feel you're never doing anything to suit him. You try to do the best you can, then your self-respect makes you start sticking up for yourself and you fight back. The first thing you know you're going yah-yah-yah-yah like a cat and a dog shut up in a cage. Then you go pfffft! And get a divorce."

"That's what you did once?"

"That's what I did," she said. "That's why you saw the card downstairs, Mr. Mason, with the name Larue crossed out. I put the guy out of my life and crossed his name off the list."

"How long ago?"

"Eight months."

"You're divorced?"

"Not yet. I just crossed the name out."

"Why aren't you divorced?"

"Because he won't pay for it and I'm damned if I'm going to put up my hard-earned dough to buy *his* freedom. He's playing around, and sooner or later some little sweetie-pie will sell him a bill of goods and want to get her hooks into his dough. He'll fall for that line of stuff and then he'll want his 'freedom.' Then he'll come to me to see about getting a divorce."

"What'll you do?"

"Probably hold him up for a little cash," she said. "After all, I lived with the guy five years. I'm entitled to something. Five years ago I had a lot to offer, now I—well, a lot of the bloom has been rubbed off now."

"You seem to be rather philosophical."

"I try to be. Tell me about Arthman. You're not kidding me, are you? This isn't a gag?"

"No. He's dead."

"Murdered?"

"I think he was murdered."

"Where's his wife?"

"Supposedly visiting her mother in Sacramento."

"When did she leave?"

"This morning."

"When did Arthman get killed?"

"An hour and a half or two hours ago."

"You check where his wife was," she said with finality. "You'll find she's the one that did it."

Mason said, "You didn't know anything about it?"

"Not a thing."

"What time did you go to bed?"

"About five o'clock this morning."

"You live here alone?"

"What does it look like?"

"You were asleep when I rang the bell?"

"That's right."

"Had been in bed ever since five o'clock this morning?"

"That's right."

"Where were you about ten o'clock this morning?"

"Right here, with my head right on that pillow. Why? Did someone intend to try to pin it on me?"

"What time does the Golden Goose close up?"

"About two o'clock."

"Where were you between two o'clock and five?"

She shook her head and said, "That's none of your business. That involves other people. I try not to be a hypocrite. I tell you the things that only concern me and that's all right, but when they concern somebody else that's different."

"You weren't alone?" Mason asked.

"No," she said mockingly, "I wasn't alone. I've had lots of things that I've paid a price for. I'm having more things that I'm going to have to pay a price for. I'm living my own life and I've earned the right to be independent."

Mason said, "Let's get down to brass tacks."

"I thought we were down to them."

"About ten-thirty this morning weren't you in a bedroom of Arthman Fargo's house at 2281 Livingdon Drive with the door closed?"

"No."

"Where were you?"

"Right here."

"You drive a car?"

"Sure."

"Didn't you drive Arthman Fargo's Cadillac out of his garage about two hours or so ago and . . ."

"Don't be silly."

"Didn't you?"

"No."

"How much do you know about Mrs. Fargo?"

"I've never met her. I've seen her—at the Golden Goose. He had her with him last night."

"How much do you know about her?"

"I don't think that needs to enter into it unless—well, unless that's true about Arthman having been murdered."

"It's true."

"How do I find it out?"

110

"You'll find it out fast enough. Unless I very greatly underestimate the intelligence of Lieutenant Tragg of the homicide detail you're going to be questioned with some thoroughness."

She said, "It's okay by me. I'm free, white and twenty-one and living my own life."

"How about his wife?"

"If Arthman Fargo is dead, Mr. Mason, he was killed by Myrt."

"Who's Myrt?"

"Myrtle, his wife."

"You seem to be very positive."

"I am."

"Mind telling me how you know, what makes you so positive?"

"She's a vain little twist. She doesn't want him herself. She would much rather be somewhere else."

"Where? Do you know?" Mason asked.

"Where what?"

"Where else?"

She shook her head and said, "She's secretive."

"You think there's someone else?"

"Of course."

"What makes you think so?"

"Lots of things."

"You haven't any idea who it might be?"

"I haven't the faintest idea, and I don't think Arthman did either."

Mason said, "Let's quit stalling. I have reason to believe that you were in the upstairs bedroom at Fargo's house this morning. I have reason to believe that you took Fargo's Cadillac and did some pretty rapid driving around the city trying to shake off someone who was following you. I think you abandoned the car some place where you feel that it won't be connected with you. I have reason to believe the body of Myrtle Fargo may be found in the trunk of that car. That's just a long, wild guess. You could have had something to do with the murder of Myrtle Fargo, or you perhaps didn't know anything about it. Would you like to talk about that?"

"I wouldn't like to talk about anything more. You're playing your cards pretty fast, big boy. I've tried to follow suit. So far, I've done pretty well. The trouble is that you know what's trumps and I don't."

"When the police find the car," Mason said, "they'll find your fingerprints on the steering wheel."

"How do you know they will?"

"Because the police have started to look for the woman in the case."

"Meaning me?"

"Meaning you, and they'll go all over that car looking for fingerprints."

"That's nice."

"And," Mason went on, "if you did kill Arthman Fargo it might be a lot better to come right out and say that you killed him and say that you had to kill him in self-defense after you had found out about the murder of his wife, rather than to try to stall around and in the end wind up facing a murder rap. Now I don't want to be your lawyer. I'm not in a position to advise you and I'm not advising you as a lawyer, but that's something for you to think over. It's just sound common sense."

She slid over to the edge of the bed, the housecoat rolling up as she slid along so that a flash of bare legs against the dark sheen of the housecoat showed she had nothing on under it. Then she stood up, smoothed the housecoat about her and said, "Look at me, Mr. Mason."

"I'm looking."

She said, "You think I'm hard-boiled. You think I've been through the mill. You think I'm working in a night club. You think I'm a gold digger. Go ahead and think all you want.

"I'm twenty-seven. I've seen a lot of the world. Every man I've known has been on the make. Lots of times I think to myself, 'Well, why not, Celinda? Why not go ahead and be on the make yourself?' And then somehow or

112

other I've always held back. I've always tried to keep on the up-and-up. I like Arthman Fargo. If he's dead it's going to be a terrific jolt to me. I can take it. I've taken lots of things in my life. I've had the rug jerked out from under me just when I thought I was sitting pretty. After you go I'll sit down here and bawl my eyes out and look like hell when I go on duty tonight. Right now I'm keeping my chin up and dealing them to you right off the top of the deck.

"I know that you're not interested in *my* feelings or in *my* grief. I suppose you had some reason for coming here. I suppose whatever your reason is you're trying to thimble-rig something that's for the benefit of your client and not for *my* benefit. I suppose I should regard you as an enemy. You look like a decent sort and you have a reputation of being a square shooter. Now then, that's my story and I . . ."

She broke off as a buzzer made insistent sounds.

"What's that?" Mason asked.

"The doorbell," she said.

"The outer door?"

"No, the apartment door right here. Some peddler probably. Don't pay any attention to it. They get in and ring for a while, then go away and . . ."

The buzzer sounded again. Knuckles pounded on the door. "Open up in there," a voice said.

Mason got to his feet, said, "Well, thanks for the interview. I think you'd better open up. That sounds like someone I know."

She walked over to the door and opened it.

Lieutenant Tragg and a plain-clothes detective stood in the hallway.

Mason said, "Celinda Gilson, Lieutenant Tragg. Celinda, this is Lieutenant Tragg of homicide. He wants to ask you some questions about Fargo."

Tragg was not entirely able to hold back his surprise. "Damned if you don't get around, Mason," he said. "Is *this* your client?"

Mason shook his head.

113

"Well," Tragg said, with elaborate politeness, "we don't want to interfere with your crowded schedule, Mason. This is one time when we *won't* detain you."

"Thanks," Mason said ironically, and walked out.

Chapter 13

It was well after two o'clock when Mason opened the door of his private office and walked in to find Paul Drake and Della Street huddled in low-voiced conversation.

"Hello," Mason said cheerfully. "You look like a couple of conspirators."

"We are," Della said.

Mason said, "I think we've got the lead, Paul. That Celinda Gilson is it. She tried to pretend she was sound asleep when I rang the bell, but she gave herself away. She's quite a cigarette smoker, yet while she was knuckling her eyes and going through all the motions of being freshly awakened, she didn't care particularly for a cigarette. Now any person who is really addicted to cigarettes has to have one the first thing in the morning on awakening. The ash tray shows she's a heavy smoker. I offered her one and she wasn't too keen about it, but hesitated a moment before she accepted it. I think she was about to say she'd smoked too much or something, and . . . What's the matter?"

Drake said, "Your theory's cockeyed, Perry."

"What theory?"

"That Fargo killed his wife."

"Why?"

"He didn't."

"Shoot."

Drake said, "We finally got the dope on the Fargos by digging up their marriage application. We got the name and address of her mother. She lives in Sacramento. We called her up just on general principles."

"The deuce," Mason said. "What did she say?"

"Said that her daughter was on the road to Sacramento on a Greyhound bus, that she'd arrive this evening."

Mason said, "Personally I don't think it's true. If it is, however, it puts us in an awful mess."

"How come, if she's your client and she's safe and . . ."

"And her husband has been neatly murdered with a knife stuck in his throat. When did that Greyhound bus leave here?"

"Probably the one that leaves here at eight-forty-five A.M."

Mason started pacing the floor. "We've got to get word to that woman somehow."

"How come?" Drake asked.

Mason said, "She's going to need an alibi, Paul."

"Well, if she's on the bus that should be a good alibi."

"She's going to need a damn *good* alibi," Mason said. "This is a murder case. You can't tell, Tragg may decide to try to pin it on her. She's going to need the names of fellow passengers who can vouch for her. . . . Della, charter a private plane. I want a fast one. Paul, get a schedule of that bus. Get a description. Della, you come with me. Grab all the data you have. Get Drake's reports. Get the mother's address. Get all the factual information we have. We're going to have to start getting proof on an alibi and getting it fast."

Della Street picked up the telephone which went through the switchboard, said, "Gertie, get us our plane rental service on the line. Tell them we want the fastest charter plane we can get to take us to Sacramento. . . ."

"Stockton," Mason amended. "We're going to Stockton."

"Stockton," Della Street said in the telephone. "As soon as you get the right person on the line put through a call to me."

"Why Stockton?" Drake asked.

"Because," Mason said, "you're going to get on the phone, telephone your correspondents in Sacramento, have them send operatives down to Myrtle Fargo's mother, and have her meet us at Stockton. We'll wait for the bus there.

116

She'll point out her daughter. We'll have operatives start circulating among the passengers, getting names and addresses. We're going to want witnesses, lots of witnesses."

"You think it's that serious?" Drake asked.

"How the hell do I know?" Mason said. "But if it *should* prove that serious I don't want to have our evidence scattered to the four winds of heaven. Let's get witnesses and let's get going."

Chapter 14

The dispatcher was just announcing the arrival of Schedule No. 320 from Modesto en route to Sacramento when Mason was accosted by a thin, professional-looking man some fifty-five years of age, dressed so conservatively as to seem almost old-fashioned. This man, after quietly sizing up the lawyer, said, "Mr. Mason?"

Mason nodded.

"I'm with the Drake Detective Agency's Sacramento affiliate. We have Mrs. Ingram here. You want to meet her now? The bus is just scheduled to come in. It's pretty crowded. This is a through bus, you know, and they won't sell local tickets except as they have seat vacancies. We have two tickets, that's all we can get."

"How long does the bus stop here?"

"Five minutes."

"Anyone with you?"

"Yes, I have one operative."

Mason said, "Okay. You take the two tickets. Get aboard the bus. Get the names and addresses of all the passengers. You'll have to use a little tact and . . ."

"Certainly," the detective said, "that's my business. We understand all that, Mr. Mason."

"All right, get those names and addresses," Mason said. "I want the through passengers in particular. Ones who have been talking with the young woman we'll point out to you."

"Here come the passengers," the detective said.

"Let me meet Mrs. Ingram," Mason ordered.

Mason moved over to meet a thin-lipped woman in the middle fifties, who seemed completely flustered.

118

"So *you're* Mr. Mason," she said. "Well, heaven knows I don't know what this is all about. They say you're a lawyer and a good one, and I certainly hope you know what you're doing. My girl is a good girl, Mr. Mason, a good girl. Now don't make any mistake about that. She can't possibly be mixed up in any trouble. I don't know what all this hullabaloo is about, but I'm certainly going to hold you responsible. The idea of gadding about this way . . ."

Mason interrupted to say, "We're not at all certain your daughter is on this bus."

"Of course she is. She said she'd be on it."

"There have been some unusual and totally unexpected developments, Mrs. Ingram. There's a chance that your daughter . . ."

"Mother, what are *you* doing *here*?"

Mrs. Ingram turned. Her eyes softened slightly but her thin-lipped mouth remained firm and hard.

"Why, Myrtle! Well, good heavens, the way you give people a start! You . . ."

"The way *I* give people a start. You're the one that's giving me a start. What in the world are you doing *here*?"

Mrs. Ingram said, "Well, you can't prove it by me. This is Mr. Perry Mason and Miss Street, his secretary."

Myrtle Fargo's eyes rested on Mason's face. For a moment her face drained of color, her eyes grew large and round.

"Mr. Mason!" she said in a voice that was hardly more than a startled whisper.

Mason said, "You know me by sight, Mrs. Fargo?"

"Yes. I . . . You were pointed out to me. . . . What in the world are *you* doing here?"

Mason said, "We haven't time for explanations now. Things are serious. Do you have your ticket stub?"

Myrtle Fargo searched in her handbag and drew out a small card. "Here it is, Mr. Mason, but why all the . . ."

Mason turned the card over quickly to note the Los Angeles teller's stamp. "Can you tell me why this stub is marked with yesterday's date, Mrs. Fargo?"

"Why, of course," Myrtle Fargo answered quickly. "I bought the ticket yesterday. I always buy my tickets ahead of time to make sure there's no delay and . . ."

"Well never mind that now," Mason said. "In which seat were you sitting on the bus?"

"The—why, let me see, the second seat from the front on the left-hand side."

"By the window, or on the aisle?"

"By the window."

"Do you know who was sitting next to you?"

"Yes, a very delightful woman. She . . ."

"Where did she get on?"

"Why, I don't know. At, oh, somewhere down the valley. She's been there for a while."

"She wasn't on when you left Los Angeles?"

"Heavens, I don't know. I didn't notice her until a while ago."

Mason said, "Do you see her here?"

"Why, yes, she's standing right over there by the news-stand."

The voice of the announcer droned, "Schedule No. 320 leaving for Sacramento. All aboard, please."

"What in the world is this all about?" Mrs. Fargo asked. "Mother, can you come with me? Can you . . ."

"You're going with me," Mason said. "We're going to drive to Sacramento in a rented car. We'll get there ahead of the bus so we can interview some of the passengers."

The passengers filed through the gates and aboard the bus. Looking through the windows, Mason could see the detective and his assistant already in circulation, smiling affably as they tactfully approached the passengers, getting names and addresses.

"Now," Myrtle Fargo said, "will you kindly tell me what this is all about?"

"Well, I should say so!" Mrs. Ingram said. "Such goings on. I'm all of a flutter. I can't seem to get organized. I never had such a rushing around in my life. People pulling

120

and hauling and rushing me around. Myrt, what in the world have you been up to?"

"Not a thing on earth, Mom."

Mason said, "Perhaps we can postpone most of the questioning until afterwards."

"Nonsense, Mr. Mason! I haven't anything on earth to keep from Mom."

Mason said, "You say I was pointed out to you?"

"Yes."

"Where?"

"In a night club. Let me see, it was . . . Why, it was only last night! Miss Street was with you. Isn't that right, Miss Street?"

Mason said, "You originally intended to take the plane this morning, Mrs. Fargo?"

"Take the *plane*!"

"Yes."

"Good heavens, no! My time isn't *that* valuable. I like bus travel. You meet a lot of interesting . . ."

"Didn't you tell your husband you were taking a plane?"

"No."

"Didn't he drive you to the airport this morning?"

"My husband drive me to the airport? Don't be silly. At that hour in the morning? Why, he wouldn't get up and lose his sleep for anything on earth. I sneaked down, got myself a little breakfast, caught a streetcar, and took the eight-forty-five bus."

"He told me he drove you to the airport."

"Arthman Fargo told you that he drove *me* to the airport?"

"Yes."

"When did he tell you that?"

"About nine o'clock this morning."

She shook her head and said, "He must have been spoofing you. He knew very well I was going to take the bus. I always travel that way, don't I, Moms?"

"Well, yes. I guess so. Most of the time. Of course, you did come up here on the plane the time before . . ."

"And was sick half the way. I made up my mind that was the end. I've traveled on Greyhound busses ever since and I enjoy them immensely."

"Yes, I guess so, but will someone *please* tell me what this is all about? I'm not a young woman any more, and I've been pushed and hauled and shoved around here until I just can't . . ."

"Mrs. Fargo," Mason said, "let's have one definite understanding. You don't need to tell me any more than you want to, but you went to a drugstore at the corner of Vance Avenue and Kramer Boulevard last night and made a telephone call, didn't you?"

She shook her head slowly, and then after a moment said, "What would *that* have to do with it?"

Mason said impatiently, "Don't lie to me. The thing is too important for that."

"Mr. Mason," Mrs. Ingram snapped, "that's my daughter you're talking to! She's a good girl. Don't you *dare* accuse her of lying. She wouldn't lie to anyone. She isn't that sort of a girl. She doesn't have to lie. She's a decent, respectable, married woman and she . . ."

Mason said, "All right. There isn't time to be tactful about it. Your husband is dead."

"What!" Mrs. Ingram exclaimed.

Myrtle Fargo swayed slightly. Her eyes became big and round. "Arthman—dead!"

"That's right," Mason said, "and as far as we're concerned we can cut out all the dramatics and all the posing. I have an idea the police are going to be moving in on the job within the next hour or two. We're going to have to cover a lot of ground and cover it fast. Now let's quit playing button, button, who's got the button."

"Arthman . . . Why, he couldn't be. He was in perfect health. He . . ."

"He was killed," Mason interrupted.

"How?"

"By someone who inserted a knife in the side of his neck. Apparently this little thrust of affection, if we may call it that, took place on the upper floor of your home sometime around ten or ten-thirty this morning. He tried to run out of the house. He made it to the head of the stairs and apparently lost consciousness, tumbled down the stairs, and sprawled out in the reception hallway within a couple of feet of the front door. Know anything about it?"

"Know anything about it! Why, Mr. Mason, *what* do you mean? You're the first one that's told me. I . . . Had you heard anything, Mother?"

She shook her head.

"Well," Mason said, "you're going to be questioned. The police are going to want to know where you were."

"What time was it?"

"Probably right around ten or half-past."

"Well, thank heavens I was all accounted for. I was on the bus at half-past ten."

"Talk with anyone?"

She frowned thoughtfully and said, "Yes, I did. There was a very delightful gentleman, an older man, a man who seemed very well informed. I think he was in the oil business or something. He got off at Bakersfield. There was a drunk sitting next to me, and there was a woman that I talked with between Bakersfield and Fresno. I don't know who she was. And I changed seats at Fresno and there was a woman sitting next to me who was going up to Sacramento to be a witness in her daughter's divorce trial. I think she said her name was Olanta. It was an odd name. I'm quite certain that was it—Mrs. Olanta. But her daughter's name was Pelham, and the case comes up for trial, that is, the divorce case, tomorrow morning. I remember she talked quite a bit about divorces and about husbands and wives and the difficulty they had getting on with each other."

Mason glanced at his wrist watch, turned to Della Street and said, "If we're going to get to Sacramento in time to do any good, we're going to have to get started."

Della Street nodded, moved over to the place where the driver of the rented car was standing. Mason turned back to Mrs. Fargo and her mother. "Now then," he said, "we're going to be in a rented car. The driver will be listening. We can't talk there. This is our last chance. Mrs. Fargo, did you telephone me last night or not?"

She met his eyes. "No," she said.

"Let's go," Mason said curtly.

Myrtle said impulsively, "I didn't telephone you last night, but *if* my husband *is* dead and *if* there's any chance—well, if I'm going to have to have an alibi or prove where I've been or what I've been doing, why, I want you to represent me. I've heard a lot about you and . . . I just can't believe, Mr. Mason, that . . ."

"Now, Myrtle, you'd just better watch what you're saying," her mother cautioned. "You don't need any lawyer. I don't know what all the idea is of trying to high-pressure you into hiring some lawyer and . . ."

"Madam," Mr. Mason said, "no one is trying to high-pressure anyone into anything. I was laboring under the mistaken impression that I was representing your daughter."

"Don't you know who your clients are?" Mrs. Ingram snapped.

"Apparently not," Mason said.

"Well, you've got my daughter off that bus, and you've dragged me down here. You've got to get us back. You've got to do that much. Land sakes, I don't know what a person's rights are, but it seems to me that a body should have some sort of compensation when you come along with a lot of detectives and push people around."

"Quite right," Mason said. "I will take you back to Sacramento if you'll just walk over to this automobile."

They walked over to the big seven-passenger car which was waiting at the curb. Mason said to the driver, "I want to catch the bus which just left here, in Sacramento. Can we do it all right?"

"Easy, the bus makes several stops."

"Okay," Mason said. "Let's go."

Mason discouraged all attempts at conversation while they drove to Sacramento. The driver, apparently curious, tried to point out various objects of local interest and quite obviously would have liked to draw out his passengers, but finally gave up his efforts when it became evident they would be fruitless.

Several times Myrtle Fargo whispered to her mother. Mason and Della Street were tight-lipped in silence.

At length they slowed for the outskirts of Sacramento, then drew up in front of the Sacramento bus station. Mason handed the driver fifty dollars then gave him a five-dollar tip.

It would be some ten minutes before the bus arrived.

Mason said to Myrtle Fargo, "There's no reason for you to wait around here. I'll pick up my operatives. You wait for me at your mother's house. I'll take a taxi out."

Mrs. Ingram and her daughter got out of the car, moved over away from the driver. Mrs. Fargo said, "I hope you don't think we're ungrateful, Mr. Mason."

"Quite all right," Mason said. "For a while I thought I was representing you, Mrs. Fargo. I thought I'd fix things so you'd have an alibi all ready and keep the police from barking up the wrong tree."

"So they could then go bark up the right tree?" Myrtle Fargo asked.

"Perhaps."

"Would you like to know who did it, Mr. Mason?"

"That might help."

"It was that mistress of his. Arthman could hardly wait for me to get out of the house to have her join him. Honestly, Mr. Mason, I'm broad-minded, but there *are* limits."

Mason said, "You don't seem particularly broken up about your husband's death."

"I'm not," she said, "if you want the truth. We've been on the point of splitting up half a dozen times. I was coming up here to see what would happen. I thought perhaps my leaving him would bring him to his senses, instead of which he obviously regarded my departure as an opportunity to bring that girl into our home. I've felt for some time that he was thinking of turning everything into cash and running away with that woman. Now I know he was."

"Do you know who this woman is?" Mason asked.

"Not specifically. I only know there's a girl somewhere. A girl he's crazy about. He was hardly home at all the last month. Always making some excuse to be out. He said it was business. That he had to see a customer and had to get listings on properties. Of course it's just a temporary infatuation. I know he won't be true to her. Why, last night when we were at that night club he was making eyes at the girl who takes pictures, and the way he was looking her over you'd have thought he wanted to wrap her up and take her home. He just couldn't keep his eyes off her legs and hips and . . ."

"Myrtle!" Mrs. Ingram snapped. "The way you talk in front of a strange man!"

Mrs. Ingram turned her back, marched over to where the driver was standing by the door of the rented car, then paused to make sure that she missed none of the conversation.

Mason said, "Regardless of how you may feel personally, it's necessary to take the reaction of other people into consideration. You'll be interviewed, police will be asking questions, and perhaps a newspaper reporter, depending on how much of a mystery they make out of the murder and how they want to play it up."

"Oh, I understand," she said. "I'll be decently mournful but I'm not going to overdo it, Mr. Mason. I'm not going to be a hypocrite."

Mason said, "I'll be at your mother's house within an hour, armed with names and addresses of corroborating witnesses and probably a written statement or two. I'll do that much for you. In the meantime you might try thinking real hard about whether or not you retained me last night."

"Oh, but I didn't."

"Try thinking some more."

"I will. And in the meantime if anyone asks me questions what shall I tell them?"

Mason said, "Tell them anything you want. If you're not my client I can't advise you."

"Not even as a friend?"

"No. The friendship is too one-sided."

"Am I supposed to be surprised when they tell me that he's . . ."

"Don't be a fool," Mason said sharply. "I met you at Stockton, took you off the bus, told you that your husband was dead."

"If they should ask me why you did that, what shall I say?"

"Just tell them I'm big-hearted, and now go join your mother. The bus is coming in."

And Mason walked away, leaving her standing, hesitating whether to follow him or join her mother.

At length she turned, and together with her mother entered the rented car and was driven away.

Mason felt Della Street at his side, pushing close to him. "Would you like exhibit A?" she asked.

"What?"

She pushed a piece of cloth into his hand. "This is Myrtle Fargo's handkerchief. I lifted it out of her purse. It has the same identical scent as that which clung to the money in that envelope."

"The deuce!" Mason exclaimed. He whirled to look for Myrtle Fargo. It was too late. She had entered the car and been whisked away.

Mason gripped Della Street's arm with long, strong fingers, piloted her to the runway where incoming passengers were entering the bus depot.

The austere countenance of Mason's detective was sternly unsmiling as the man hurried ahead in the vanguard of the passengers. Catching Mason's eye he drew him to one side.

"You have the names of witnesses?" Mason asked.

The man nodded.

Mason said, "All right, let's get some written statements

127

from them. Do you suppose we could pick up a few of these witnesses, offer to compensate them for their time and ..."

"I have half a dozen written statements in my pocket," the man said, "They're pretty badly scrawled on account of the motion of the bus, but they're all in order and signed. Here they are."

"That's fine," Mason said, pushing the statements into his side coat pocket.

"Perhaps it isn't."

"What do you mean?"

"That bus left at eight-forty-five in the morning," the detective said. "We found people who sat with her from Fresno. We found a woman who spoke with her at Bakersfield. We don't find anyone that was on the bus from Los Angeles who ..."

"That's all right," Mason said. "She was talking with a man who got off at Fresno and ..."

"Just a minute," the detective interrupted quietly and courteously but with an air of grim finality. "We found *one* woman who happened to notice her particularly and who is willing to swear that she wasn't on the bus when it left Los Angeles, that she came tearing up in a taxicab and barely caught the bus by the skin of her teeth at Bakersfield."

"That woman must be mistaken."

"She's the type that doesn't make mistakes, not in her own mind."

"Hang it," Mason said, "that could cause complications. Did you get a statement from this woman?"

"Yes. It's in the bunch I gave you."

"Where does she live?"

"Los Angeles. Her address is in the report."

"And your office is here?"

"Yes."

"Let me have one of your cards. Now I don't know just what this situation is developing into, but I want you to keep your mouth shut, do you understand?"

128

The man nodded.

Mason said, "Do you bill me or do you bill the Drake Detective Agency?"

"The Drake Detective Agency."

"You can trust your men?"

"Sure, but let's not misunderstand each other, Mr. Mason. If the police start asking me specific questions I'll give them specific answers."

"Fair enough," Mason said, "and in the meantime, I take it you didn't give *your* name to any of the passengers."

"I'm employed to get information, not to give it."

"That's fine."

"Of course the police will learn that someone was on the bus asking questions. That is, if they make an inquiry."

"I understand."

Mason piloted Della Street back toward where the taxicabs were parked, said, "I guess we were just a little too optimistic, Della."

"You have those written statements?"

"Yes."

Della Street said, "It might be a good plan to give them to me, then if anyone should ask you where they are you wouldn't have them."

Mason silently passed them over.

Mason gave a taxi driver the address of Mrs. Ingram's residence. The driver pulled down his flag and started the car.

Della Street squeezed Mason's hand as the taxi twisted through the traffic. "After all, she denied being a client, Chief."

Mason nodded silently.

It was as they pulled up in front of a neat bungalow that Della Street said quietly, "She won't want to talk in front of her mother."

"That's only half of it," Mason said, handing the taxi driver a bill. "Come on, Della."

They ran up the steps to the porch. The taxi driver

looked at the bill, grinned and shut off the motor to sit there, waiting. Mason thumbed the bell button.

Mrs. Ingram came to the door. "Well, hello," she said. "You don't seem to have been of very much help."

"What do you mean?"

"I thought a lawyer was supposed to advise his client."

"Well?"

"Well, you weren't here when the police came. You left my daughter to face it all alone."

"The police have been here?"

"They were waiting for us."

"Where did they go?"

"I don't know. They drove away."

"Well, that's fine," Mason said. "I'll talk with your daughter and . . ."

Mrs. Ingram said angrily, "That's the thing I'm trying to tell you."

"You mean the police took your daughter . . ."

"The police took Myrtle with them. She left you this note."

She handed Mason a sealed envelope, on which appeared the penciled words, "PERRY MASON, ESQ."

Mason tore open the envelope and took out a sheet of paper on which had been written simply:

> I'm sorry, Mr. Mason. I had no idea it was going to turn out like this. I hope you'll understand.
>
> *Myrtle Fargo*

Mason thrust paper and envelope into his pocket. "Your daughter wrote this, Mrs. Ingram?"

"Yes, of course. Now then, I want to know what this is all about. I want to know . . ."

The telephone bell interrupted what threatened to have been a monologue.

She said, "Just a minute," turned on her heel and went to answer the phone. She was back in a moment, saying,

"It's long-distance calling you. They say it's very important."

She led the way to the telephone, stood near by so that she could hear the conversation.

Mason said, "Hello," and heard Drake's anxious voice on the other end of the line.

"Thank the Lord I got you, Perry," Drake said. "There's hell to pay in that Fargo case."

"What about it?"

"Police have located Myrtle Fargo's car."

"Where?"

"At the parking station at the Union Terminal depot. It just happens that the parking attendant remembers the person who parked it, or thinks he does."

"A good description?"

"Better than that," Drake said, "or worse than that, whichever you want to call it. He's identified a photograph of Mrs. Myrtle Fargo, the dead man's widow, as being the girl who got out of the car. He noticed her because he happened to see her walk over and try to flag a taxi. The driver told her that it was against the rules to pick passengers up in the front of the station and the witness referred her to a taxi-loading place on the south side.

"Police picked up her trail where a male accomplice rented a plane for her saying she had to be downtown in Bakersfield before one o'clock. They had a tail wind and made good time to Bakersfield. At Bakersfield, she picked up a taxi at the airport and told the driver she simply had to catch the one-ten bus out of Bakersfield. He got her up to the bus depot just about two minutes before the bus pulled out."

"The police," Mason said, "have evidently been working fast."

"They have. I thought I'd warn you so you wouldn't get your feet wet."

"They're wet."

"How wet?"

"Just as wet as they can get," Mason said, and hung up, to face the snapping, beady eyes of Mrs. Ingram.

"Now then, Mr. Mason," she said, "I'm this girl's mother. You and I had just better have a frank talk. Just *what* are you going to *do* for my daughter?"

"If I could get my hands on your daughter at the present time," Mason said grimly, "I'd break her damn neck."

Chapter 15

Perry Mason, tilted back in the swivel chair at his desk, read the newspaper accounts which Della Street had carefully clipped from the various papers and placed on his desk.

The consensus seemed to be that a certain lawyer had tried to build an alibi for Myrtle Fargo and had fallen down on the job rather badly.

Inasmuch as the police seemed to hold all the trumps in their hands, and have a perfect solution to the murder of Arthman D. Fargo, real estate operator, who had been stabbed to death in his residence at 2281 Livingdon Drive, the faces of police officers on the homicide squad were singularly free from worry.

One newspaper account went on to state that:

> The face of a well-known trial lawyer, however, is not exactly wreathed in smiles. It is difficult to ascertain exactly what happened from the standpoint of the lawyer because he is answering all inquiries with a terse, "No comment."
>
> However, it seems that this attorney was firmly convinced that Mrs. Fargo took the Greyhound bus, No. 320, leaving Los Angeles at eight-forty-five A.M. and scheduled to arrive in Sacramento at ten-five that same evening. So convinced was he that such was the case, or that such could be made to appear to be the case, that he whisked the woman off the bus at Stockton in order to drive her to Sacramento in a rented car, and placed detectives aboard the bus to gather the "evidence."
>
> The detectives duly gathered the evidence. That evi-

dence indicated that the woman had not boarded the bus in Los Angeles but had boarded it in Bakersfield at ten minutes past one in the afternoon.

Police appropriated the lists of names and addresses taken by these private detectives.

The murdered man left his widow, Myrtle Fargo, and a son, Stephen L. Fargo, aged ten years. The boy is in one of the better known junior preparatory schools near Sacramento, and is very popular with both pupils and faculty. He is considered highly intelligent, loyal and cooperative.

Mrs. Fargo's primary concern seems to be with the effect her arrest will have upon her son.

Stephen L. Fargo yesterday was a happy young lad. He had been commended by the faculty for his scholastic standing, and had been elected president of his class. Today he finds that his father has been murdered, that his mother is being held by police under suspicion of murder, and that a certain amount of unwelcome publicity has attached itself to him and to the school where he is studying.

Members of the faculty have arranged to keep the young lad in virtual isolation where he is not available to the press. They make no secret of their annoyance at the fact that so much notoriety has attached itself to the pupil and to the school. However, other students, friends of Stephen Fargo, who were available for newspaper contact, stated that Fargo's personal popularity was undiminished and his friends, among both the faculty and the students, were standing by.

Mason pushed the newspaper clippings back to one side on his desk, got to his feet and started pacing the floor, slowly, thoughtfully. He hooked his thumbs in the armholes of his vest and walked with steady, monotonous regularity back and forth across the office.

Della Street, seated in her secretarial office, kept pounding away at her typewriter, glancing up at her employer from time to time but making no comment.

The telephone on Della Street's desk jingled softly. She picked it up, said, "Hello," and heard the voice of the girl at the office switchboard conveying a message.

After a moment she said, "All right, Gertie. I have it. Thanks."

She hung up the telephone, arose from her desk and stood quietly in the doorway of her office, waiting.

Mason continued pacing for almost a minute before he suddenly noticed her standing there, then he brought himself up with a jerk, raised his eyes to regard her with a frowning concentration which was the aftermath of the thought he had been devoting to the case.

"What is it, Della?"

"Mrs. Fargo has now been booked at the local bastille."

"That," Mason said, "means that they've wrung her dry, extracted a lot of written statements and are tossing the husk back into circulation so an attorney can advise her in regard to her 'constitutional rights.' "

Della Street, knowing Mason and understanding his moods, remained discreetly silent.

"That, of course," he said bitterly, "follows the usual pattern. They have a warrant for the arrest of some person whom they apprehend in Sacramento. If the person doesn't talk it takes them ten days to get the prisoner back here to be booked in the county jail.

"If, however, the prisoner falls for the police line that they don't want to prosecute an innocent person and are only too anxious to be convinced of the prisoner's innocence, they charter a plane and book their prisoner almost before the ink is dry on the written statements."

"Here's an early edition of the afternoon paper," Della Street said. "It came in a few minutes ago but I didn't want to disturb you."

Mason took the newspaper from her, stood with his feet spread far apart, his shoulders set. He snapped the paper open, looked at the picture of Myrtle Fargo which was

135

spread over the front page, together with photographs of the house where Fargo had been murdered, a diagram showing the premises, and a photograph of the interior of the office with the safe door swung wide open and the litter of papers on the floor.

Mason skimmed through the article, then paused and turned to Della Street.

"Listen to this," he said.

Police are looking for a male accomplice. Some person who was sufficiently friendly with Mrs. Fargo to risk his life on a charge of being an accomplice in a murder.

The aviator who flew a woman, whom he insists was Mrs. Fargo, to the Bakersfield airport, states that he was employed by a "middle-aged man." His passenger sat in an automobile until all arrangements had been made. Then the man paid the aviator in cash and beckoned to the woman.

It wasn't until the plane was out on the runway, the motor all warmed up and ready to start, that the woman, who was heavily veiled, appeared and took her place in the rear seat of the plane. She didn't speak during the entire flight to Bakersfield.

A taxi driver who picked up this woman at the Bakersfield airport and rushed her to the Greyhound bus depot also states there was no conversation during the entire trip, and that the woman kept her veil down over her face. He assumed that there had been a sudden death and the woman was masking her grief, and he therefore respected her silence.

It is interesting to note that between the taxicab and the Sacramento bus this veil, together with the hat, seems to have been discarded.

Attendants at the Bakersfield bus station report having found a hat with a heavy, dark veil in one of the refuse receptacles. Since the hat seemed to be in excellent condition it was turned in to the Lost and Found Depart-

136

ment, and it wasn't until police made a detailed inquiry that the significance of the hat and veil was discovered.

This bit of evidence was located and preserved, due to excellent police work on the part of the Bakersfield police, in co-operation with Lieutenant Tragg of the Metropolitan Homicide Detail.

Police have a description of the male accomplice who seems to have engaged the plane. He is a man in the sixties, apparently remarkably well-preserved, with a well-modulated voice and gray eyes. He is short, chunky and rather well dressed. Police believe this man 'mastermineded' the fake alibi.

Oddly enough this alibi might have worked if it had not been for the zeal of a prominent attorney whose attempt to gather evidence not only defeated its own purpose, but placed in the hands of the police a list containing the names and addresses of several persons who were passengers aboard the northbound bus.

Mrs. Newton Maynard, thirty-one, residing at 906 South Gredley Avenue, is particularly positive that Mrs. Fargo boarded the bus at Bakersfield.

"I distinctly remember seeing her drive up in a taxicab," Mrs. Maynard stated to the police. "I was particularly impressed because she wore a black hat with a heavy black veil, and she handed the cab driver a bill and didn't wait for change but hurried into the rest room in the bus depot.

"I felt she must be someone who had sustained a loss, and was overcome by grief. I made up my mind that I would try and comfort her if I had an opportunity while she was on the bus.

"Imagine my surprise when this woman emerged from the rest room to join the line of passengers waiting to board the bus. She seemed somewhat excited, but she was not depressed. The hat and veil had vanished, and she was wearing a small, black velvet beret which could very well have been folded and concealed in her purse.

137

I noticed that she made it a point to start talking with various passengers before we had arrived in Fresno.

"That woman was Mrs. Fargo. I am just as positive as I am of the fact that I am standing here. I have a very good memory for faces and I was naturally curious because I had seen her drive up in a taxicab when she was heavily veiled. I studied her very carefully, wondering just what was back of the abrupt transition from a heavily veiled, quiet woman who seemed intent upon avoiding people, to the vivacious, sociable young matron who was so anxious to cultivate the acquaintance of other persons aboard the bus.

"Moreover, I am one of the few passengers who boarded that bus in Los Angeles. Quite a few of them got off at Bakersfield, some got off at Fresno, some got off at Stockton. Mrs. Fargo was not on the bus when it left Los Angeles. I like to talk with people when I travel, and I looked over the passengers who were waiting in line to board the bus at the Los Angeles Terminal; I looked them over after I got aboard the bus and I am absolutely, thoroughly positive that Mrs. Fargo was not on that bus when it left Los Angeles, but that she boarded it in Bakersfield."

Mason folded the paper, tossed it over on his desk, said, "Well, there you are, Della."

"There *she* is, Chief."

Mason said, "Della, have you noticed that the description of the man who helped charter the plane ties in with that of someone we know?"

She thought that over. "You don't mean Pierre, the headwaiter at the Golden Goose?"

"*I* don't exactly mean him," Mason said. "But the description sure fits."

"It surely does," she admitted. "Chief, do you suppose that . . ."

Once more Della Street's telephone rang. She picked up

138

the receiver, said, "Hello," and then said, "Just hold on, Mr. Sellers. I think he wants to talk with you."

She said to Mason, "Clark Sellers, with a report on that handwriting."

Mason moved over, picked up the telephone, said, "Yes, Clark. What is it?"

The handwriting expert said, "I have made a careful examination of the writing on the envelope you gave me, and the exemplars written by Myrtle Fargo. They were both written by the same person."

Mason hesitated a moment, then said, "Meaning Myrtle Fargo wrote 'PERRY MASON, ESQ.' on that envelope?"

"*If* she wrote the exemplars, she did. They were all written by the same person. Of course, I can't vouch for the identity of individuals, only for identity of writing. Where does that leave you, Perry?"

"Behind the eight ball, I'm afraid," Mason said, and hung up.

"Bad?" Della Street asked.

"Bad," he said. "We're in the Fargo case up to our necks. She sent that money."

"You don't have to accept it."

Mason shook his head. "It was that terrified voice that got me. She was in trouble and now she's in worse trouble. It's my business to represent people who are in trouble and do the best I can for them."

"What do you mean? You can't afford to represent her in court. She's absolutely guilty, she . . ."

"How do you know she's guilty?"

"Well, take a look at the evidence," Della Street said.

"That's just it," Mason said. "Let's take a look at the evidence and forget her story. Suppose she was locked in the bedroom in that house when I was there. She had intended to take the eight-forty-five bus. Her husband quarreled with her. She let him know she knew about his mistress. He tried to choke her. She ran to the bedroom and locked the door.

"After I left, she tried to escape. He tried to grab and choke her once more. She stabbed him.

139

"That's what the real evidence indicates. But she thought she could get out from under. So she ran to the car, drove it to the depot, parked it, called on some friend and got him to charter a plane for her."

"A boy friend?" Della asked dubiously.

"I doubt it, probably the same messenger whom she used to take the money to the Golden Goose.... Her *story* makes her seem guilty of murder. The *evidence* indicates a woman who was terrified of her husband, who acted in self-defense, and then made a mistake in trying to avoid publicity.

"We'll start Paul Drake working to try and find that messenger. Now that Clark Sellers says that the address on that envelope containing the money is in the same handwriting as the note she left for me with her mother, I have no choice in the matter. She's my client. I started to represent her, and I'm going to keep on."

He was silent for a moment, then said, "The interesting part of it is that Myrtle Fargo's alibi just might have worked if I hadn't been so damned efficient. Passengers would have remembered her as getting on the bus, the police never would have been able to find out all of the passengers who were on the bus and ..."

"Wouldn't they have come forward when the case received notoriety?" Della Street asked.

"About ten per cent of them," Mason said. "Suppose *you* had been on that bus. The average citizen doesn't fancy becoming involved in a murder case and letting himself in for a lot of cross-examination by attorneys on a question of identification. Suppose you were riding on a bus. You'd probably remember the person who was sitting next to you if you engaged in conversation, but could you positively identify some fellow passenger whom you hadn't noticed particularly? And if you felt that you could, would you feel that your identification would be sufficiently positive so that it could stand up against the browbeating cross-examination of some attorney who was trying to discredit you?

"For instance, suppose he should say, 'Very well, Miss Street, since you've been able to identify the defendant as one of the passengers on the bus, suppose you now describe *all* of the passengers who were on the bus. Start in with the two who were in the front seat on the left-hand side and go on back. Let's have a complete description, please.' What would *you* do?"

"I'd probably faint," Della Street said, grinning.

"You'd have a hell of a time with your descriptions before you got very far," Mason said.

"Then the lawyer would turn to the jury and say, 'There you are. She's hypnotized herself into believing that she remembers all about this defendant because she saw her pictures in the paper, because she was called on to identify her in the jail and because of the testimony of other witnesses, but as a matter of fact she can't remember clearly what *anyone else on that bus looked like*. Take for instance the man who occupied the seat directly behind her. She only remembers him as an oldish sort of man, with a gray suit. She can't remember whether he had a stubby mustache or didn't, whether he wore glasses or didn't, whether his hair was gray or dark, whether he smoked or didn't smoke, what color shirt he wore, what color tie he had on.

" 'The woman in the seat in front of her, she says, had hennaed hair and that's all she knows about *her*. Yet she comes into court and identifies this defendant who could at most have been only one other passenger on the bus whom she must have noticed equally casually . . .' "

"Save it," Della Street said, as Mason almost automatically started making gestures. "You have me convinced."

Mason grinned. "I thought for a minute I was arguing to a jury. But that's the answer, Della. Many of those passengers would have gone on about their business and wouldn't have cared to face the ordeal of cross-examination. Many of them could only have identified the defendant as a fellow passenger, but been unable to swear as to where she boarded the bus."

"Weren't the police planning to question the other passengers when they got off the bus in Sacramento?" Della Street asked.

"Apparently not. Their idea at the time was simply to arrest Myrtle Fargo. They had some sort of a telegraphic warrant which Lieutenant Tragg had rushed up to them and they were supposed to grab her as she got off the bus. The idea of her building an alibi hadn't occurred to them."

"Specifically, and in view of this report from Clark Sellers, just what are you going to do now, Chief?"

He reached for his hat.

"I'm going up to call on my client, and see what can be saved from the wreckage. . . . And that probably will be damned little."

Chapter 16

Perry Mason faced the newspaper reporters with a grin.

"Hold it," one of the photographers said.

The flashlight blazed into swift brilliance.

"Aren't you rather leading with your chin, Counselor?" one of the reporters asked.

"What difference does it make?" Mason said. "My chin is already in the ring, so I may as well lead with it."

"Not your *most* vulnerable spot, anyway," the reporter told him.

One of the other reporters said, "Definitely, Mr. Mason, we want an answer. Are you or are you not representing Myrtle Fargo?"

"No comment."

"You're calling to see her?"

"That's right."

"And under the regulations of the jail you have to be a person's attorney in order to see them?"

"Wrong."

"Well, you have to be an attorney."

"I am an attorney."

"All right, have it your way. You went to Stockton to represent Myrtle Fargo, didn't you?"

"No comment."

"You did hire detectives to get witnesses who were on that bus?"

"Right."

"You thought at that time she had asked you to represent her, didn't you?"

"No comment."

"You went to considerable expense in order to get up to Stockton?"

"Right."

"You paid these detectives out of your own pocket?"

"Right."

"Have you at any time received any money from Myrtle Fargo by way of a retainer?"

"Not that I know of."

"Has someone else paid you to represent her?"

"Not that I know of."

"You're not accustomed to interesting yourself in a case unless you have been retained, are you?"

"No."

"Then can you explain your unusual interest in the Fargo case?"

"No."

"You mean you don't know what it is or you can't explain?"

"No comment."

"You're not being very helpful."

"There's not much help I can give."

"If she wants you to represent her, will you do so?"

"She hasn't asked me yet."

"You're going to see her now to find out if she wants you to represent her?"

"I'm not soliciting business, if that's what you mean."

"You know that's not what we mean."

"What do you mean then?"

"I've already asked the question."

"Then I've already answered it."

"Do you know anything about Mrs. Fargo's male accomplice?"

"She couldn't have had an accomplice unless she's guilty, could she?"

"Assuming that she is guilty, do you know anything about her accomplice?"

"No."

"Assuming that she is guilty, would you represent her?"

"A lawyer can never assume a client is guilty. It's like asking a newspaper reporter to assume that if he had a scoop he wasn't going to publish, would he do this, that or the other."

"You never assume that a client is guilty?"

"Why should I?"

"You can form an opinion, can't you?"

Mason said, "Many people misunderstand the duty of an attorney. It's an attorney's duty to see that a defendant has a fair trial. If the attorney makes up his mind that the defendant is guilty and therefore won't represent that defendant, that's asking an attorney to substitute his own prejudices, his own judgment for the judgment of a Court and a jury."

"Suppose you *know* a client is guilty?"

"That's different."

"Do you know that Mrs. Fargo is guilty?"

"No, I assume she is not."

"Do you know she is not guilty?"

"I know only that she is accused of crime, that she is entitled to a fair trial before a jury, and in order to have such a trial it will be necessary for her to have counsel. If counsel should refuse to appear for a defendant, there couldn't be any trial."

"The Court would order counsel to represent a prisoner under those circumstances, wouldn't it?"

"Then the person would still be represented by counsel."

"Aren't we talking around in circles, Mr. Mason?"

Mason's smile was disarming. "I think so."

They took a few more pictures, then left him alone. Mason found himself sliding into a chair opposite the long meshed screen which ran the length of the divided table. A matron brought Myrtle Fargo in and she dropped into the other seat.

Her face was white and lined. There were dark circles under her eyes. Her lips, without lipstick, seemed about to tremble.

Mason said, "I take it you didn't get any sleep."

145

"They had me up all night questioning me, browbeating me, making me tell my story, wheedling me, signing statements, and then they loaded me in a plane and brought me down here and we went through the same thing all over again. I haven't had a wink of sleep."

Mason said, "Did you telephone me and ask me to take a message to Medford Carlin?"

She met his eyes. "No."

"Did you kill your husband?"

"No."

"Did you send me any money?"

"No."

"Do you understand that you're charged with murder?"

"Yes."

"Do you understand that you don't have much of a defense?"

"Apparently not. I thought I did but I guess I haven't."

She went on. "Mr. Mason, I'm in a horrible predicament. I had absolutely nothing to do with my husband's death. I can realize the position that I'm in but what bothers me more than anything is the effect all of this is going to have upon Steve, my son."

Mason's nod was sympathetic.

She said, "I've sacrificed everything for him. I've—I can't tell you how much I've sacrificed in order to give him the breaks. To think what is going to happen now is more than I can bear."

Mason said, "The question is, do you want me to represent you?"

"Mr. Mason, I haven't any money to squander. My uncle had died and left me some money that my husband was investing. I think he falsified the account. I want whatever estate there is to pay for my son's education. There's some insurance but I can't get that so long as I'm . . . well unless I'm cleared of the murder charge."

"Do you have any ready cash?"

"Very little. I had five hundred dollars when they arrested me, but they took it away from me."

146

"You had five hundred dollars when they arrested you?"

"Yes—it belonged to me."

"Do you want me to represent you?"

"I tell you that I have no money to squander on lawyers."

"Do you want me to represent you?"

"Yes."

"All right," Mason said. "You are lying to me about a lot of things. You *did* telephone me; you left a piece of paper with the safe combination written on it in the telephone booth. You *did* send the money; it was your handwriting on the envelope."

"No, no," she repeated dully.

"But even if I can't make you tell the truth, I'm going to represent you. Now here's what I want you to do. I want you to sit absolutely tight and make no statements to anyone. They'll probably leave you alone and probably won't ask you for much because they already have you crucified. You signed statements?"

"Yes."

"In front of a notary public?"

"Yes."

"You made statements that were taken down in shorthand?"

"Yes. I told them everything."

"All right," Mason said. "Balance up for it by telling them nothing for a while. Now do you know anything that could help me in handling your case?"

"No."

"Your husband had a real estate business?"

"Yes."

"Anything else?"

"No, that was all."

"Was he doing much good in the real estate business? Was he successful?"

"Fairly so, but things have been quiet lately."

"I understand. Now, Mrs. Fargo, I'm going to tell you

something frankly. I'm going to tell you something as your attorney. I'm going to tell you what I *think* happened."

"Yes, go on."

Mason said, "I think you called me up at the Golden Goose, I think you gave me a job to do and . . ."

She interrupted him by slowly shaking her head.

"Let me finish, please," Mason said. "I think you sent me all the money that you had, money that you'd been saving up against an emergency. I think you had encountered some emergency. I think that in some way your husband found out what had happened, and I think the next morning in place of taking the bus for Sacramento as you had planned you found yourself engaged in a showdown with your husband. I think you became afraid of him and locked yourself in your bedroom. I think your husband finally persuaded you to open the door and I think that he tried to choke you. I think you had a knife and stabbed at him in self-defense. Then I think you got in a panic because of the feeling that a lot of newspaper notoriety would make things difficult for you and your son, and tried to fake an alibi. You originally had intended to be on that bus at eight-forty-five in the morning, you knew that your mother was expecting you to arrive on that bus, you felt that if you could find some way of getting aboard the bus and arriving in Sacramento on that bus you would be all right.

"I think you killed your husband but I don't think you murdered him. I think you acted in self-defense. I think you have all but put yourself behind the eight ball trying to tell a story that won't hold water.

"Now then, that's my idea about the case."

She kept shaking her head.

"Is it true?"

She avoided his eyes. "Mr. Mason, I—I wish . . . Oh, I do wish I dared tell you what . . ."

"What are you afraid of?" Mason said. "Anything you tell your attorney is in confidence. Isn't that the way it happened, Mrs. Fargo?"

"I—no."

"It isn't?"

"No."

"How did it happen?"

"I told the truth all along. I left on that . . ."

"Didn't you kill your husband in self-defense?"

"No."

"Why don't you admit you rang me up at the Golden Goose and . . ."

"I didn't!"

Mason said, "You're making it very difficult for me to represent you."

"I've told you everything I can."

"All right," Mason said, "I'm going to represent you. Now I want you to understand one thing."

"What?"

"If I represent you I'm going to try to get you acquitted."

"Naturally."

"No jury on earth is going to believe the story that you've told so far."

"I'm sorry. I can't help it."

"Therefore," Mason said, "I'm going to try to give the jury something that they *will* believe."

"But I can't help you, Mr. Mason, I can't. . . ."

"Of course you can't," Mason said, "you've already committed yourself. You've made affidavits, you've signed statements, you've put yourself in such a position that you're completely bound hand and foot. You're lashed to a set of circumstances that are going to send you up for life if they don't send you into the gas chamber, but *my* hands aren't tied."

"What are you going to do?"

"What I think will be for your best interests."

"But, Mr. Mason, you can't—in view of what I've said you can't found a defense on a lie."

"I can found a defense on anything I want to," Mason

149

said, "and it isn't a lie unless you tell it. Now then, you've got yourself in a mess. I'm going to try to get you out. Remember that under the law the prosecution has to prove that you're guilty beyond all reasonable doubt before the jury can convict you. You understand that?"

"Yes."

Mason said, "I'm going to raise a reasonable doubt in the minds of the jury."

"How's that?"

"I'm going to make it appear that you killed your husband in self-defense."

"I didn't."

"Yes, you did. You're afraid to admit it on account of certain facts that you want to keep from the public, facts that you think will disgrace your son."

"No, Mr. Mason, honestly, I'm telling you . . ."

"I'm going to keep you off the stand, I'm going to let them throw all those affidavits that they want in front of the jury. I can't stop them, but I'm going to raise a reasonable doubt in the minds of the jurors as to what happened. That's all I can do, and the only way I can do it is by utilizing the testimony of the prosecution's own witnesses. Now then, I want you to keep quiet from now on. Do you understand?"

"Yes."

"Can you do it?"

"I think so."

"Try it then," Mason said, and nodded to the matron that the interview was over.

Mason took the elevator down to the lower floor of the Hall of Justice, where he found a telephone booth and called Paul Drake.

"Paul," he said, "I'm up against it on this Fargo case."

"Are you just finding that out?" Drake asked.

Mason said, "I'm stuck with it."

"Don't do that, Perry, get out from under. Don't have anything to do with that case. It's dead open-and-shut."

Mason said, "Just the same, I'm stuck with it, Paul, and I'm going to need some ammunition that I can shoot when I get to court."

"Anything you can get will sound like a firecracker popping back against a sixteen-inch gun," Drake told him.

"Never mind, Paul. I have to take the case as it is. Now Mrs. Maynard is the most deadly witness. I want you to find out about Mrs. Maynard's eyes."

"What about her eyes?"

"She's around thirty-one or two. The picture of her in the paper shows her without glasses. Now there's just a chance she's accustomed to spectacles. She may have a pair which she wears when she isn't particularly concerned with the impression she's creating. Whenever she appears in public, however, she takes off her spectacles."

"A lot of women do that," Drake said.

"But," Mason said, "if a woman witness is going to identify a client of mine and has her glasses in her bag instead of on her nose, I intend to make a point of it."

"I get you," Drake said.

Mason said, "As a matter of fact it's an utterly cockeyed and false impression that a woman doesn't look well wearing glasses but some women have built up a complex on it and I just have a hunch that Mrs. Maynard may be one of those women."

"I'll find out."

Mason said, "I want you to find out everything you can about her, everything about her past, her present, her tastes, her likes, her dislikes, where she goes, what she does. . . ."

"Better take it easy, Perry," Drake said. "You know what'll happen. They'll claim you're tampering with witnesses for the prosecution."

"I don't give a damn what they claim," Mason said. "I'm not threatening her. I'm simply trying to find out facts. Now get busy and see what you can do. She must be back

151

in Los Angeles. Start asking questions around the neighborhood. Get a general line on her."

"And particularly about her glasses?" Drake asked.

"*Very* particularly about the glasses," Mason told him.

Chapter 17

It was early the next afternoon when Paul Drake had a report ready for Mason on the prosecution's star witness.

"This Mrs. Maynard," Drake said, thumbing through the pages of a report, "is a woman who keeps very much to herself. No one knows very much about her. She's a widow and apparently has a little insurance that enables her to live quietly and simply without having to ask favors of anyone. She keeps pretty much to herself and has a little car, wears pretty fair clothes, and is away from home a lot."

"Working?" Mason asked.

"No, not working, because she leaves at irregular hours, and sometimes she is away for days at a time. She has a telephone that's not on a party line, but . . ."

"Well, you can find out where she goes from now on," Mason said. "Shadow her everywhere she goes."

"We're doing that," Drake said, "but since my men have been on the job she hasn't been out very much. However, here's something that you *can* use, Perry."

"What?"

"Yesterday there were some glasses delivered to her from an optometrist."

"How do you know? You weren't on the job then."

"No, but this morning one of my men talking to her next door neighbor discovered that yesterday a delivery boy rang and rang Mrs. Maynard's bell and it didn't answer, and finally the neighbor called out to him to leave his package with her. He did. She remembered the label because she knew the name of the optometrist, whose shop was only a few blocks away."

"That's a break, Paul!"

"Yeah. *If* her glasses were broken when she was making this trip and she . . ."

"Now we're getting somewhere!" Mason exclaimed. "Let's follow up that lead. Who's the optometrist?"

"Dr. Carlton B. Radcliff. He has a little shop where he sells binoculars, optical goods, does fitting for glasses and . . ."

"What sort of a chap?"

"An oldish man, around seventy, I'd say. He lives up above his shop. Apparently he knows his way around—a quiet, patient man who's making a little living out of his shop. Want me to try to find out more about . . ."

"I'll tackle him myself," Mason said. "That may be very important."

Drake said, "I have something else for you."

"What?"

"You wanted me to get a line on Celinda Gilson."

"What do you have, Paul?"

"The card on her apartment reads 'Celinda Gilson Larue.' The Larue has been scratched out and . . ."

"I saw that," Mason said.

"And," Drake went on, "the last name of the headwaiter of the Golden Goose happens to be Larue."

"Pierre?"

"That's right."

"Pierre Larue," Mason repeated.

"That's right."

"Good Lord, Paul, you don't mean he's the husband?"

"Apparently he is. I can't find that they're formally divorced. However, they're separated and—well, anyway, that's the story. Apparently in place of any kind of a property settlement, Larue got his wife a job with the photographing concession there at the Golden Goose. Now then, try putting all that together and what sort of an answer do you get?"

"An answer that doesn't fit in with the problem."

"You'd better change the problem, then," Paul Drake said. "Facts are stubborn."

154

"Damned if they aren't," Mason admitted. "Did you find out where Pierre lives?"

"No one knows," Drake said. "When he leaves the Golden Goose he's gone."

"All right," Mason said, "if he's tied up in the case that much, if he's the husband of the Gilson girl, put a shadow on him. Let's find out where he goes when he quits work."

"You're going to be spending a lot of money before we get done," Drake warned.

"That's all right," Mason told him. "I want results. Let's go see that optometrist."

"My car or yours?"

"Mine. It takes you all day to get there."

"Well," Drake said, "riding with you is always an experience. Let's go."

Mason told Della Street where he was going, then he and Paul Drake drove to the office of Dr. Carlton B. Radcliff.

Despite his various qualifications, Dr. Radcliff quite evidently was seeking retirement in his little shop.

A sign over the counter at the back of the store which could be read by everyone on entering proclaimed:

"I WON'T BE BULLIED AND I WON'T BE HURRIED."

There was a watch-repair counter at the front of the store, and as Mason and Drake entered Dr. Radcliff was seated at the counter, a loupe over his eye, assembling the component parts of a watch.

"Just a minute," he called over his shoulder and went on with his work, carefully picking up a small jeweled wheel with a pair of tweezers, fitting it into position in the movement of the watch.

After a few moments he pushed back his chair, came to the counter and surveyed the men with patient eyes in which there was a glint of quizzical humor.

"What can I do for you gentlemen?" he asked.

Mason smiled. "We want some information."

"Information you can get better some place else."

"I think this is information you can give us," Mason said.

"I am an old man; I have studied but few things. The world has moved rapidly and now there are many things I don't know."

"We want information about glasses," Mason said.

"Now glasses are different," the man conceded. "Glasses and watches I know. Those two things I have studied. I have studied them a lifetime and a lifetime has been too short. What can I do for you?"

Mason said, "We want to know something about Mrs. Newton Maynard's glasses."

"Maynard, Maynard, her glasses. . . . Oh, yes, the broken pair. But I delivered them to her already. She was in a great rush."

"I want to know something about the glasses themselves," Mason said. "They were broken?"

"One of the lenses was chipped. Both of them were scratched badly from—but what is this you wish to know?"

"I want to know whether she could see without those glasses."

"Whether *she* could see?"

"Yes."

"Gentlemen, why is it you want this information?"

"It is necessary that we have it."

"You are friends of Mrs. Maynard?"

Mason hesitated. Drake said, "Yes."

The jeweler smiled urbanely. "Then it is easy. You will get the information from Mrs. Maynard herself."

"Dr. Radcliff, I'm an attorney," Mason said. "I'm trying to get certain facts. I want . . ."

The man was shaking his head even before Mason had finished the question. "Information about a patient or a customer I don't give out. No."

"But," Mason said, "this is information which may be important. It might mean that as a witness . . ."

"As a witness, yes. You are a lawyer, you know the law. I am only an optometrist, a jeweler and a watchmaker. I do not know law. But this I *think* I know. I think that as a witness you give me a paper and I come to court, then you put

156

me on the witness stand, I take an oath to tell the truth and I tell the truth. Then I answer questions. Then the judge will tell me I have to answer questions. Now I do not answer questions. I do not have to. Do we understand each other?"

There was smiling courtesy in the man's eyes but an inflexible something in his manner which was hard as a granite cliff.

"We understand each other. Thank you just the same," Mason said. "Come on, Paul."

They turned and walked out.

Back in Mason's car Drake said, "Don't you think we could have found out a little more if . . ."

"No," Mason said. "All we could possibly have done was to have antagonized him. But this much we do know, there was a chipped pair of glasses with scratches on both lenses brought in by Mrs. Maynard. Now then, Paul, when we get her on the witness stand I'm going to cross-examine her about her eyes and about her glasses, how well she can see without them, and then try to prove that she couldn't have had them on when she was traveling because she'd been carrying them in her purse and they'd become scratched and chipped."

"You think she'll be wearing them in court?"

"I think she'll wear them every minute from now on," Mason said, "but I don't think she *was* wearing them when she was on that Greyhound bus."

"It's going to be hard to prove," Drake said.

Mason said, "That's the reason I didn't question Dr. Radcliff any farther."

"I don't get you, Perry."

"If I had been insistent he would have gone to Mrs. Maynard and told her that we were making inquiries. As it is, the chances are fifty-fifty that he won't even mention it. We didn't make an issue of it and the glasses have already been delivered, so he'll go back to his watch repairing. He isn't the sort of man who will do any gossiping. He's a tight-lipped, skilled workman who wants only to be let alone to do his job."

Drake nodded. "I guess you're right at that, Perry."

"We will, however," Mason said, "serve a subpoena on him just as soon as the date for the preliminary hearing is set."

"When will that be?"

"That," Mason said, "may be very soon indeed."

Drake said earnestly, "Perry, you don't stand a ghost of a chance in that case, and you know it. Why don't you back out of it?"

Mason said, "I'm not much good at backing out. I'm going to make the prosecution prove every element of this case beyond all reasonable doubt. The truth may be one thing, Mrs. Fargo's story may be another—but they're going to have to *prove* she's guilty, Paul."

"They can do it," Drake said. "I wish you were out of it, Perry."

"We'll see if they can do it," Mason said, and then added, "I'm not too happy about being in it myself, Paul, but I'm in it. Don't make any mistake about that. I'm in it all the way."

Chapter 18

The preliminary hearing of Myrtle Fargo for the murder of her husband had attracted little public interest.

Courthouse attachés who had followed the spectacularly successful career of Perry Mason suspected that the cross-examination of Mrs. Newton Maynard would be the highlight of the case and it would be well worth watching to see if the astute cross-examiner could shake her testimony, but those who had talked with deputies in the District Attorney's office were betting as high as twenty to one that her story couldn't be broken down in any important particular. Mrs. Maynard was going to be a positive, skillful, sharp-tongued witness capable of matching wits with any attorney.

So far as the general public was concerned Mrs. Fargo was guilty and that was all there was to it. She had tried to manufacture an alibi and had been caught red-handed. The case was hardly worth wasting time over.

For that reason Mason found himself for one of the few times in his career in a courtroom which was not crowded to capacity. Outside of the first four or five rows of seats, the courtroom was empty of spectators.

All this was to the annoyance of Hamilton Burger, the District Attorney, who had taken the case out of the hands of his deputies and decided to handle it himself. Those who were in the inner circle of the courthouse knew that Burger had taken this case not because he considered it particularly important, but because he wanted to gratify a lifelong ambition to achieve a smashing triumph over Perry Mason.

Because that triumph would be so sweet to a district attorney who had smarted under a series of defeats, Burger was prolonging this case as much as possible.

Patiently he called witnesses to build up the case, yet at the same time tried to keep from disclosing too much information.

Burger introduced a plan of the premises where the murder had taken place, photographs of each room in the house. An autopsy surgeon testified as to the cause of death. The murder weapon had been found and introduced in evidence. It was a kitchen knife, well sharpened and honed, covered with sinister stains, but devoid of fingerprints.

Burger had even found a witness who testified that he had paid Arthman D. Fargo five hundred dollars in currency the night before the murder took place, that in his presence Fargo had placed this money in the safe and had given the witness a receipt. The witness was interrogated as to the denominations of the bills. The bills, he explained, were ten fifty-dollar bills, making a total of five hundred dollars. He had drawn those bills from the bank that same afternoon.

Then Burger introduced evidence of the open safe, the contents piled on the floor where they had been dumped out of the safe. Then, as a crowning touch, a police officer testified that at the time of her arrest Mrs. Fargo had in her purse ten fifty-dollar bills.

Then started the procession of the dramatic witnesses, the ones who were to show flight from the scene of the crime. Burger called Percy R. Danvers, the parking station attendant at the Union Terminal.

Danvers testified that about eleven o'clock on the morning of the murder a woman had parked an automobile in his section. She had received the usual parking station ticket. The other section of the ticket had been placed under the windshield wiper of the automobile. He had gone off duty two hours before the police had found the car.

The witness gave the license number and the engine

number of the automobile and the name on the certificate of registration, the name of Myrtle Ingram Fargo.

Then came the dramatic question, "Could you identify the woman who left that car with you?"

"I could. Yes, sir."

"Did you see her again?"

"I did. Yes, sir."

"Where?"

"In a shadow box at police headquarters."

"How many women were in that shadow box?"

"Five."

"All of approximately the same height, weight, age and complexion?"

"Yes."

"And did you pick the person out whom you had seen parking the car?"

"I did. Yes, sir."

"Who was it?"

The witness pointed a dramatic finger. "Mrs. Fargo, the defendant there."

"Cross-examine," Burger said triumphantly.

Mason smiled reassuringly at the witness. "Mr. Danvers, you did that very nicely," he said.

"Did what?"

"Point your finger."

"Oh."

"How did it happen that you pointed directly at the defendant when you identified her?"

"Because she was the one I saw."

"But you didn't need to point your finger. You could simply have said that the woman you saw was the defendant."

"Well—I didn't want any mistake about it. I pointed."

"I know you pointed," Mason said. "Now who told you to point your finger?"

The man seemed suddenly uncomfortable.

"Come, come, Mr. Danvers," Mason said, "your gesture was hardly spontaneous. There was a studied something about it as though it had been rehearsed. Now remember you're on oath. Did someone tell you to point your finger when you were asked to identify the witness?"

"Yes."

"Who?"

"Oh, Your Honor," Hamilton Burger said, his voice carefully modulated to show that his patience had been taxed far beyond human endurance, "all of this petty embroidering of irrelevant details, *that's* not proper cross-examination. The witness identified the woman. The question is whether that's the woman or whether she isn't the woman, not whether he was told to point when he identified her. . . . Why, I'm perfectly willing to stipulate that *I* told this witness, in my office, when I was discussing the case with him, that if the defendant seated in the courtroom was the woman he had seen he was to point to her so there would be no misunderstanding. *I'll* take the responsibility of that."

And Hamilton Burger beamed at the spectators as much as to say, "See, this bombshell of Perry Mason's was very much of a dud after all."

"Thank you," Mason said to Hamilton Burger. "I'm quite certain you told the witness to point, and I'm quite certain that your desperate attempt to make it appear as a casual, everyday occurrence hasn't really fooled anyone."

Mason turned back to the witness. "So the District Attorney told you what to do in giving your testimony. Now then did he tell you what to say?"

"Oh, Your Honor," Hamilton Burger shouted, "that is entirely out of order! It is incompetent, irrelevant, and immaterial. It's not proper cross-examination."

"Objection overruled. Answer the question."

"Well, he told me to point out this woman and to point to her when I indicated who she was."

Hamilton Burger, his face flushed, slowly sat down, but remained poised on the edge of his chair, showing plainly that he was ready to rise militantly to protect the rights of the People on the one hand and the dignity of the District Attorney on the other.

"What color stockings did this woman have on?" Mason asked.

"I don't know. I didn't notice how she was dressed."

"What sort of a skirt?"

"I tell you I didn't notice, but I think it was some sort of a—oh, a darkish color—I can't say."

"What color shoes?"

"I don't know."

"Did she wear a hat?"

"Yes, I think she did."

"Do you know what color?"

"No."

"You didn't notice her very closely, did you?"

"Well, I didn't notice her clothes, but I did notice her face. She parked the car and then wanted to get a taxi and that was a little unusual, so I just happened to remember her. Usually people who park their cars go right into the station."

"You don't know what percentage of the people park cars in your parking lot and then take a taxi, do you?"

"No. All I know is that this woman *asked* me about getting a taxi."

"Don't you know as a matter of fact that a great many people who dislike to drive in traffic utilize the parking facilities at Union Terminal and then use taxicabs to do their running around in the city?"

"Well, I suppose so, yes."

"Don't you know?"

"Well, I don't know because I don't know—I don't ask them."

"So in this case when this person asked you about getting a taxi it made an impression on your mind?"

"Yes."

"And that was the first time you really noticed the person whom you now identify as the defendant?"

"Yes, sir."

"Coming out of the space allotted for parking automobiles?"

"Yes, sir."

"A good many automobiles were coming in at that time?"

"We had quite a brisk little business, yes."

"Now, as I understand it, Mr. Danvers," Mason said, "the customers drive up in front of the entrance to the parking place. You give them a ticket and place the stub under the windshield wiper of the automobile, then you collect some money and then the customer drives into the parking lot, finds a parking place, locks the car and walks back out."

"That's right."

"So there's some little time consumed between the time the stub is first given and the time the person walks out."

"A minute or two."

"Sometimes more than that?"

"Oh, yes."

"Now the first time you noticed this person whom you now identify as the defendant was when she emerged from the parking lot and asked you about where to get a taxicab. Is that right?"

"Yes, sir."

"And you noticed her then?"

"Well, not well enough to tell you everything she had on, but well enough to be pretty sure that this defendant is the woman."

"Oh, you're *pretty* sure," Mason said.

"Yes, sir."

"You're not absolutely sure?"

"Well, I think I am."

"Why didn't you say so then? Why did you say you were pretty sure?"

"Well, I am pretty sure."

"Are you absolutely sure?"

"Well, I think so, yes."

"Which is it? Pretty or absolutely?"

"Well, I guess it's absolutely."

"You *guess* it's absolutely?"

"I'm sure."

"Then why did you say you were pretty sure?"

"Well, I wanted to give the defendant the benefit of all the doubt."

"Oh, then there is a doubt."

"Well—I didn't say I had a doubt. I said I was giving the defendant the benefit of any doubt."

"What doubt?"

"Any doubt."

"Then as I understand it, you did have a doubt, and it was to resolve this doubt in favor of the defendant that you said you were *pretty* sure. Is that right?"

"I guess so—yes."

"Now then," Mason said, "if you're only *pretty* sure that it was the defendant who emerged from that parking place, and if when she came out was the first time you took particular notice of her, you can't be absolutely sure that she was the woman who drove the Fargo automobile into that parking space, can you?"

"Well, it stands to reason she had to be."

"I'm not talking about what stands to reason," Mason said. "I'm asking you if you know."

"Well, if you want to put it that way, I assume that she's the same person. She must have been."

"But you don't know?"

"No, I don't *know*."

"You aren't sure?"

"Well, I'm not absolutely sure."

"Are you *pretty* sure?"

"Well, I'm—I just acted on the assumption that . . ."

"I know you did," Mason said. "You acted on the assumption that she must have parked that car, but you didn't particularly notice the driver of that car when it came in, did you?"

"Not particularly, no."

"You simply followed your usual routine of handing the driver a stub, getting the money necessary for the parking

165

privilege and putting the other end of the ticket under the windshield wiper. Isn't that right?"

"Yes."

"And under those circumstances you don't take any particular notice of the drivers, do you?"

"Well, sometimes."

"All right, Mr. Danvers," Mason said, "now describe the drivers of the two cars who came in before the defendant."

"I can't remember them now."

"You don't even know whether they were men or women, do you?"

"No."

"And at that time there was no particular reason for you to notice the woman who you now claim is the defendant. She hadn't said anything or done anything that had attracted your attention."

"No."

"This person was in the parking space for several minutes. During that time other cars came in?"

"I think so. I would assume so."

"You can't remember?"

"No."

"Then you saw some woman coming out of the parking place, who asked you something about a taxicab."

"That's right."

"And the District Attorney told you that when you got on the witness stand you were to point at the defendant and say, 'That was the woman.'"

"Yes," the witness said before Burger could get an objection in.

Burger said, "Your Honor, I ask that that answer be stricken so that I can interpose an objection. That's assuming a fact not in evidence. It's a misquotation of the previous evidence."

"The witness has already answered," Mason said.

"And I'm asking that the answer be stricken out so that the Court can consider my objection."

"The witness said 'Yes,' " Mason said. "He was under oath. Do you claim that answer was incorrect?"

"I claim that I want to have the answer stricken out so I can interpose an objection on the ground that that's assuming a fact not in evidence."

"I think it's proper cross-examination," the Judge said. "I'll let the answer stand."

"But that isn't in accordance with the facts," Hamilton Burger said. "That's not . . ."

"Hamilton Burger can be sworn and testify if he wants to contradict his own witness," Mason said.

"Oh, after all, it's a petty matter," Burger yielded with bad grace, sitting down.

Mason's voice lost its formality, assumed an easy conversational tone. "Let's see," he said casually, "the police came to you first and asked for a description of this woman, didn't they?"

"That's right."

"You gave them a description?"

"Yes, the best I could at the time."

"And then they showed you several pictures of the defendant?"

"Yes."

"You studied those pictures carefully?"

"Yes."

"You didn't just glance at them?"

"No, I studied them carefully."

"Did you tell the police that those were pictures of the woman who had parked the car?"

"I said there was something familiar about her face."

"And what else?"

"I said she could have been the woman—that it might be her."

"You didn't say positively it was her?"

"No."

"Then later on when you saw the defendant in a line-up you recognized her at once from her pictures, didn't you?"

"Yes, of course."

"And when you saw her in that line-up you can't be absolutely sure whether you picked her out because you remembered her face from the encounter at the parking lot or because of having seen her picture, can you?"

"Well, of course . . ."

"Can you?"

"Well, it could have been a little of both."

"Exactly, and even then you didn't identify her positively, did you?"

"Well, I said she looked like someone I'd seen before."

Mason smiled at the witness. "That's all," he said.

"Any redirect-examination?" the Court asked.

"Getting back to what I told you," Hamilton Burger said, "isn't it a fact that all I told you was that when you indicated the defendant, you were to point?"

"Yes."

"That's all."

"Just a moment," Mason said as the witness started to leave the stand. "There's some recross-examination."

The witness settled himself.

"How long were you at Hamilton Burger's office the time he told you to point to the defendant?"

"Oh, half an hour I guess."

"What did you talk about?"

"Just a moment, Your Honor, just a moment," Hamilton Burger said. "That's not proper cross-examination. It's incompetent, irrelevant and immaterial. It calls for a privileged communication that has nothing to do with the testimony of the witness."

Mason said, "Your Honor, on redirect-examination Hamilton Burger asked him about what was said. That was redirect-examination. Under the familiar rule that when counsel asks a question calling for part of a conversation the other party has the right on recross-examination to ask for all of the conversation, I want to know everything that was said."

Hamilton Burger's face was now the color of raw liver. "Your Honor," he shouted, "I simply refuse to have confi-

168

dential conversations pried into in this manner! I have a right in my capacity as District Attorney to investigate all phases of a case and ..."

"But you did ask a question on redirect-examination calling for a part of a conversation," the Court said, "and this man isn't a client, but only a witness. The objection is overruled."

"Go on," Mason said. "What did you talk about?"

"Well, we talked about my testimony."

"And what was said?"

"Well, I told Mr. Burger what I've said here."

"And what did Mr. Burger say to you?"

"Well, he told me about pointing, and that's about all."

"Now then," Mason asked, "wasn't there something that he told you you didn't need to mention unless you were specifically asked about it?"

"Well—yes."

"And what was that?" Mason asked.

"About the woman not carrying a traveling bag."

"Oh, I see," Mason said. "When this woman left the parking lot she was not carrying any traveling bag?"

"No, sir."

"Nothing in her hands?"

"Nothing except a little leather purse."

"You're certain of that?"

"Yes."

"And Hamilton Burger told you that you weren't to say anything about that, didn't he?"

"Well, not unless I was asked."

"Thank you, Mr. Danvers," Mason said sarcastically. "That's all."

"No questions," Hamilton Burger muttered, and then tried to cover his discomfiture by hurriedly calling his next witness.

That witness was the pilot who testified that he had been hired by a man to fly a woman to Bakersfield, that it had been represented to him that it was necessary for the woman to be at the Pacific Greyhound Bus Depot in

Bakersfield by one o'clock in the afternoon. He had agreed to get her there in time and had done so. The woman had been heavily veiled and he hadn't seen her face, but he remembered the manner in which she was dressed. He had paid some attention to her clothes because of the fact of the veil. He had also particularly noticed the woman's figure and general appearance.

"Do you see anyone in this courtroom whose figure and general appearance are about the same as the figure and general appearance of the woman you flew to Bakersfield in the airplane?" Hamilton Burger asked.

"Yes, sir."

"Where is she?"

"If Mr. Burger told you to point, go right ahead and point," Mason interposed.

"He didn't tell me to point," the witness said, "he just told me I was to say 'the defendant.' "

There was a burst of laughter from the courtroom.

Hamilton Burger shouted angrily, "But you had previously seen her in the matron's office and had told me she looked like the woman. Isn't that right?"

"Just a moment," Mason interposed, "that's objected to as leading and suggestive, an attempt to cross-examine his own witness, and an attempt on the part of the District Attorney to testify."

"It's leading and suggestive," the Court said. "It also may be an attempt at cross-examination of your own witness. However, the objection is sustained on the ground of its being leading."

"Well, had you seen her before?" Burger asked.

"Yes."

"And that woman was the defendant?"

"It looked like her."

"Cross-examine," Burger snapped.

"How many times had you seen the defendant before seeing her in court this time?"

"Once."

"That's all. Thank you," Mason said.

170

"Just a moment," Burger shouted. "The witness misunderstood the question. He means that he saw her once for purposes of identification. He saw her twice. Once when he identified her, once when she got in the airplane. That's right, isn't it?" Burger said, turning to the witness.

The calm tranquillity of Mason's tone was in sharp contrast to that of the District Attorney. "I object, Your Honor," he said, "on the ground that this is leading, on the ground that it assumes a fact not in evidence, and on the further ground that it is quite palpably an attempt on the part of the District Attorney to coach the witness as to the answer he is to make in response to the question the District Attorney has just asked."

"The District Attorney will please confine his statements to direct questions asked of the witness," the Court ruled.

"Very well," Hamilton Burger said, controlling himself with difficulty. He turned to the witness. "When you had previously testified that you had seen the woman once before, you meant—or—well, tell us *what* you meant."

"Oh," Mason said, "I'll stipulate that the witness isn't so stupid that he hasn't already got the point of the District Attorney's coaching. I'll stipulate that he would testify that he meant he had seen her once before for purposes of identification."

"I guess that's it," the witness said.

"That's all," Burger said.

"Just a moment," Mason said. "Before you leave the stand perhaps we should find out a little bit more about this man who made arrangements to charter the airplane. Would you know him if you saw him again?"

"Yes."

"Have you ever seen him again?"

"No."

"Now can you describe him a little more particularly?"

"Well, he was around sixty, somewhere around there, and he seemed to be a little uncertain in his movements. He—I thought he might be drunk but I didn't smell any liquor on his breath. He may have been drugged or something. He seemed to be sort of feeling his way and—well, I just noticed him, the way he walked and the way he looked, sort of uncertain like."

"Was he tall?"

"No, he was short and thickset and—well, he was around sixty. I don't remember too much about him. I just took it for granted he was the girl's father."

"Now about this identification. Did you see the defendant in a line-up?"

"No, just by herself in the matron's office."

"And did Mr. Burger point her out to you?"

"Answer that by either yes or no," Burger interposed.

"No."

"Did the police?"

"Not exactly."

"What do you mean by that?"

"Well, they told me they had the woman for me to identify. They took me into the matron's office. There was only one woman there except for the matron."

"Exactly," Mason said. "Now didn't they also tell you that there could be no doubt on earth but that this was the woman you'd taken to Bakersfield, to go in there and identify her, and to be sure you didn't make any blunder in what you said?"

"Well, something like that. They told me not to get fainthearted or act like I wasn't sure, or some smart lawyer would rip my guts out when I got on the stand."

"So you said you were sure?"

"No, I didn't. I wasn't sure. I said I thought she was the one. Actually I had to wait until the next day before I was absolutely certain."

"And in the meantime, the police kept talking to you?"

"I'll say they did."

"That's all," Mason announced.

"No further questions," Burger said. "I'll call my next witness."

The next witness was the taxi driver from Bakersfield who had transported the heavily veiled woman from the air-

172

port to the Pacific Greyhound Bus Terminal. He admitted, however, that he could not identify her, that she was heavily veiled, that he had not seen her face, that he had not noticed in particular how she was dressed. He only knew that she was a woman about five feet three, or three and a half, who weighed about a hundred and twenty or a hundred and twenty-five pounds.

"You have heard the defendant, Myrtle Ingram Fargo, talk?" Hamilton Burger asked.

"Yes, sir."

"And did you notice any dissimilarity between the voice of Mrs. Fargo, the defendant in this case, and the woman whom you transported to the bus depot at Bakersfield?"

"No, sir."

"You may inquire," Burger said.

"You didn't notice any dissimilarity?"

"No, sir."

"Can you pick out any particular points of similarity?"

"Well, their voices sounded something the same."

"But you can't identify the defendant from her voice as being that woman, can you?"

"Not absolutely."

"You can't identify her from her voice at all, can you?"

"Well—just like I said, I can't notice any points of difference particularly that I can swear to."

"In other words," Mason said, "you, too, have had a talk with Hamilton Burger, haven't you?"

"I told him what I knew, sure."

"And he asked you if you could identify the defendant from her voice, didn't he? And you told him that you couldn't?"

"Well, yes."

"So then he said to you, 'I'm going to put you on the stand and ask you if there were any particular points of *dis*-similarity, and you can say that you didn't notice any points of dissimilarity.' Isn't that the way it happened?"

"Well, I—I don't exactly remember."

"The suggestion that you testify as to whether there were any points of *dis*similarity came from Hamilton Burger?"

"Yes."

"That's all," Mason said.

Hamilton Burger said, "That's all. My next witness is Mrs. Newton Maynard, and I hope, Mr. Mason, that you cross-examine *her* at some length."

"That will do," the Court interposed. "There will be no side comments from counsel."

Mason smiled at Burger's angry countenance.

As Mrs. Maynard came forward, it was apparent that she had suffered some injury. Her left eye was tightly bandaged. She held up her right hand and settled herself comfortably on the witness stand.

Hamilton Burger asked her a few preliminary questions, then inquired, "Where were you on the twenty-second day of September of this year?"

"I was in Los Angeles and then I was in Sacramento; both places on the same day."

"Yes, Mrs. Maynard, and how did you go from Los Angeles to Sacramento?"

"By Pacific Greyhound bus."

"And do you know what time you left Los Angeles?"

"I do. Yes, sir. I left Los Angeles at eight-forty-five."

"And what time did you arrive in Sacramento?"

"At about ten minutes past ten in the evening. We were due in Sacramento at five minutes past ten but we were five minutes late."

"Did you on that twenty-second day of September have occasion to talk with the defendant in this case, Myrtle Ingram Fargo?"

"I did. Yes, sir."

"When did you first see her?"

"I first saw her when she got out of a taxicab at Bakersfield."

"Had you seen her before that time?"

"No, sir."

174

"You were on the bus between Los Angeles and Bakersfield?"

"I was. Yes, sir."

"Was the defendant on that bus?"

"She was *not*!"

"You're certain of that?"

"I'm positive, absolutely positive."

"If she had been on the bus would you have seen her?"

"I would have seen her and I would have noticed her. That woman was not on that bus between Los Angeles and Bakersfield. She arrived at the bus depot in Bakersfield wearing a heavy veil and she arrived by taxicab. The cab was driven by the man who has just testified on the witness stand."

Mrs. Maynard clamped her lips together in a firm line of self-righteous assurance and glared at Mason as much as to say, "Now, take that. Let's see you shake *my* testimony."

"Did you talk with the defendant?" Burger asked.

"I did. Yes, sir."

"At some length?"

"Yes, sir."

"Will you explain to the Court just how that happened, Mrs. Maynard?"

"Well, I suppose I'm curious. Perhaps I am, but I never was a body to keep to myself. When I travel I feel that I want it to be a broadening experience and you don't get broadened simply by sitting down and wrapping yourself up in your own personality and . . ."

"We understand," the District Attorney interrupted, "but please let's get to the point, Mrs. Maynard. Will you tell me just how it happened that . . ."

"That's what I am telling you. Now please don't interrupt me," she snapped.

There were titters throughout the courtroom and the Judge smiled broadly.

"Go ahead," Hamilton Burger said lamely, "but try and make your testimony as concise as possible."

"We'd save a lot more time if you didn't interrupt me,"

she said truculently. "Now, let's see, where was I? Oh, yes. I was telling you that when I saw this person get out of the cab all heavily veiled and everything, it made me curious. I watched her and she went in the women's rest room and when she came out she didn't have the veil.

"When the call came to get aboard the bus and I saw that she was going to board the bus, I managed to get next to her in line and started talking with her, and then some passengers got off at Fresno. When we got aboard the bus there at Fresno it just happened that I had an opportunity to get in the seat next to her. I dropped into that seat and we started talking.

"I'm perfectly willing to admit that I was trying to draw her out. I was curious to find out why she had worn that heavy veil."

"Did you ask her?" Hamilton Burger inquired.

"I tried to but I didn't have a chance. That is, I started to lead up to the question and she told me with her own lips that she'd been on that bus all the way from Los Angeles and I thought to myself, 'Why, you little liar, you. You . . .'"

"Never mind what you thought to yourself," Burger interrupted, but there was a note of triumphant satisfaction in his voice. "Just say what she told you."

"Well, that's it. I started to ask her something about the trip she was making and wanted to find out how it had happened she had been so heavily veiled and in such a rush to get to the bus depot and . . ."

"Well, suppose you tell us, not in generalities, but just as specifically as you can, just how this conversation came up," Hamilton Burger said.

"Well, as nearly as I can remember, I said something about I hoped she didn't think I was trying to pry into her private affairs, but I was naturally curious—and she interrupted me to say that she didn't mind at all, that she was glad to have someone to talk with, that she'd been seated next to a man coming out from Los Angeles and he'd been a little tipsy. I asked her if he'd been fresh and she said no,

176

just drunk, and she was afraid she'd become intoxicated from the smell of his breath."

"Anything else?"

"Yes, sir. I just tested her. I said, 'Well, where is that man? I didn't notice him,' and she made a point of looking all around and said, 'Well, I guess he must have got off at Bakersfield.' Got off at Bakersfield!" Mrs. Maynard snorted. "He wasn't on the bus. I guess I know. I was on the bus all the way from Los Angeles, and there wasn't any man that was intoxicated like that, and she wasn't on the bus herself."

"Are you positive of that?"

"I'm positive."

"Now what else happened on the trip?"

"Well, we sat next to each other all the way then from Fresno to Stockton and then she left the bus and two men got on. One of those men tried to get me to swear that she'd been on the bus all the way from Los Angeles. I knew right away there was something fishy and . . ."

"Now never mind your conclusions," Hamilton Burger said, "and we don't want any conversation that took place without the presence of the defendant. Never mind about those men at the moment. We may ask you about that later, but I want to know now how long you occupied the seat on that bus next to the defendant."

"All the way to Stockton. Of course, we got off at the stations, sometimes there'd be a long stop and sometimes a short stop, but while the bus was traveling I was seated next to her all the way up from Fresno, and we talked along quite a bit of the time."

"Did you notice how she was dressed?" Burger asked.

"I noticed everything about that woman," Mrs. Maynard said with the finality of one who is absolutely certain of herself.

"How was she dressed?"

"Quietly, the same as I was, in fact I think I commented that our clothes looked very much alike and she said yes, she liked to dress quietly when she traveled, but in good taste, and she made some compliment about my clothes. I don't remember what it was except that they were in good taste, only she did mention something about my being an older woman and I didn't like that. I might be a year or two older but not a great deal older and I've been told that I don't look my age, I . . ."

"I'm quite certain you don't," Hamilton Burger said, and then, turning to Mason with a sardonic little bow, said, "Now would you care to cross-examine, Mr. Mason?"

"Oh, yes, indeed," Mason said, arising from his chair at the counsel table and smiling affably as he walked around the table to stand within some ten feet of the witness. "Indeed you don't look your age, Mrs. Maynard," he said.

"How do you know?" she snapped. "I haven't told you yet how old I am."

"Exactly," Mason said, smiling. "Whatever it is, you don't look it."

"I don't think I care for that," Mrs. Maynard said. "That has all the elements of being a nasty dig."

"I didn't mean it that way," Mason said. "I notice you are having trouble with one eye, Mrs. Maynard."

"Yes, sir, I have an infection in that eye. I injured it and the eye became infected. I have to keep it tightly bandaged."

"Why tightly?" Mason asked.

"So I can keep my glasses on," she said. "If it were a bulky bandage I couldn't get my spectacles on over it. But by fastening it tightly with adhesive tape I am able to wear my spectacles."

"Oh," Mason said, "so you have to wear spectacles."

"I don't have to. I want to."

"But you do wear them?"

"I do. Yes, sir."

"How long have you worn them?"

"For some ten years, I guess."

"Do you always wear them?"

"No, sir."

"No?"

"No."

"When do you take them off?"

"When I go to sleep and when I wash my face."

There was laughter from the courtroom.

Mason waited for the laughter to subside. "You find that wearing glasses improves your vision?" he asked.

"Well, I don't wear them to try and keep my nose in line!" she said.

The Judge rapped with his gavel. "The witness will try to answer questions," he said, "and avoid being facetious."

"Then let him ask questions that make sense, Your Honor," the witness snapped angrily at the Judge.

"Proceed, Mr. Mason," the Judge said, smiling slightly.

"You can see quite well with your glasses on, Mrs. Maynard?"

"Certainly."

"How about when you have your glasses off?"

"Naturally I don't see so well."

"How much trouble do you have with your eyes?"

"I don't have any trouble. I just don't get along well without glasses."

"Now that clock, for instance," Mason said, "the clock at the rear of the courtroom, you can tell the time?"

"Certainly."

"Now take your glasses off and see if you can tell the time."

"Oh, just a moment," Hamilton Burger said. "Your Honor, I think I can see what Counsel is trying to lead up to, but there seems to be no foundation whatever for this line of questioning. If he is going to make any such showing as he apparently is trying to make there should first be a preliminary proof that the witness did *not* have her glasses on at the time concerning which she is testifying."

"Well, I did have my glasses on," Mrs. Maynard said. "I had them on every blessed minute of the time and . . ."

Mason said, "If the Court please, I think I'm entitled to have the witness answer the question. I think it is important to ascertain the extent of her vision with her glasses off."

The Judge hesitated, then said, "Mrs. Maynard, do you have any objection to removing your glasses temporarily?"

"Not at all."

She took her glasses off and, holding them in her hand, looked up at the Judge.

"Now then," Mason said, "can you tell what time it is by the clock in the back of the courtroom?"

She blinked her unbandaged eye. "Very well, if you want to know, I'm just as blind as a bat without my glasses. Now wait a minute, I'm under oath. I don't mean that I'm blind either, I just mean that I can't see good enough to do very much good for myself, but I just want you to understand that I had my glasses on every minute of the time I was on that bus. I had my glasses on all the time I was riding from Los Angeles to Sacramento."

"I understand," Mason said. "Put your glasses back on, Mrs. Maynard. Since you are quite dependent on your glasses I take it that you have more than one pair?"

"What do you mean by that?"

"You carry a spare pair with you in the bag that you're holding on your lap, so that in the event one pair should break . . ."

"What's going to break my glasses?" she said. "Certainly not. A pair of glasses isn't like an automobile tire. They don't puncture on you so that you have to carry a spare all the time."

"You mean you have only the one pair of glasses?"

"That's all. That's enough, isn't it? You can't see any better with two pair than with one. Not as well, I guess."

"But occasionally you do break glasses or injure them, do you not, Mrs. Maynard?"

"No."

"And your glasses were in good condition on this twenty-second day of September?"

"Yes."

"Are those the same glasses that you have on now that you wore then?"

The witness hesitated.

"Are they?"

"Is there any reason why they shouldn't be?"

"I don't know," Mason said. "I'm asking you, Mrs. Maynard. Are those the same glasses?"

"Yes."

"Then," Mason said casually, "how does it happen that you went to Dr. Carlton B. Radcliff to have the lenses in those glasses replaced about the twentieth of September?"

For a moment it seemed as though the witness couldn't have been any more disconcerted if Mason had suddenly hit her.

"Go on," Mason said. "Answer the question."

The witness looked around her as though seeking some physical means of escape from the witness stand. She moistened her lips with her tongue, then said, "I didn't take in *these* glasses."

"Well, then," Mason said, "since you don't have any spare glasses what glasses *did* you take to him, Mrs. Maynard?"

"Just a moment, Your Honor," Hamilton Burger interposed hastily, trying to give the witness time to collect herself. "I think this is not proper cross-examination. After all, there was nothing said about her glasses and . . ."

"Objection overruled," the Judge interrupted, his eyes on the face of the witness, and at the same time motioning the District Attorney to his seat. "Let's see what this witness has to say in answer to that question without a lot of interruptions. Can you answer that question, Mrs. Maynard?"

"Why, of course, I can answer that question."

"Well, please do so then."

"Well, I—I guess I don't have to account for everything I do."

"The question was," Judge Keith said, "what glasses did you take to this doctor in the event you don't have any extra glasses of your own?"

"They were glasses that belonged to a friend."

"What friend?" Mason asked.

"I—I—that's none of your business."

"Are you going to answer the question?" Mason asked.

Hamilton Burger was on his feet. "Your Honor," he said, "I submit that this is going far, far afield. The witness has stated positively that she had her glasses on at the time she made the identification, she has stated that she had her glasses on at all times during the period concerning which she has testified. Now Counsel has tried to show what would have happened if she had not had her glasses on. And now he is going even farther afield in an attempt to show what happened some time after the occurrence in question."

"For the purpose of raising at least an inference that she did *not* have her glasses on at that time," Mason said.

"Well," Judge Keith ruled, "I think that Counsel has made his point and *if* there is any evidence which he has which would indicate this witness did not have her glasses on at that time, he is at liberty to present such evidence as part of his case."

"Exactly," Hamilton Burger said. "The witness has given him all of the information that could possibly pertain to this case."

"I think I will sustain the objection to any further cross-examination along those particular lines," Judge Keith said. "You have made your point, Mr. Mason, and if you have any evidence which you can produce tending to show that the witness did not wear her glasses at that time, or could not have worn them, that, of course, will be pertinent."

"What I want is to impeach the witness," Mason said.

"You will have to impeach her upon a matter that relates to the relevant portions of her testimony—in other words, to the presence or absence of glasses at that specific time, not at a later time. Proceed."

"Now when you first saw the defendant she was heavily veiled?" Mason asked.

"Yes, sir."

"That veil prevented you from seeing her features?"

"Yes, sir. That was the object of it. That was why she wore it."

"But when she emerged from the rest room in the bus station at Bakersfield she was not wearing the veil?"

"That's right."

"Then that was the first time you had seen the defendant's face?"

"Yes, sir."

"Then how did you know that the person whom you then saw was the person who had gone into the rest room wearing a veil?"

"Well—by her clothes, I guess."

"Can you describe those clothes?"

"Well, I can't particularly. I—I just know it was the same woman who came out, that's all."

"You don't know how many women were in the rest room at that time?"

"Well, no."

"You simply saw a woman go in heavily veiled, and then you saw this defendant come out, and by some process of mental reasoning on your part you reached the assumption that it was the same person?"

"Well, I know it was the same person."

"How?"

"Well, I recognized her."

"By what?"

"By her clothes."

"How was she dressed?"

"Well, at this date I can't tell you *exactly* how she was dressed, but I can come pretty close to it. I can tell you exactly what I had on, and I remember that she was dressed very much the same way. We commented about it on . . ."

"I understand that," Mason said. "You made that statement on direct-examination, but can you tell us *exactly* how the defendant was dressed?"

"Only because I remember that her clothes were just about the same color as mine and we made some comment on it and I know how I was dressed and . . ."

"I am asking you now," Mason said, "if from your memory you can tell me *exactly* how the defendant was dressed."

She said, "And then if I tell you that, why you'll ask me how the woman in the seat in front of me was dressed, and how the woman in the seat behind me was dressed, and when I can't answer those questions you'll make a monkey out of me."

The courtroom roared with laughter.

Judge Keith pounded for silence but was smiling broadly as he said to Mason, "Proceed."

"So you can't then remember how the defendant was dressed?"

"All I can remember is that we talked about our clothes being about the same color. Now if you want to know how *I* was dressed . . ."

"I don't," Mason said. "I'm simply trying to test your recollection to see if you can remember how the defendant was dressed."

"I can't."

"Then how can you be certain that it was the defendant you saw entering the rest room and wearing a heavy black veil?"

"Well, it stands to reason she had to be the one. She's the one who came out—I can't remember exactly what her clothes were, but I do know that the woman who came out of that rest room without the veil was the same woman that went in wearing the veil. I'm swearing to that."

"Now," Mason said, "if you were mistaken about wearing your glasses at that time, if you hadn't had your glasses on, you couldn't have made an accurate identification, could you?"

"I was wearing my glasses."

"But if you hadn't had them on, you couldn't have made an accurate identification?"

"No."

"Thank you," Mason said, "that's all."

"And that," Hamilton Burger announced, "concludes our case. The prosecution rests."

184

The move came as a distinct surprise to Judge Keith and to most of the courthouse attachés who had filed in to listen to Mason's cross-examination of Mrs. Maynard.

"Court will take a ten-minute recess," Judge Keith said, "before the defense starts putting on its case."

"Gosh, Perry," Paul Drake said in a low voice to the lawyer during the intermission, "isn't that a sketchy way to put on a murder case?"

"That's a damn skillful way of putting on a murder case," Mason said. "He has enough in there to convict my client of first-degree murder if there isn't any defense, and we're faced with the choice of either putting Mrs. Fargo on the stand or not putting her on the stand."

"Both bad?" Drake asked.

"Both terrible," Mason said. "If we don't put her on the stand the Judge will bind her over. If we *do* put her on the stand and she tries to substantiate her alibi, she's sunk.

"Her only real chance would be to tell what *I* think is the real truth. A story which for some reason she tried to avoid telling."

"What's that?" Drake asked.

Mason said, "She intended to take that bus up to see her mother, but she had some trouble with her husband. He was investing some of her separate property she'd inherited from a rich uncle who had died, and I think it's pretty evident now that Fargo had been juggling accounts around and was short about twenty-five or thirty thousand dollars. I *think* Mrs. Fargo caught him at it and I think there was quite an argument. I think probably she threatened to tell the police and I think Fargo locked her in her bedroom and kept her there a virtual prisoner. I think she was in there while I was looking at the house pretending that I wanted to buy it, and I think Fargo was intending to skip out."

Drake said, "And then you think they had a fight?"

"Then I think Fargo unlocked the door and I think that he probably tried to choke her and I think she had a knife and stabbed him, not intending to kill him but simply trying

185

to defend herself, striking out blindly. She stabbed Fargo in the neck, severed an artery, realized what she had done, and in a panic ran downstairs, climbed in the car and started running, all the time with the feeling that if she could only catch this bus she could manufacture an alibi for herself. I think she had really intended to take the six o'clock plane, and the bus was something she resorted to as an alibi. I think she phoned her mother to corroborate the bus story."

"Suppose you put her on the stand and have her tell *that* story?" Drake asked. "It would be self-defense and . . ."

"And the fact that she'd tried to manufacture an alibi and had made a false affidavit in order to make that alibi stand up would hopelessly prejudice the public against her. There's some reason she won't tell the true story. If I could only find that real reason and bring that into the evidence I'd stand a chance."

"Isn't it an attempt to protect her son?"

"No. I thought it was for a while but now I don't think so. It's something else, a most persuasive, powerful reason."

"Can't you force her to tell the true story?"

"No."

"Can't *you* tell the Judge what the true story actually is?"

"If I only had that reason which is sealing her lips, I could do it. Without that reason, I'd just be getting her in deeper than she is now. The public would think I'd given her a good story, but that she actually killed her husband in order to get the insurance."

"How much insurance?"

"Twenty-five thousand dollars. Just about enough to cover the shortage in her husband's accounts."

"In her favor? Or is the estate the beneficiary?"

"She's the beneficiary."

Drake said, "You're in something of a dilemma now, Perry."

"Damned if I'm not," Mason said. "The only satisfaction is that this is a preliminary hearing. If I can do something to shake the testimony of that Maynard woman I'll know a lot better what to do by the time we get to the Superior Court."

"Are you going to try to have your client released on this preliminary hearing?"

"No," Mason said, "I'm going to let the Judge bind her over. I don't dare put her on the stand; I don't dare do a thing until I can get her to tell me exactly what did happen."

"You're satisfied her alibi is faked?"

"Sure, it's faked," Mason said. "The District Attorney has punctured that. However, I *may* be able to discredit that Maynard woman after we find out about the glasses. Notice that she doesn't have any spare glasses, therefore we *may* be able to make a point. I'm going to put on a defense just long enough to put Dr. Radcliff on the stand and see what he has to say."

Della Street moved up close to Mason, said, "Chief, I have one more contribution to the evidence."

"What?"

"Mrs. Ingram uses the same scent her daughter does."

Mason digested that information. "I don't see that it gets us anywhere, but it's an interesting point. However, Clark Sellers says that it's Myrtle Fargo's handwriting on the envelope that contained the money.

"She still swears she didn't address that envelope with my name, send me money, or . . . Here comes the Judge."

Judge Keith returned to the Bench, said to Mason, "Any defense?"

"Yes, Your Honor. I wish to call one witness."

The District Attorney's face lighted with anticipation at the idea of an opportunity to cross-examine Mrs. Fargo, but Mason said, "Dr. Carlton B. Radcliff who is under subpoena by the defense. Will you please take the stand?"

A choking, almost strangled cry sounded loud in the silence of the courtroom.

Everyone turned to where Mrs. Maynard had started to get to her feet. "You can't do that," she shouted. "You can't dredge out my private life and hold it up. . . ."

Judge Keith pounded his gavel.

"Silence," he roared. "Order in the court. Spectators will be silent. The rights of the parties will be amply protected by respective counsel."

Mrs. Maynard swayed, was seized with a fit of coughing and then dropped back into her chair.

Mason was frowning thoughtfully as he asked Dr. Radcliff the usual preliminary questions, then said, "You are a duly licensed and qualified optometrist, Doctor?"

"I am. Yes, sir."

"And you are acquainted with Mrs. Newton Maynard, the witness who has recently testified?"

"I am. Yes, sir."

"It is part of your business to prescribe, grind and fit lenses?"

"It is. Yes, sir."

"Now did you see Mrs. Maynard on the twenty-first day of September of this year?"

"I did not. No, sir."

"You did not?" Mason asked.

"No, sir."

"On the twentieth?"

"No, sir."

"I thought she delivered some glasses to you to be repaired?" Mason said.

"She did. Yes, sir."

"When?"

"On the twenty-second day of September."

"The twenty-second!" Mason exclaimed.

Mason turned to the Judge. "I beg the indulgence of the Court. This witness is not exactly hostile, but he has refused to make statements on the ground that to do so would be betraying the interests of the patient, that he would only make such statements in answer to questions if he were subpoenaed and called to the witness stand."

"Very well," Judge Keith said, leaning forward and showing his interest.

"At what time on the twenty-second?" Mason asked.

"At about eight o'clock in the morning."

"Was your place of business open at eight o'clock?"

"No, sir, but I live over my store with a telephone extension from the store. She called me at eight o'clock and told me she had an emergency rush job and wanted to know how soon I could grind a pair of lenses."

"What did you tell her?"

"I told her that I could not possibly have the lenses ground before the next day, and she asked me to have the glasses delivered to her home the moment they were ready."

"And this was at eight o'clock."

"Yes—within a minute or two. I had just started my breakfast. I always eat breakfast at eight o'clock."

"And then she brought the glasses around to you personally?"

"She did not. They came by messenger a few minutes later."

"Who was the messenger?"

"A boy. I haven't seen him before. He had the glasses wrapped up in a package."

"The new glasses were delivered to Mrs. Maynard when?"

"On the twenty-third, as I had promised."

"As I understand it, then," Mason went on triumphantly, "Mrs. Maynard had her glasses delivered to you soon after eight o'clock the morning of the twenty-second and did not receive them back until the next day. Therefore, if she didn't carry a spare pair of glasses she couldn't possibly have been wearing her glasses on the twenty-second. I think you may inquire, Mr. Burger."

"Just a minute," the witness said. "I don't know whether you are asking me a question, but it was not at all impossible for her to have been wearing *her* glasses on the twenty-second. These weren't *her* glasses."*

*I am deeply indebted to S. J. Goldstein, O.D., Optical Salon, Hotel Laurentien, Montreal, Canada, for some of the technical material in this

"Weren't her glasses!" Mason said, trying to conceal the disappointment in his voice.

The District Attorney smiled broadly.

"No, sir," Dr. Radcliff said, "these were entirely different glasses."

"You're sure?"

"Of course I'm sure. These were glasses for a person around sixty years old. They were not Mrs. Maynard's prescription at all."

"Do you mean," Mason asked, "that you know Mrs. Maynard's prescription?"

"I don't know her prescription, but I know that these were not her glasses."

"How can you tell that if you don't know what her prescription is?"

"Because I can take one look at her eyes and the general construction of the glasses and tell that these are an entirely different prescription. She has the characteristic large pupil and very clear sclera, or white of eye, which is associated with shortsightedness, or myopia. These are of the opposite type of glasses and are for a person about sixty years old."

"You can tell a person's age from the prescription of the glasses?"

"Generally. You can, in fact, tell a lot about a person from his glasses. These glasses were probably for a person of Slavic descent. I would say they were for a man rather than a woman because of the nose measurement. There was rather a bulbous nose and . . ."

"Will you kindly tell us," Mason said, venting his irritation now that the triumph which had seemed in his grasp was slipping through his fingers, "how you can tell that a man was of Slavic descent simply by an inspection of his spectacles?"

---

book as well as for a vast storehouse of material indicating the remarkable things which a competent optometrist can tell from such a prosaic thing as a pair of glasses.

"Well, I can't tell absolutely. I said probably," the witness stated.

"And what caused you to believe that he might be of Slavic descent?"

"A great deal can be told by glasses," Dr. Radcliff said. "There is not only the prescription of the lenses themselves, but there are the shape, style and construction of the frames. For instance, on the present glasses there was a very wide nose measurement which indicated a bulbous nose, there were very short 'temples,' as we call them, the side pieces holding the frame on the ears, approximately three and a half inches from the hinge to the beginning of the curve of the bow. That indicated a person with the type of skull usually found in persons of Slavic descent. The average temple measurement is four, four and a half and even five inches. Other types have a greater distance from ears to eyes. Then in addition to that there were indications that the left ear was approximately half an inch higher than the right ear. Furthermore there were parallel scratches on the outside of the lenses indicating that the person who wore the glasses quite frequently took them off and placed them face downward on a desk. Ordinarily particles of grit will not scratch optical glass, but if the glasses are placed on a hard surface containing grit and particles of perhaps sand, the tendency will be for the lenses to be scratched. This is particularly true in the case of the present glasses which have an inside curvature of ten diopters giving an exceptionally deep dish, so that these glasses when placed on a table with the lenses down would be quite apt to receive scratches. The average inside curvature is six diopters."

"And you noticed all of these things from the glasses?"

"Yes, sir. The glasses and the frames."

"Why did you take such a particular interest in them?" Mason asked.

"Because that's my business."

"And what did you do with these glasses?"

"I replaced the lenses with fresh lenses and had them delivered by messenger on the morning of the twenty-third to Mrs. Maynard's Los Angeles address."

"I guess that's all," Mason said.

"That's all," the District Attorney announced, grinning broadly. "No questions."

"Any further testimony?" Judge Keith asked Mason.

Mason shook his head. "Under the circumstances, Your Honor, we will probably not put in any further defense. We will have no objection to the Court making an order binding the defendant over. However, since it is near the hour of adjournment, I would like to have until tomorrow to give the matter consideration."

The District Attorney was on his feet. "We object to the matter going over for another day. . . ."

"I may decide tomorrow to put the defendant on the stand," Mason interrupted.

Hamilton Burger cleared his throat. "Under the circumstances, I will withdraw my objection. We will make no objection to an adjournment until tomorrow morning."

"Very well. Tomorrow at ten," Judge Keith said. "Court's adjourned."

Chapter 19

Perry Mason, Paul Drake and Della Street sat in Mason's office.

"Where," Drake asked, "do we go from here?"

Mason, pacing the floor, said, "Hang it, Paul, we're going at this case all backwards."

"How come?"

"I'm going by what my client tells me and my client is lying—probably in order to protect her child."

"She's lying about her alibi," Della Street said. "That much is certain, but we don't know she's lying about . . ."

"She's lying about having sent me that money," Mason interposed.

Drake said, "Surely admitting that she had sent you the money wouldn't compromise her. She's in a position now where she needs your services. To have paid for them in advance would be all to the good so far as she's concerned."

Mason shook his head impatiently and said, "That's the trouble, Paul. We're looking for reasons before we have the facts. Let's try and get the facts and then we'll learn the reasons."

"Well, what *are* the facts?"

"The facts," Mason said, "are all tied up in a crazy quilt of events and we're going to have to analyze that crazy quilt in order to find out where the pieces of material came from. And when you remember that the material represents human emotions, human lives, human hates, human fears, you can begin to get an understanding of the problem."

"Where's your starting point?" Della Street asked.

Mason said, "You can start any place, but so far as *we're*

193

concerned the start was when we walked into the Golden Goose. Now let's begin piecing together what must have happened from that time on. In the first place this woman and her husband must have been in the Golden Goose. Somebody must have pointed me out to the woman but not to the husband. I'm willing to swear Arthman Fargo had no idea who I was when I called on him the next morning pretending to be looking for a good buy in real estate."

"Well," Drake said, "it must have been Pierre who pointed you out. The more we find out about Pierre the more we realize he's tied up in something which won't stand investigation. He's simply disappeared into thin air. He walked out of that night club shortly after you talked with him, and he's never been back."

"All right, *that's* a significant fact," Mason said. "Now when this woman telephoned me she was terrified of something."

Drake nodded.

"And," Mason went on, "a short time after I'd talked with her and immediately after Pierre had been seen talking with me, a woman who was a complete and utter stranger approached us with a story about her baby having been stolen and placed out for adoption."

"Well," Drake asked, "how the devil are you trying to get any connection between those two?"

Mason, pacing back and forth across the floor, suddenly started snapping the fingers of his right hand. "There," he said, "is the answer. There's the key clue that I overlooked. That has to be it."

"I don't get it," Drake said.

Mason said excitedly, "Paul, I want to find out about that old Helen Hampton blackmail case—you know the clipping that came in the envelope. I want to get the fingerprints. . . . No, wait a minute, there isn't time. We don't even know when it happened. I'm going to have to short-cut it. . . . Wait a minute now, let's think fast. Let's get this thing where we can nail it down. We can't afford to fumble this one. Now let's see."

194

Mason paused in pacing the floor to stand poised, thoughtful. "Helen Hampton, Helen Hampton," he kept repeating aloud.

"Those spectacles," he said almost musingly. "Mrs. Maynard almost went through the floor when I brought up the matter of those spectacles. . . . And Arthman Fargo's girl friend is a girl who works at the Golden Goose and was formerly the wife of Pierre. . . ." Again Mason snapped his fingers. "I've got it," he said triumphantly. "By George, I've got it."

"*What* have you got?" Drake asked.

Mason whipped a notebook from his pocket. "This is the number of Celinda Gilson's telephone, Della. Put through a call. Now when you have her on the line I want you to make your voice sound just as excited as you can. Make it appear that you've been running and that you're out of breath, that you're frightened and trying to rush through a message. Think you can do it?"

"I can try," Della Street said.

Mason said, "Get Celinda Gilson on the line. Tell her that you're a friend of Helen Hampton; that under the guise of testing her reactions, the police have given Helen a truth serum and that she's talking. Then hang up the telephone with a little exclamation as though someone had either caught you at the phone or was approaching the phone and you had to get out."

"Good grief," Della Street said, "I should have studied to be an actress."

"You are, and a darned good one," Mason told her. "Come on, let's run through this act once for effect."

Della Street said, "I should have some sort of a script."

"Type it out if you want," Mason told her. "You're going to have to pour these words into the telephone. It has to sound like an emergency. You can't falter, you can't stumble, you're going to have to sound frightened to death."

"I don't get it," Paul Drake said. "What the devil are you trying to get at, Mason?"

Mason grinned. "I'm trying to get the man with the glasses."

Della Street ratcheted paper into the typewriter, her fingers played a tune over the keyboard. Mason stood behind her, looking over her shoulder, nodding a couple of times, then said, "That's okay, Della."

Della Street whipped the paper out of the typewriter, stood over by the telephone and ran through the hastily improvised script.

"A weak point right here," Mason said, with his pencil in hand, leaning over the script. "It doesn't sound quite urgent enough."

He crossed out a couple of words, then a whole sentence, then made one short interlineation. "Let's try that."

Della Street ran through it again.

"Perfect," Mason said, pointing to the telephone. "Put through the call."

They were tense and silent as Della Street's fingers spun the dial of the phone.

"If they only answer," Mason said, half under his breath, "if they *only* answer."

Abruptly Della Street said into the telephone, "Hello. Celinda Gilson? . . . Never mind who this is. I'm a friend of Helen Hampton, more than a friend. I share things with her. We have no secrets. Get this, get it straight. They can't see me at the telephone. No one must know I'm telephoning. Police came to the apartment. They made an excuse, I don't know what it was, I was out of the room. They gave Helen a hypodermic. The poor sap took it, thought it was some sort of a reaction test. It's sodium amytal—truth serum. She's beginning to talk. I don't know what she's saying, but my God, she's certainly talking. Sounds like she's talking in her sleep but she's pouring out a blue streak. I thought you should know. I—*oh!* . . ." Della Street lowered

196

her voice to a half-whisper. "I've got to get out of here. . . ."

She gently slipped the receiver back on the hook.

"That," Mason said, "is fine," and walking over to the coat closet grabbed his hat and whipped out of the door.

Chapter 20

Mason's knuckles tapped gently on the door of Celinda Gilson's apartment.

"Who is it?" she called.

"Me," Mason said gruffly.

"Well, don't be so coy. The door's unlocked, and . . ."

Mason pushed open the door and entered the apartment. Celinda Gilson, standing nude in front of the full-length mirror, turned to face him.

The smile on her face froze into a look of horror. "Damn you!" she exclaimed, and with one swift step reached the chair over the back of which was draped a robe. She flung the robe around herself and, with eyes blazing, said, "You've got a crust to come in here this way. . . . I'm dressing."

"You invited me in," Mason said.

"Well, I thought you were someone else."

"Who?"

"None of your business."

Mason walked over to the overstuffed chair, from the back of which she had taken the robe, settled himself comfortably and took the cigarette case from his pocket. "Have one?" he asked.

"Say, what do you think I am?"

"A very attractive young woman," Mason said.

"You're not even getting to first base."

"First base doesn't interest me at all," Mason said.

"What does?"

"Home plate."

"You're playing on the wrong diamond."

Mason lit a cigarette. "Just on the wrong team. Sure you won't have one?"

"Look, will you tell me just what you're after?"

Mason said, "Since you want to talk baseball, I'm going to let you keep on pitching until I find the one I like and then I'm going to knock it over the fence for a home run."

"I'm not going to pitch."

"Oh yes you are," Mason said, crossing his long legs. "You have to."

"Will you kindly tell me just what in hell you think you're doing here?"

"I'm hiding out."

"Hiding out?"

"That's right."

"Who from?"

"Believe it or not," Mason said, "I'm hiding from the police."

"*You* are?"

"That's right."

"Well, you came to the wrong place to hide."

"I don't think so."

"Well I do. Probably you don't realize it, Mr. Mason, but you've just put yourself completely in my power."

"Have I?"

"You know you have."

"How?"

"By telling me you're hiding from the police. All I have to do is to walk over to that telephone, pick it up, ask for police headquarters, and I'll be the fair-haired baby."

"Go ahead," Mason invited.

"Well, don't think I won't."

"I don't know what's stopping you. Go right ahead."

"It's just that I hate to be a rat."

"I know," Mason told her. "You're not accustomed to calling the police."

"Why are you hiding out? What do the police have against *you*?"

Mason said, "I tried to pull a fast one and my foot slipped."

"What?"

"I had a brain storm that I thought would pay off. It didn't."

"Why?"

"Because I took too long a chance. I had private detectives get in touch with a girl from whom I wanted to get some information and they pulled a fast one."

"Who was it?"

"Helen Hampton. We waited until we caught her driving a car and accused her of drunken driving. She indignantly denied it. We told her we were state police in plain clothes and wanted a sample of her blood. Since she was cold sober she agreed to take any kind of a test we wanted. That gave us the chance to do what *we* wanted."

She was watching him with eyes that were filled with puzzled curiosity. "What did you want?"

"We gave an injection of sodium amytal," Mason said, "on the pretense of taking some of her blood, and—well you know sodium amytal. It's a truth serum."

"Why, you—you . . ."

"Exactly," Mason said. "It was tricky but I simply *had* to have the truth."

Her eyes were cold with caution now. "Did you get it?"

"Get it?" Mason said scornfully. "We got it in the neck. She was just beginning to talk when one of her close friends, a roommate, I guess, who was a pretty smart little cookie, sneaked down the hall and telephoned. We caught her at it and she put it to us right on the line, said she was telephoning the police."

"So what happened?"

"What do you suppose happened?" Mason said. "We cleared out. We couldn't stand a rap like that. It's put me in one hell of a position. I've pulled a lot of fast ones but this is about the most desperate chance I ever took."

"Why did you do it?"

"Because I thought her testimony would give us the key clue we're after in this murder case."

"Helen Hampton? What does *she* know about it?"

"From the way she was talking before the blow-off," Mason said, "I think she knows plenty."

"And you want me to believe that with something like that happening you didn't stick it out until the last minute?"

"Oh, we stayed as long as we dared," Mason said. "She was getting pretty sleepy at the last. I guess we gave her a little too much. However, I got a clue which I can work on if I can only keep out of the way of the police."

Celinda Gilson regarded him thoughtfully. "You can't stay here."

"Be a sport," Mason said. "I could hole up here."

"You mean stay here *permanently*?"

"Until the thing blows over. Until I can . . ."

"Why you're just as crazy as . . ."

"After all," Mason interrupted, "*you* have some interest in this."

"I have an interest in what? . . . Say, what do you think you're trying to pull? What kind of a bluff is this?"

Mason merely smiled and blew out cigarette smoke.

Abruptly she said, "Look, there's somebody else coming up here. I've got to head him off."

She started for the telephone.

Mason grabbed her wrist.

"Let me go," she said, struggling with him. "I'll scream, I'll call the police, I'll . . ."

"That's exactly what you're trying to do now," Mason told her. "If you get to that telephone you'll call the police and . . ."

"No, no. I swear I won't. Honestly. In fact I *may* give you a break. I might be able to put you up here for a while, but I can't let this other person know that you're in the apartment. I . . ."

"No telephone," Mason said. "Meet him at the door and tell him you're busy."

"He'd cut your heart out."

201

"Like that?"

"Like that."

Mason said, "I'll watch the number you dial. If it's a police call I'll jerk the phone out by the roots."

"Fair enough, fair enough," she said.

She started for the phone, Mason following her. Then halfway to the telephone she stopped and said thoughtfully, "Say, that sounds fishy."

"What does?"

"That story about you giving Helen a shot of truth serum. You wouldn't have been that desperate. And she wouldn't have fallen for it. You . . . Say, how the hell did you know her name was Helen Hampton? Whose mail have you been reading? You . . ."

Knuckles tapped on the door.

She glanced at Mason like a trapped animal.

Mason got up, crossed the room with two quick strides and jerked the door open.

Medford D. Carlin stood on the threshold, a fatuous grin on his face which changed into an expression of startled surprise as his eyes blinked recognition.

His right hand swung toward his hip pocket and Mason hit him flush on the point of the jaw.

Chapter 21

Mason pulled down the wall bed, jerked off the sheets, tore them into strips, calmly fashioned a gag for the unconscious figure whom he had dragged in from the corridor. He then tied the hands, arms and feet with the strips of torn sheeting, taking great pains to make certain that there was no slack, and that the man was bound securely.

Celinda Gilson stood over at the far corner of the apartment biting her knuckles. Twice she started to speak, caught herself both times before saying a word.

Mason arose from the carpet, brushing dust from the knees of his trousers.

"Just what do you think all this is going to get you?" she asked.

Mason grinned. "How do I know? I might win a murder case."

"Don't be a fool. This has nothing to do with that murder case. His bitchy wife killed him, and you know it."

Mason contemplatively regarded the trussed-up figure that was beginning to twitch with returning consciousness. "And just where does *this* fit into the picture?"

"It's another picture altogether."

"Or," Mason said thoughtfully, "it could be another frame."

On the floor, Carlin, regaining consciousness, gave a smothered moan which came as a strangled, inarticulate noise from behind the gag. He opened his eyes, blinked a couple of times, then suddenly started struggling.

Mason watched him with a casual, detached interest until he saw that none of the knots were slipping, then he turned back to Celinda Gilson.

"Of course," he said, "you mustn't expect Carlin to stand by you. He's smart. He's left himself an out all the way along the line. Pretty smart chap, Carlin."

On the floor, Carlin tried to talk. The result was an inarticulate gurgling of sounds behind the gag.

Mason walked over to the telephone, picked up the receiver, dialed "Operator" and said, "Get me police headquarters, will you please?"

That did it.

Celinda was over at his side, her arms around his neck. "Please, Mr. Mason, *please*! For God's sake! Give a girl a break, can't you? You ..."

"Get some clothes on," Mason said over his shoulder. "While you're dressing you can decide whether you want to talk."

She said, "I haven't done anything, Mr. Mason. Only— well, a girl has to live."

"Was it a good living?"

"No."

"I thought not," Mason said. "You're good-natured and you're friendly. They used you and probably only gave you enough to get by."

"I suppose that was all I wanted."

"Better get dressed."

The figure on the floor made gurgling, inarticulate sounds, rolled his head from side to side in a gesture of negation.

"He'll kill me if I talk," she said.

"Suit yourself," Mason told her. "Right now you have a break. He has a gag on and *can't* talk. If you tell your story first it may be that you can get Lieutenant Tragg to buy it."

"Who's Lieutenant Tragg?"

"Homicide. You met him the other day."

"I tell you this has nothing to do with the murder."

"Which one?" Mason asked.

"Why—the only one, of course."

Again Carlin struggled with the strips of torn sheeting.

"Don't be silly," Mason said. "There were two."

204

"Two what?"

"Two murders."

"I know, but one was—one was . . ."

"What?"

"Fargo," she said.

"Naturally," Mason told her.

"No, no. I mean . . ."

"What do you mean?"

"Nothing, I guess."

"Better get some clothes on," Mason said.

She started for the closet, then suddenly turned. "All right," she said, "you win. It wasn't murder, it was a baby racket. A switch on the old shakedown."

Carlin on the floor raised his legs and pounded his heels down hard.

Mason walked over, prodded him in the short ribs with the toe of his foot, said, "Don't interrupt when a lady is talking, Carlin. I'll have to kick the wind out of you if you aren't polite! Go ahead, Celinda, what were you saying?"

"A modification of the old baby racket," she said. "Carlin got babies—illegitimate babies. I don't even know how he handled his source of supply, but he apparently had a swell contact. He'd wait until the new parents had become very much attached to the child. Then he'd see that they got word that the real mother was employed at the Golden Goose.

"That was about all he had to do. Once people have taken a child and have become really attached to it they have an irresistible desire to get a look at the mother, particularly if they think they can steal a look without being detected.

"So people would come to the Golden Goose and Carlin would tip off Pierre. Pierre would handle things very smoothly. There'd be just a little flicker of a signal when he was hovering around the table, and shortly after that Helen Hampton would come over to sell cigars and cigarettes. Then she'd break down, start crying, and sob out

205

her story about having had her baby stolen and being Japanese."

"How much Japanese blood has she?"

"Don't be silly. She's no more Japanese than you are, but she has those peculiar high cheekbones and dark eyes and—well, the rest of it was just good clever make-up. If you'd take a good look at her under a bright light you'd find that she'd done some very clever work slanting the eyes."

"Then what?" Mason asked.

"Then the suckers are fed just enough information so they realize that they've got Helen's supposedly stolen baby. They think the adoption papers are illegal, and from then on it's a smooth shakedown."

"Didn't the parents ever want to let the child go when they heard the story about the Japanese ancestry?"

"Only once that I ever heard of. You see it was a carefully engineered story. Just a mere fraction of Japanese blood. No one would ever have known it or need ever to know it. But it made a bulletproof scheme. The new parents couldn't go to court with the person they thought was the real mother because then the child's future would be forever blasted. The way the new parents looked at it, Helen would give testimony that would show the child was part Japanese, and after that—well, you know how it would be. People wouldn't want their sons to marry a girl who was part Eurasian, and nice girls wouldn't want to marry a boy who had a similar mixture of blood in his veins. It was all handled so cleverly no one ever, ever suspected a shakedown."

"But they paid money?"

"Sure they paid money—but the big money came after the slip-up."

"You said they slipped up once. What happened that time?"

"They picked the wrong man. Four years ago Carlin tried to pull it on the Fargos."

"The Fargos!"

"Yes. The Fargos' boy is adopted. Three years ago they tried to blackmail Fargo, but he got wise. Instead of tipping off the police, Fargo forced Carlin to take him into partnership, and they've worked together ever since.

"Fargo, pretending to be a private detective masquerading as a real estate man, would start snooping around their neighborhood asking questions about the adopted child, and the parents would become convinced that the mother knew that they had her baby. From then on Fargo and Carlin would whipsaw the new parents for as much as the tariff could bear, and a lot of it went for fictitious lawyers and detectives who, the parents thought, were working for them."

"And Mrs. Fargo?"

"Doesn't know anything about it. When Fargo discovered what the game was, he kept his mouth shut. She still thinks the boy has Japanese blood. That's one of the holds he had over her."

"So that's it!" Mason burst out. "That's why she won't talk! But she must have known Fargo was mixed up with Carlin."

Celinda shrugged. "I guess she knew he was in some racket, but she didn't know what it was all about." Then her eyes narrowed. "Or maybe she found out! Now if you're looking for a nice hot motive for Myrt killing her husband . . ."

"I'm not," said Mason grimly. "Were you really Fargo's girl friend, or just an accomplice in the racket?"

"I started out being an accomplice," she said, "and then—oh hell, I guess I'm a pushover."

"And were you in Fargo's house on the morning of the twenty-second of September?"

"Don't be silly."

"Weren't you in that upstairs bedroom that he didn't dare to open when I was in the house?"

"Are you nuts?"

"Weren't you?"

"No," she said, "and what's more I don't want to hear any more of that kind of talk. I don't know what you're trying to pin on me, but I don't like it. I'm going to put some clothes on."

Chapter 22

Lieutenant Tragg said, "What the hell's coming off here?"

Mason indicated the tied, gagged man on the floor and said, "Another corpse."

"This one looks like a live corpse to me," Tragg said.

Mason went over and untied the piece of sheeting which held the gag in place.

Carlin spat out the piece of damp cloth and said to Mason, "You son of a bitch!"

"Who is it?" Tragg asked.

"Our esteemed friend, Mr. Medford D. Carlin," Mason said.

"So I suppose you want me to be surprised," Tragg said.

"Aren't you?"

Tragg merely grinned. After a moment Tragg said, "Well, I know a lot about you, Mr. Carlin, if you *are* Mr. Carlin."

"Take his fingerprints," Mason suggested.

"Oh thank you *so* much," Tragg said with heavy sarcasm. "I'd *never* have thought of that if you hadn't suggested it."

Carlin said, "You haven't a damn thing on me. I have a record, that's all."

"I'll bet you have a record," Tragg said, "and while you're making explanations, who was the charred corpse that was so conveniently found in the bedroom?"

"How would I know? Ask Mason. He seems to be masterminding the whole thing."

"How does this girl fit in the picture?" Tragg asked, jerking his thumb toward Celinda Gilson.

"How do you fit into the picture, Celinda?" Mason asked her.

"I don't fit," she said.

"How'd you like to take a little ride?" Mason asked.

"That's a hell of a return for my hospitality."

"Just a ride," Mason told her, "nothing else—not yet."

Tragg said, "Let's not have any misunderstanding, Mason. I'm running this thing."

"Sure you are," Mason told him, "but you're anxious to clear up the case, aren't you?"

"I'm driving to headquarters. Let's take these rags off the guy and put on some handcuffs. Mason, I'll take your word that this is Carlin. I'll play along with you that far, but that's as far as I'm going."

"Keep an eye on him," Mason warned, "I have an idea he might even go through a window."

Tragg fitted handcuffs to Carlin's wrists, said apologetically, "I don't ordinarily do this, but I'm handcuffing your wrists behind your back on account of Mason's build-up."

Carlin said, "Sure, let Mason do the talking, you do the listening. You'll wind up behind the eight ball. Why the hell do you take *his* word for everything? Why don't you ask me for my story?"

"I asked you," Tragg said. "I didn't get much of an answer."

"Because Mason was doing all the talking."

"Mason was giving information," Tragg said.

"Sure," Carlin said sarcastically. "Mason's trying to get you a promotion. That's all *he* thinks about. The client who hired him to save her neck in a murder case means nothing to *him*. The only thing Mason wants is to see that good old Tragg gets the case solved no matter who's guilty."

"Keep talking," Tragg said.

"Mason knocks me out, ties me and gags me so I can't say a damn word and then gets you on the job. That gives him a swell opportunity to sell you on his side of the case."

"What's *your* side?" Tragg asked.

Carlin said, "I left my home to go on a business trip—

out on a mining deal. Someone entered my house as soon as I'd left, set fire to it and apparently planted a corpse so it would seem I'd been burned to death. How much co-operation do the police give me in trying to find out what's happened? Not a damn bit."

"I didn't see you down at police headquarters asking for any co-operation."

"I was going down there as soon as I found out what had happened. I just this minute got back to the city."

"And came calling on your girl," Tragg said.

"Why the hell don't you grow up?" Carlin asked belligerently.

"I'm wearing long pants now," Tragg told him. "Come on, buddy, we're going places. You can talk then."

"I demand that you take these handcuffs off," Carlin said.

"I'm hard of hearing in that ear," Tragg told him, pushing him out into the corridor. "You'll have to move to the other side if you want to make any requests."

"Don't you worry," Carlin told him, "I'll move to the other side all right, and it'll be your blind side when I do."

Mason made an elaborate gesture of offering his arm to Celinda Gilson.

She said, "No thank you. I can get along very well without *your* help."

"Indeed," Mason murmured.

"From now on," she said.

They crowded into the little elevator, rattled down to the first floor, and Carlin, walking awkwardly with his hands behind his back, was assisted by Lieutenant Tragg down the steps to the waiting squad car.

Tragg said to the officer who had driven him, "You sit in back, Joe. I'll do the driving. Keep an eye on this guy. Clout him hard if he tries anything."

"Your face is going to be red over this," Carlin warned. "You take these handcuffs off. Take me into headquarters like this and you'll be on the carpet tomorrow."

Tragg said, "Wrong again, Carlin. I'm paid by the taxpayers to bring every live corpse I find down to headquarters. Now officially you've been murdered, and that makes you part of the spirit world. We have to take extra precautions with people who have been murdered and then come to life. That's the way the department wants it."

"Go ahead, crack wise," Carlin said. "When I get down to headquarters, I'm going to make you look foolish as hell."

Tragg said, "Please don't. If you make me bust out crying my eyes will be all red and swollen, and I have to do a lot of fast driving."

Tragg saw that his passengers were seated in the car, turned on the blinking red spotlight, switched on the siren and started traveling with constantly accelerating speed, screaming through intersections, detouring around frozen traffic, skillfully picking openings through which he could send the speeding car, never slowing speed now, never accelerating, but keeping a steady, sustained high speed.

"Might I suggest one more stop?" Mason asked.

"Where?" Tragg inquired.

"Where you can find a witness who . . ."

"Don't let this guy keep bamboozling you," Carlin pleaded. "Go on down to headquarters if you want and listen to *my* story, then make up your mind. You let Perry Mason start putting candles on your cake and there won't be any birthday."

"*Your* story is full of holes like Swiss cheese," Tragg said.

Carlin snapped, "Well, do you think I want to spill all the details in front of this slick mouthpiece?"

Tragg shot Mason a quizzical glance, then suddenly shut off the siren, slowed down the car to a speed that was little more than a crawl.

"What's the idea?" Mason asked.

"Shut up," Tragg said. "I want to think."

"I don't know why you want to bother doing that now," Carlin said. "You've let him do your thinking for you so far. You might as well give him your badge and . . ."

212

"Shut up!" Tragg said. "I've told you I want to think."

The officer in the back seat reached over and placed his thumb on the nerve center where Carlin's jaw joined the neck. He exerted sudden pressure.

"*Ouch!*" Carlin screamed.

"The Lieutenant wants you to keep quiet," the officer told him.

Tragg drove slowly, being careful to observe all of the traffic regulations, to yield the right of way at intersections when necessary.

Twice Carlin started to say something. Each time the officer in the rear seat promptly shut him up.

Mason smoked a cigarette. Celinda Gilson sat absolutely silent, her face completely dead pan. Once or twice Lieutenant Tragg, while waiting for a signal light to change, stole a thoughtful glance at her.

As far as Celinda was concerned she might not have known Tragg existed.

Abruptly Lieutenant Tragg slowed the car to a full stop, and pointed across the street to where a yellow cab was standing at the curb.

"See that, Mason?" he asked.

"What?"

"The cab."

"Yes. What about it?"

Tragg smiled. "You're a busy man, Mason. You have a lot of irons in the fire, you have a great many things to do. I wouldn't want to interfere with your activities in any way. You've given me a lot of time. You've been more than generous. I simply can't accept any further sacrifice."

"Meaning?" Mason asked.

"Meaning that that cab will take you back to your office or wherever you want to go."

"Now you're getting some sense," Carlin said. "You . . ."

"Shut up," the officer commented, clamping more pressure on Carlin's neck.

Carlin, after one startled exclamation of pain, subsided into silence.

Mason said, "You'd like to get the answer in this case, wouldn't you, Tragg?"

"I'm getting it."

Mason said, "Let's suppose it was self-defense."

"How do you mean?"

"Suppose Fargo was tied up with Carlin. Suppose Mrs. Fargo found out about it. Suppose the whole thing is a pretty rotten mess. Suppose her husband found out she knew about it and tried to kill her."

"It's okay by me," Tragg said, "but you can't make it stick."

"I think that's what happened."

"This is a hell of a time to start thinking so," Tragg said. "You can't swap horses in the middle of the stream."

"I'm not in the middle of the stream."

"Perhaps not," Tragg said, "but you're way over your head."

Carlin said, "This guy is nuts."

The officer holding Carlin asked, "You want him to talk, Lieutenant?"

"Not now," Tragg said. "Mason is a busy man. He hasn't time to listen to Carlin's story. It's too bad, but he's got things to do and places to go. We won't *think* of detaining him."

Mason said, "If I get the answer, Tragg, and it's self-defense, will you ride along with me?"

"I won't ride with anyone on anything," Tragg said. "It's up to you and the District Attorney and the Judge. I'm getting evidence."

"If it should be the truth you won't throw anything in my way?"

"I always like the truth."

Mason said, "It's the answer that fits into the picture. Myrtle Fargo was trying to protect the kid. She found out her husband was mixed up in a slimy racket. She wanted to handle it her way. She wanted Fargo to step out of the picture and release custody of the kid and then she'd get a divorce on the ground of desertion or some . . ."

Carlin said, "This guy makes me sick."

Tragg pointed to the taxicab and said, "On your way, Mason."

"Because I'm making your prisoner sick?" Mason asked.

"Because you're talking too damn much," Tragg said. "Save your arguments for the Judge."

The officer reached across and opened the door of the car. Mason stepped out to the pavement and the door slammed.

Mason watched the police car speed away, then walked across the street to where the driver of the yellow cab had been watching the police car with curious speculation.

Chapter 23

Morning newspapers had announced the discovery that the corpse found in the building occupied by Medford D. Carlin was not that of Carlin, but was at the moment unidentified. Carlin, who had been found to be very much alive, had stated he had been away on a business trip inspecting mining interests in a remote section of the state. He was being held by the police for further questioning. And rumor around the courthouse had it that perhaps the arson case and the Fargo murder case were not unconnected.

All of this had caused a sudden surge of interest in the case of the People of the State of California versus Myrtle Fargo, and Mason found the courtroom crowded as he entered and sat waiting for the bailiff to bring the defendant into court.

A matron ushered Mrs. Fargo to the door of the courtroom. A deputy sheriff escorted her to her chair.

Mason leaned forward for a brief, whispered conference. "Carlin is alive," he said.

"So they told me." Her voice was level, dispirited and showed no interest.

Mason said, "You sent me that money."

"No."

"You killed your husband."

"No."

"Was it in self-defense, or was it because of what you had found out?"

"I don't know what you are talking about."

"You knew your husband was mixed up in a racket with Medford Carlin."

"No."

216

Mason said, "You're trying to protect your son. You'd do a lot better by ..."

"No, no, please, Mr. Mason. I've told you everything." She deliberately turned away from him.

Judge Keith entered the courtroom and called court to order.

Mason said, "Your Honor, I was cross-examining one of the prosecution's witnesses, Mrs. Newton Maynard. I would like to resume that cross-examination, particularly in view of the fact that there have been rather startling developments since court adjourned."

"Developments which, however, have absolutely no bearing on *this* case," the District Attorney interpolated.

"That," Mason pointed out, "remains to be seen."

"Mrs. Maynard will resume the witness stand," Judge Keith ordered.

Mrs. Maynard's attitude had undergone a subtle change. She was wary, careful and as cautious as a skillful boxer sparring for an opening. She seated herself on the witness stand, placed the tips of her fingers against the patch over her eye, then turned to regard Perry Mason.

"Mrs. Maynard," Mason said, "I'd like to know a little more about the injury you sustained to your right eye."

"What does that have to do with it?" she asked.

"Oh, Your Honor," Hamilton Burger said, "this seems rather trivial. I think it is conceded by all concerned that this injury occurred *after* the twenty-second of September. She had both eyes at that time and it is quite apparent that she can see with *one* eye now."

"Many persons," Mason said, "can see with one eye who can't see with two."

"What do you mean by that?" Burger asked.

"A lack of co-ordination," Mason said. "I think it is a matter which can be demonstrated by the evidence of an expert."

"Does it have any application in this case?" Judge Keith asked.

"I think it does," Mason said. "I think Your Honor will

217

find that this witness is unable to see with both eyes, although she can see with one, but for purposes of appearance she naturally dislikes to go about in public with one eye completely covered."

"That's not so," Mrs. Maynard snapped. "I can see perfectly."

"I don't think you can," Mason said, smilingly confident.

"Why, certainly I can. I never heard of such a thing. This injury is the result of an infection. The doctor told me to keep my eye covered."

"What doctor?" Mason asked.

"A—a doctor whom I consulted."

"After all," Burger said, "this is going far afield. This is completely extraneous."

Judge Keith regarded the witness meditatively.

"I am willing to challenge the witness," Mason said. "I will venture to say that with both eyes open she cannot make an identification of an individual previously known to her who will stand up in the courtroom. I make that as a challenge to the prosecution."

"Oh, that's absurd," Burger said.

"I shouldn't remove my bandage," Mrs. Maynard said.

"Not even for a brief interval?" Judge Keith asked suspiciously.

"Oh, I don't suppose it would hurt for just a brief interval, but it's all foolish. If I can see with one eye why couldn't I see with two?"

Hamilton Burger said, "Your Honor, it seems to me that this is very plainly a desperate attempt on the part of counsel to take advantage of an unfortunate situation in which the witness finds herself. She's suffering from an infected eye which should be kept bandaged. There is no question but what she was able to see clearly enough to travel when she was on that bus and . . ."

"Clearly enough to travel," Mason said, "but that doesn't necessarily mean she could identify persons."

"No?" Hamilton Burger asked sarcastically. "Not clearly

enough to see persons who were seated right next to her on a bus? Don't be ridiculous, Mr. Mason."

Mason smiled, glanced at his watch, and said, "After all, Your Honor, we've consumed several minutes with this objection. All that would be necessary would be for Mrs. Maynard to remove that bandage temporarily and be called upon to identify a person in the courtroom who will arise at a given signal."

"Some person who is known to her?" Judge Keith asked.

"Some person whom I feel quite certain she has seen under circumstances at least on a par with the circumstances under which she claims to have seen the defendant in this case."

"Is there any reason why such a test should not be carried out," Judge Keith asked, "so that the matter can be disposed of?"

"*I'm* quite willing," Mrs. Maynard snapped. "If you think you can trap me that way, Mr. Mason, I'll give you the surprise of your life. Anyone I've ever seen before, I can identify. I have a very, *very* good memory for faces. That's one thing on which I pride myself. If I've once had a good look at a person I never forget that person."

Mason said, "Just a moment." He whispered to Della Street, who was seated at a point within the mahogany rail and directly behind his counsel table.

Della Street nodded, moved out into the audience.

Mason said, "I can assure the Court that I am not making this test idly. I think that the witness is unable to see with both eyes although she may be able to see with one."

"That's absolutely *absurd*," Mrs. Maynard snapped. "I'm quite willing to show how absurd that is."

"Will you then," Mason asked, "kindly remove your bandage?"

Della Street, moving through the spectators near the middle of the courtroom, passed a note to the parking lot attendant, Percy R. Danvers, who was sitting on an aisle seat.

On the witness stand Mrs. Maynard was fumbling for a moment with the bandage over her eye.

"May I help you?" Hamilton Burger asked, hovering about her solicitously.

"If you please," she said, "and I'll want my glasses left on. Remember I'm blind as a bat without my glasses. I told you that. I want to put my spectacles on and then I can see perfectly."

"All right," Burger said, "let's have your spectacles ready, Mrs. Maynard. Now let the record show that the bandage is being removed. Here are your spectacles, Mrs. Maynard. Let the record show that the witness has now adjusted the spectacles. Now, Mr. Mason, go ahead."

There was a smile of triumphant satisfaction on the face of the District Attorney.

Mason nodded toward the courtroom and motioned.

Percy Danvers got to his feet.

"Who is that person?" Mason challenged.

Mrs. Maynard peered at him intently for a moment, said, "I don't know his name but he's the man who has the parking station there at the depot."

"You're certain?" Mason asked.

"Quite certain," she snapped.

"You've seen him there?"

"Yes."

"And recognize him as the person you have seen at that parking station?"

"Certainly, I—I . . ." Her voice abruptly trailed into silence.

"Go ahead," Mason said.

"I—I made a slight mistake," she said. "I meant to say that I had had him pointed out to me in the corridor as one of the witnesses in the case who was to testify that . . ."

Mason said suddenly, "Now, Danvers, I want to ask you a question which you can answer from right where you stand. Isn't *this* the woman who parked the automobile on the morning of September twenty-second; the person who asked you about taking a taxicab? Think carefully and . . ."

"I did no such thing," Mrs. Maynard snapped. "I wasn't

there. I never saw this man before I came to court. He's never seen me. I . . ."

"Then why did you just now say you saw him *at the parking station?*" Mason asked.

"Because I—I was confused. I—and then again, I've parked my car there before. I've seen him there on other occasions long before the twenty-second of September."

Mason turned to Danvers. "Is this the woman you saw?"

"By gosh, I don't know," Danvers blurted. "It sure looks like her."

"It could be?" Mason asked.

"It could be."

"Just a moment," Hamilton Burger shouted. "This is getting entirely out of hand. Counsel is examining two witnesses at once. We're getting nowhere. We're . . ."

"On the contrary," Mason interrupted, raising his own voice to drown out that of Hamilton Burger. "We're getting to a solution of this case, Your Honor; the only solution which actually fits the facts in this case."

Judge Keith pounded with his gavel. "Let's have an orderly procedure here. We . . ."

Mrs. Maynard started hastily adjusting the bandage over her eye.

"Just a moment," Mason said, "before you put on that bandage, Mrs. Maynard, we happen to have a good eye doctor here in court. Perhaps you wouldn't mind having Dr. Radcliff look at that eye."

"I don't need any doctor to look at it."

"I didn't notice any evidence of inflammation," Mason said.

"Surely, Your Honor, that's beside the point," Hamilton Burger said.

Mason laughed. "No, it isn't, Your Honor. The witness testified under oath that she had an inflammation of that right eye, an infection. I think the court had an opportunity to observe that eye and I know Dr. Radcliff did, and I think everyone will agree that there is certainly no evidence of infection, no redness, no inflammation, or . . ."

"It's gone down. It's ever so much better now," Mrs. Maynard said.

In the moment of silence that followed Percy Danvers said quietly, "Come to think of it, I think that *is* the woman."

Chapter 24

Mason, entering his office, scaled his hat in the general direction of the shelf in the hat closet, grabbed Della Street around the waist and gleefully started to whirl her around.

"What happened?" Della Street asked.

"Well," Mason said, "we finally got the whole story and it's so darned simple that I should have known what it was even sooner than I did."

"It's clear as mud to me," Della said.

"Here's what happened," Mason told her. "Carlin, Fargo and Pierre Larue were all in cahoots in a baby-blackmail racket.

"They used Helen Hampton in their main shakedown, too, but the racket was far more intricate than she knew about. It involved getting illegitimate children, putting them out for adoption at a fat fee, and then, after the new parents had become attached to the child, steering them into the Golden Goose and letting Helen Hampton do her stuff. Helen would get the tip-off from Pierre. Then she would put on her act, and vary the age of the infant and the circumstances in her story to suit the occasion.

"Myrtle Fargo found out that her husband was mixed up in some racket with Carlin, but she never associated it with the blackmailing she'd been subjected to three years ago. Until today she still thought her adopted son had Japanese blood. Talk about compelling reasons for not telling the truth! She secured the clipping showing Helen Hampton's criminal record and was foolish enough to think that she could frighten Carlin into letting her husband out of the partnership—the poor kid had no idea just how deep the thing went."

"And Carlin killed Fargo?" Della Street asked.

"There's where Carlin's girl friend entered the picture," Mason said. "But in order to understand that you have to know exactly what happened. Mrs. Fargo has come clean and filled in all the gaps. And Helen Hampton has confessed."

"I'm listening."

"Myrtle Fargo was ready to call for a showdown," Mason said. "She didn't know just how she was going to do it because she wanted to avoid publicity. Then that night in the Golden Goose the girl in the powder room told her who I was. Myrtle immediately made an excuse to go home, get the money she had been saving and send it to me, together with the clipping.

"That clipping was her ace in the hole. She opened her husband's safe to get it and then slipped out of the house. She got a man who runs a nearby delicatessen store, whom she knew and trusted, to deliver the envelope at the Golden Goose, and then went to the drugstore to telephone me.

"Fargo had gone up to his bedroom, saying he had an important real estate agreement he wanted to prepare, but when his wife didn't appear he got suspicious. He found she had left the house. He checked on the safe. His money was there, but things were disturbed and he found the Helen Hampton clipping was missing. He suspected she might have gone to the drugstore to telephone—her mother, the police—he didn't know who, but he was frightened. He didn't know how long she had been gone, and when he caught up with her at the drugstore he thought he had headed her off before she had had a chance to put through the call.

"On the way home there was a scene, and Fargo notified Carlin that his wife was going to make trouble, and he also notified Pierre.

"Then that package came for me at the Golden Goose,

and Helen Hampton, seeing Pierre in conference with us, got her signals mixed. They'd been waiting for the parents of one of the adopted babies to show up at the Golden Goose, and she thought we were the new victims!"

"How delightfully intimate," Della Street said.

"Wasn't it? Well, you can imagine what happened. Pierre got Helen Hampton away from our table as soon as he saw what was happening, but it didn't take him long to find out that he had been too late.

"Pierre gave us credit for being able to put two and two together as soon as we had the facts, so Pierre slipped out of the night club the moment he could and rushed out to Carlin's house. He was in a panic. He wanted to divide all the money in the business and start making tracks.

"Carlin felt certain he could wait it out. Carlin and Pierre got in a fight and, according to Carlin's present story, he hit Pierre on the chin, not too hard. But evidently Pierre's arteries were brittle. The blow brought on a cerebral hemorrhage, and Pierre died."

"You mean he was dead when we called on Carlin?" Della Street asked.

"I mean he'd been killed and was lying on the bed in an upstairs bedroom all the time Carlin was making coffee for us and talking about the beauties of nature."

Della shuddered.

"So Carlin then knew he *did* have to get out from under. He telephoned his girl friend, Mrs. Maynard, to join him, but to park her car out of sight of the house. He then proceeded to fix up a time bomb which would set off a gasoline fire and destroy the house.

"You'll remember that Pierre Larue was a chunky Swiss about sixty years old, about the same age as Carlin and with almost the same build. Carlin felt certain Pierre's body would be found and the police would naturally assume that Carlin had died in the fire.

"However, you will remember that Pierre didn't wear glasses. Carlin not only wore glasses but, because of the peculiar lopsided facial development, one ear was about an inch higher than the other. He took his own glasses off and put them on Pierre, hoping that even after the fire there would be enough of them left for the police to clinch the identification. Then they both slipped out of the back door before Paul's second man got on the job. Carlin holed up somewhere.

"Mrs. Maynard had an old pair of Carlin's discarded spectacles at her house, and she was to rush through a new pair for Carlin."

"How about Fargo?"

"Fargo wouldn't go for murder," Mason said. "He was willing to go for blackmail but he was scared of murder. He wanted to clear out, and fast. His wife had left and he didn't know what she was up to because of the night before and because that morning before she left she had taken the five hundred dollars from the safe. So Carlin sent Mrs. Maynard out to reason with him. She was in the upstairs bedroom when I called. After I left she and Fargo had a showdown. She stabbed him. She was desperate. Fargo had told me his wife had taken the six o'clock plane for Sacramento because he didn't want anyone to know where she really was, but he told Mrs. Maynard the truth—that she'd taken the morning bus. Mrs. Maynard figured that by impersonating Mrs. Fargo she could leave a trail that would make it appear that Myrtle Fargo had committed the crime, and tried to build a fictitious alibi.

"At two places we almost ruined the whole scheme for Carlin. The first time was when our detectives, who were watching the house, put in a fire alarm so promptly that the fire department was able to get the fire extinguised before the evidence had been obliterated. (And, of course, the fact that Carlin had taken everything from his safe and put in charred papers was really the pay-off on the whole thing.) The second time was when we put detectives on that Greyhound bus. It just happened that luck played into the conspirators' hands in that there weren't any other through passengers traveling all the way through from Los Angeles to stop them, and therefore Mrs. Maynard was able to get by with her deception.

"That, of course, was purely a matter of luck, but, on the other hand, the fact that we rushed detectives aboard the bus was also a matter of luck. If their plans had gone through, no one would have thought to look for witnesses until after the passengers had scattered to the four winds of heaven."

"But how did you trap Carlin?" Della Street asked.

"Carlin," Mason said, "was keeping in touch with Celinda Gilson, Larue's former wife. She didn't know anything about the murders, and wasn't involved personally with the blackmail. She had been playing around with Carlin, too, on the side and didn't know about Mrs. Maynard. When Carlin went underground after the fire, she thought he was trying to hide out from a woman and she was only too glad to help him. And when you called her up and said that Helen Hampton was talking, she immediately notified Carlin. So Carlin came rushing up to see what it was all about and ran into me. If I hadn't hit him first he'd have pulled his gun on me."

Della Street said, "How did you know Mrs. Maynard was the one who boarded the bus in Bakersfield?"

Mason laughed. "It was so simple I should have known it a lot earlier. But I was blinded by the conviction that Myrtle Fargo had killed her husband in self-defense. In the first place, Mrs. Maynard was about the same size, the same build and the same age as Myrtle Fargo. Furthermore, she herself kept insisting that they were dressed very much alike.

"The testimony of the pilot about the man who arranged to charter the plane, and his uncertain, groping movements should have suggested someone who couldn't see well and should have been connected with Mrs. Maynard's ordering glasses for a friend, and the description of the glasses pointed to Carlin—especially when I remembered that they had an unusual inside curvature to accommodate a person with protruding eyes. The woman who boarded the bus at Bakersfield wore a veil, and when Mrs. Maynard came to court she had one eye bandaged in such a way that the strips of adhesive tape pulled the skin over her forehead, so that it distorted the expression in the other eye. I should have realized she was trying to avoid identification!

"By trapping her into believing I was making a point that she couldn't see with *both* eyes, I got her to take off the bandage, and by defying her to recognize the parking station attendant, I got her to betray herself."

Della Street's eyes were sparkling. "You certainly squeezed out of a tight corner on that one, Chief," she said.

Mason made a little grimace. "I used a certain amount of ingenuity to get my client out of it, but using ingenuity to take the place of good sound police technique is like trying to walk a tightrope over Niagara Falls without a balancing pole. It takes footwork, ingenuity and luck."

"I don't see that police technique did so much in this case," Della Street said.

Mason grinned. "It turned out afterwards that Tragg managed to get fingerprints from the corpse in Carlin's burnt house. He checked those fingerprints with police records and found the dead man was really John Lansing alias Pierre Larue who had been implicated with Helen Hampton in the first blackmail racket."

"You mean he knew all that," Della Street said, "and would nevertheless have let Myrtle Fargo be convicted of murder?"

Mason said, "What he didn't know was whether the name Medford D. Carlin was simply another alias. Moreover, he assumed that I'd opened Fargo's safe and removed documents which I was afraid would incriminate my client. Therefore, he wasted a lot of time following the trail of a red herring."

"But you must admit you did open the safe."

"Tut, tut," Mason said. "You must use more careful reasoning. I merely unlocked the safe."

228

"Pardon me," Della Street said demurely.

"Gosh, how I wish I'd known about those fingerprints earlier."

"Well, after all," Della Street told him, "you had to do something to earn your $570."